DEADLY
INTENT

DEADLY INTENT

a reggie da costa mystery

laraine stephens

First edition

ISBN: 978-1-68512-130-3

Cover art by Level Best Designs

This book was professionally typeset on Reedsy.
Find out more at reedsy.com

For my darling Bob

Praise for DEADLY INTENT

"In this delightful historical crime novel, Australian author Laraine Stephens delivers an enthralling page turner in *Deadly Intent*. Readers will enjoy being transported back in time with an intriguing set of characters, led by Reggie, and a great setting to contrast and go hand in hand with the specter of a fiendish killer on the loose."—R. Barri Flowers, award-winning criminologist and author of *Chasing the Violet Killer, Exposed Evidence,* and *The Big Island Killer.*

"Chock-full of delightful details and cinematic settings, Stephens paints an enthralling picture of Australia in the 1920s. Her protagonist—the flamboyant, well-dressed, moustache-smoothing, investigative reporter Reggie da Costa—is quite the charming rogue. He meets his match in the spirited Dotty, who finds she rather enjoys the darker side of Melbourne that Reggie introduces her to. Together, they puzzle through an alarming number of local murders. When his editor demands that he stick to reporting instead of sleuthing, this only fuels da Costa's determination to continue seeking what he views as his mission…bring criminals to justice with the printed word as his sword! This is a charming and wonderfully atmospheric novel, full of riddles and flirting and endearing characters; but prepare yourself for a good dose of gritty, early-twentieth-century crime, too. Grab a cuppa, sit in a comfy armchair, put your feet up, and get ready to drift into another time and place."—Kerry Peresta, author of the Olivia Callahan Suspense series.

Prologue

June 1919

Edmund Stout awoke into darkness. He was lying on his back in some sort of box made of rough-hewn timber, his head wedged into a corner, chin on chest, knees drawn up. His first thought was that he'd been buried alive. He cried out but silence was the only answer.

Lying still, his eyes grew accustomed to the dark. He sniffed. The air smelled fresh, not humid and dank as he expected.

Minutes ticked by. The first glimmer of light broke through the gaps between the wooden slats; the stirring of the dawn. A prayer of thanks brushed his lips, in gratitude that he wasn't underground.

Arms and legs compressed, with an unpleasant tingling stretching out to his fingers and toes, he could feel panic intensifying. Encompassed in this one small space, with senses heightened, Edmund Stout felt his awareness of the world constricting as his fears grew.

His breathing grew laboured, short painful gulps of air squeezing through his contracting throat. The pounding of his heart was amplified, hammering against his chest. He willed himself to stay calm, to wait out the time till he was discovered.

Dread gripped him. That weird but familiar sensation was returning, the one that had inexplicably assailed him after dinner. Its arrival was imminent, stronger this time. Shutting his eyes tight, with fingernails digging into palms, he tried to put his mind elsewhere.

His stomach lurched, the sour taste of bile rising up into his throat, tickling his tongue. Waves of blood pounded in his ears; roaring in the stillness;

drowning him. His vision was distorted, like peering through a fish-eye lens, corrupting the straight lines of the coarse timbers, the right angles of the corners.

Words formed on parched lips, but were strangled at birth on his tongue, now coated, thick, and pasty. His jaw felt strangely tight, like it had been wired shut. Cold sweats oozed from moist skin, signalling the advent of tremors, creeping their way out from his core, and spreading out to the extremities.

Only a whisper of air entered his lungs as the cramps gathered pace, twisting and turning and knotting his insides. Gripped by muscle spasms, he writhed in agony, lashing out, clawing at the wood, tearing fingernails. Blood dripped from his knuckles, splinters like needles ripping through skin. Thoughts like scythes slashed away at his perilous grip on sanity. His back arched involuntarily; his vertebrae crushed against the timber. His mouth opened in a silent scream.

The climax over, the spasms receded. Spent and exhausted, Edmund Stout lapsed into blissful unconsciousness.

* * *

It was dark when he awoke. Through the feverish haze in his brain, he could hear voices, whispering, laughing.

'Help.'

'Would you believe it? He's still alive.'

The cold hand of disappointment pressed on his heart.

There were grunts, swearing. The box tilted. His head rammed hard against the timber.

There was a splash, and then the sound was muted. The temperature dropped. Edmund Stout was descending, head first, towards the river bed.

The box settled on the bottom. Water, muddy and chill, gushed in through the gaps in the timbers. Icy water sloshed from side to side, seeping, drenching, choking. He flailed like a madman, powerless in his confinement, his eyes wide and staring in the inky darkness. With nostrils flared, and lips drawn back in a hideous grin, Edmund felt the water rise, soaking his back. A warm sensation spread through his pants; he had pissed himself.

This was it. The last hurrah. The waters lapped at his jawline. He took a deep breath and held it. His face was rigid, his mind focused, as he willed himself to hold on. With his strength ebbing away, the realisation came that all was lost.

He inhaled involuntarily, then coughed and gagged as the filthy waters swamped his lungs, scalded his insides, consumed him. The corners of his vision started to blacken as he surrendered himself to the inevitable: to the embrace of the cold, cold waters.

The last thing that Edmund Stout would know was that death was merciless.

* * *

And yet, the Yarra River treated him with a respect that others had not. He did not remain in the murky depths for long, in that muddy graveyard that held the detritus of past years, dumped and forgotten.

Around midnight, beneath the Church Street Bridge, whirlpools formed, making strange sucking noises. The heavy stones, which had been used to weigh the box down, broke away, allowing it to rise to the surface. It bobbed up and down as it was taken by the river, travelling along the tops of little eddies, not unlike a small boat heading for the harbour.

From the banks it would have appeared innocuous at first sight, although the heavy six-strand wire that encircled it hinted at the guilty secret within. Finally, it came to rest, wedged into the mud on the river bank, water draining from the cracks in the timber.

If anyone had been a witness to the interior of the box, they would have been hard-pressed to recognise what lay within, such was the strange arrangement of the corpse. The body had been laid on its back, the legs bent forward, and then doubled back at the knee joints. Again, to make room, the head was twisted into the left corner of the box, the chin almost touching the collar bone. A thick layer of sticky mud had adhered to the torso and limbs, creating a quasi-mattress on which the corpse lay.

In the early morning light, at high tide, the river surged again. As they passed beneath Princes Bridge, the waters encircled and embraced the box, dislodging it from the river's edge. The makeshift coffin was lifted up, and resumed its journey along the river, bobbing along the crest of the waves, as if borne on the shoulders of pallbearers. As threads of silver sunlight glimmered across the whitecaps, the box reached its final resting place: the entrance to Port Phillip Bay. The water eased its way into the cracks between the boards, filling the space around the corpse, and expelling the remaining air. The box listed sideways, then rose up on its end.

Encased in his coffin, Edmund Stout slid slowly and solemnly beneath the waves into a watery grave.

Chapter One

October 1923

T he rain started to hammer on the roof of his automobile. Reggie
da Costa wound up the side window of his pride and joy, a 1923
two-seater Citroen 5CV 'Torpedo' tourer, and closed his eyes. He
let his mind travel back to the previous night, reliving his evening in the
company of Joseph Theodore Leslie 'Squizzy' Taylor, Melbourne's most
notorious criminal. The liquor had flowed as Reggie listened to the gangster
waxing lyrical about his accomplishments, complaining about harassment
by the coppers, and reminiscing about his feud with 'Long Harry' Slater's
Fitzroy gang. It had been a productive evening for the crime reporter, giving
him plenty of fodder for his articles in *The Argus*, and some excellent stories
to tell at dinner parties, mostly at Squizzy's expense.

He smiled to himself. The little criminal was a joke, all five feet two of him,
with his silk shirts and silk socks, the rakish angle of his bowler hat, his gold
teeth, and his swagger, when in reality he was nothing but a reckless, loud-
mouthed thief with a lust for violence. Sure, Squizzy had animal cunning,
but eventually he'd find himself either at the end of a rope or dead in a gutter
from a rival's bullet.

Reggie opened his eyes. The weather was clearing, a welcome break from
the steady drenching rain that had lashed Melbourne for the past week. On
his way, he had driven across the Yarra River, pausing on the bridge to watch
all manner of debris pass beneath him: tree roots, branches, old bicycles,

furniture, and building materials. The residue of past years had disengaged itself from the river bottom, and was borne by the floodwaters out towards the mouth of the Yarra and into Port Phillip Bay, where it would presumably sink from sight or be washed up on bayside beaches.

The sudden rise of the river, and the steady downpour of rain, had flooded many low-lying streets. Drains backed up and overflowed, choking gutters, and swamping footpaths. In some cases, basements and cellars filled with water as the entrances to buildings were breached.

And, it was at one of the latter that Reggie now found himself, directed by his editor to file a report on the impact of the flood on the lives of everyday Melburnians. He would have to grit his teeth and deal with the mundane, rather than his usual assignment of recording murder or armed robbery by the gangs of Fitzroy and Richmond.

He ran his fingers through his mane of thick black hair, and stared morosely out of the window. Across from him were three terrace houses built around 1900, hawthorn brick with a plain rendered parapet above the balcony roofline. In front of the property was a depressing array of sodden furniture and personal possessions, rescued from the deluge that had flooded the property.

A repair gang from the Melbourne and Metropolitan Board of Works walked past, carrying long hoses and pumping gear.

Reggie wound down the window. 'What's up?'

A worker with a tomahawk replied, 'Basement's sealed in number 1039. Have to break down the door.'

Reggie lit a cigarette and exhaled slowly, then loosened his tie and undid the top stud on his shirt. He checked his watch. Midday. He yawned and stubbed out the cigarette, then munched his way through some sandwiches whilst reading yesterday's newspaper.

He looked up. The last of the water was being pumped from the basements, and was emptying into the gutters, snaking its way to the drain. Reggie put the newspaper away and walked around to the back of his car. It really was a beauty. Worth every penny. The Citroen had a four-cylinder engine and a boat-tail, painted pale yellow with black mudguards. Flashy yet classy, he thought, much like himself.

He smiled as he opened the boot. Inside was what he called his 'reporter's kit,' containing the quintessential equipment that every journalist needed at his fingertips. Along with spare notebooks, a typewriter, and blank paper for writing up reports on the fly, he kept a camera and spare film in case his photographer couldn't make it. A bottle of whisky, cigarettes, and the latest copy of the *Victoria Police Gazette*, courtesy of a member of the constabulary, helped pass the time during a stakeout, along with a change of clothing and a shaving kit if night passed into day. Gumboots, a raincoat, and umbrella were insurance against bad weather. And then there were the bribes—tickets to sporting events, films, shows, and dances—to grease the palms of police and those who gave him access to crime scenes. He was always prepared. Anything to keep him ahead of the press pack.

Taking a torch from his kit, he slipped it into his coat pocket and returned to the scene. A man in a dressing gown and pyjamas, unusual attire for an afternoon, was staring dejectedly at the terrace house.

'Reggie da Costa, from *The Argus*. Who lives here?' he asked him, a notebook and pen in hand.

The delicate man barely acknowledged him; his gaze fixed on the terrace. 'Miss Brockelbank lives in number 1035. Mr and Mrs Morris, and the Collinses are in 1037. The Adlers and me are in number 1039.'

'And you are?'

He looked properly at Reggie for the first time. 'The name's Frank. Frank Feely.' A racking cough escaped his lips. He covered his mouth with a checked handkerchief.

'Mind if I take a look around?'

'Go ahead. I'm in the upstairs flat. The Adlers are away.'

The front door was wide open. Reggie peered in and sighed. The place was neglected, the flocked wallpaper peeling away from the cornices, the carpet runner on the staircase almost threadbare.

Off the hallway was the door to the basement. It was hanging open, the lock broken. Reggie pushed the door aside. Then he stepped down into the cellar.

He switched on the flashlight and directed the beam around the main room. There were actually two rooms, joined by an open doorway. The walls were brick; the floor earthen. A thin ray of light penetrated through the slit of a ventilation grill on the outside wall. Large puddles of muddy water pooled across the floor. A line of dirt formed a rim on the walls, about three feet above the floor, indicating the height to which the waters had risen.

Reggie sniffed the air. It smelled dank and musty. Time to go.

He swept the beam around the basement one last time. As he did, he heard a movement behind him, and saw a shadow dart out from under the stairs. The light from his torch caught the tail of a rat disappearing into the adjoining room. Reggie made his way tentatively across the floor, the soles of his shoes squelching in the sticky mud.

He looked down, his nose wrinkling in disgust. 'Damn.' His expensive wingtip shoes, cream and tan, were smeared in sludge.

From the corner of his eye, he noticed a large steamer trunk, pushed up against the wall. It was about four feet long, two feet high by three feet deep, anchored to the ground by a thick layer of mud. The brown leather exterior, reinforced with metal studs, was showing its age. The lid was attached with two broad leather hinges.

'Treasure chest.' He smiled to himself, despite the state of his footwear. He stepped forward and grabbed the large brass padlock which secured the trunk. It was locked.

Back at the car, Reggie took a claw hammer and a chisel from the toolbox, and returned to the basement of number 1039. The padlock looked invincible, but the trunk itself was showing signs of wear and would be easier to breach. He wedged the chisel in the gap between the latch and the body of the trunk, and then hit it hard with the hammer. The latch broke off, the padlock still attached.

Reggie lifted the lid and reeled back, almost slipping over in the mud, as a loathsome stench wafted heavily through the restricted space of the basement. He dry-retched, his eyes watering, and his stomach heaving. He retreated to the steps and sat down heavily on the bottom one.

'Bloody hell.'

Slowly and deliberately, he took deep breaths, calming himself. He took out his handkerchief and tied it around his nose and mouth, then approached the trunk again. He switched on the torch and leaned over the trunk. In his celebrated career as chief crime reporter for *The Argus*, he had seen many bodies, but never had he witnessed one that looked like this. It was extraordinary.

The body had been compressed into the space. It was lying on its side, its knees tucked up against the torso, the arms wrapped around the body as if it were hugging itself. The head had been twisted so that it fitted into a corner of its coffin. Judging by the clothes that clung to the remains, the corpse was male. The remaining flesh, in an advanced state of decomposition, had been bloated by the flood waters.

A glint of gold caught his eye. A putrefying hand extended from the sleeve of a checked shirt; its little finger adorned by the smooth curve of a signet ring.

Reggie backed up again, breathing heavily. He leaned against the wall, assigning to memory what he had just witnessed. He felt nauseous, yet excited. It was worth ruining his shoes for a story this big. In the depths of the building was the body of a murdered man, who would have remained undiscovered if not for the floods. How long he had lain there would be determined by the medical examiner but, in Reggie's experience, a body in that state would have been there at least a year or two.

What a fillip! Instead of a boring article on the human cost of the deluge, he had been gifted access to a murder scene, a crime reporter's dream come true. Nothing like being the first, he thought, smiling despite the churning of his stomach. There was nothing like the smell of death to brighten his day. A death, in suspicious circumstances.

He went outside and stood on the front step, leaning against the door jamb, breathing in the fresh chill air.

'What's up, mate?' asked Mr Feely. 'You look like you've seen a ghost.'

'How right you are,' said Reggie. 'We need a copper. There's a body in the basement.'

Chapter Two

Reggie da Costa resided with his mother in a modest weatherboard terrace house in the working-class suburb of Richmond. It was a far cry from where he wished to be, which was living by Port Phillip Bay, in affluent Brighton. With his innate good taste and appreciation of the finer things, he would fit right in. The only thing he lacked was the money. It was the recent, fortuitous death of a distant relative that had provided Mavis da Costa with enough to buy a permanent home but, unfortunately, the inheritance had not been sufficient to purchase an abode in one of the leafy suburbs of upper-class Melbourne.

If you'd asked Reggie what he really wanted, apart from a change to his residential status, he would have told you that marriage to an attractive (preferably beautiful), well-connected woman in her twenties with money, and lots of it, would have made him feel so much better about life. Such a wife would restore him to the social class which was his birthright, and which was now denied to him. Such a wife would have provided the material things of life that he enjoyed: clothes, cars, travel, good food, and wine. Despite his best efforts, such a wife remained elusive.

Reggie da Costa settled into his armchair. It was getting on to dinnertime and he was hungry. He poured himself a glass of Bordeaux and smacked his lips in satisfaction, reflecting on his recent good fortune. What had started as an unedifying task—reporting on the damage done by the excessive rain—had surprisingly turned out to be a blessing. A corpse had been hidden in the basement, and he had been the sole witness to its discovery. With luck, this might lead to another Death Mask Murders case, which had cemented his reputation back in 1918 as the premier crime reporter for Melbourne's premier newspaper, *The Argus*.

It was only five years since a psychopath had embarked on a bizarre killing spree, strangling his female victims and creating death masks of their faces. Reggie's role in his capture had featured in all the major newspapers, and provided him with the kudos that, in his view, he undoubtedly deserved.

Since then, the pickings for good stories had been thin. He had been relying on the antics of Squizzy Taylor, and his gang of thugs, to provide material for his stories and reports. But now, fate had intervened in the form of a body in a trunk, and he wasn't about to let a golden opportunity go begging.

Clawing his way up from lowly office boy to a member of the press had been difficult and slow. His education had been cut short at the age of thirteen. He had been thrown into the alien world of the newsroom, surrounded by the clatter of typewriters and printing presses; a male environment full of colourful language and excessive drinking, with conversation centred around the subjects of crime, politics, gossip, and deadlines. It was nothing like his previous life of polite conversation and the company of his mother. But slowly, his reputation as someone who could ferret out a good story, and who could string a sentence together, bore fruit, with the result that he was given more challenging assignments. Once his by-line appeared in *The Argus* beneath his report, he realised that he was well on the way to greater things.

And now, his inside story on The Basement Murder was in the hands of the typesetters, and would be on newsstands the following morning. He perused his copy of the report. It read well, he thought:

GRUESOME DISCOVERY
THE BASEMENT MURDER

By REGGIE DA COSTA, Senior Crime Reporter

Melbourne's recent heavy rain has wreaked havoc throughout the city

and suburbs. Sightseers have flocked to see the Yarra River in flood, while damage to homes, schools, parks, sporting fields, and businesses has been unprecedented. But one of the strangest stories, to come out of the greatest deluge to engulf Melbourne since 1891, is the discovery of a body in the basement of an East Melbourne apartment house.

As the flood waters receded yesterday, a repair team from the Melbourne and Metropolitan Board of Works was sent in to pump out the basements of three attached terrace houses in Punt Road. It appears that the basement of Number 1039 concealed more than just gallons of water: it contained a brown leather steamer trunk.

The trunk was a coffin!

First on the scene was Reggie da Costa, crime reporter with this newspaper, who called in the police. He discovered the body when he prised open the lid.

'It was a repulsive sight,' he said. 'The body had been arranged to fit into the trunk. The deceased man must have been dead already, when he was placed there. The perpetrator locked the basement, hoping that it would discourage others from discovering the corpse. The passage of time would make it more difficult for the police to track down the killer. It was clear that this murder was premeditated.'

Foul play!

A preliminary examination by a doctor at the scene indicated that the body had most probably been stored in the trunk for between one and two years. The man was estimated to be in his early fifties. It was found that his skull had been fractured, possibly by being struck with a blunt instrument.

The other point of interest was that someone had tried to remove a signet ring, worn on his little finger, by sawing into the bone.

The residents of the terrace houses were shocked by the discovery. Mr Frank Feely, tenant of the upstairs apartment, said, 'I never would have guessed that there was a dead body down there. The basement was locked when I moved in. It's frightening to think that something could happen like that, just two floors below where you live.'

The tenants of the ground floor flat are away, and will be questioned on their return. There is no suggestion that they are involved in the murder.

The body has been removed to the Morgue. A post-mortem examination will be held today.

At this stage, police enquiries into the identity of the man are continuing. Members of the public are asked to contact either *The Argus* or Detective Sergeant Michael O'Flanagan, of the Criminal Investigation Branch, Victoria Police, if they have any information that might help in the investigation.

[*The Argus* October 15, 1923]

Reggie looked at his fob watch. It was after seven o'clock, and dinner was still not on the table. The smell of food drew him into the kitchen, where his mother was dishing up dinner, prepared by the daily 'help.'

Mavis da Costa was a plump little woman with innocent blue eyes and rosy cheeks in a round face, framed by a froth of fair curls.

Reggie frowned. 'That woman made stew again? Is that all she can cook?'

Mavis stared accusingly at her son. 'She's all we can afford. If you would only—'

'Yes, yes. Find a rich wife.'

'You're not getting any younger, Reggie,' she sighed. 'If only your father was still around, everything would be fine.'

'You seriously believe that? You live in a fantasy world. We'd have even less in the bank if he were.' His eyes narrowed as he thought of his father. Twenty-two years before, Italian-born Mario da Costa had taken off with the maid, leaving them in dire straits, after frittering away his wife's inheritance on women and horses.

Mavis stared out the window, her thoughts far away. 'Mario was so handsome. Smouldering eyes, coal-black hair, and white teeth. He could make that violin sing.' She turned back and faced her son. 'He swept me off my feet, you know.'

'Yes, yes. I've heard it before.'

It was a source of irritation to Reggie that his mother had softened her view of her absent husband, coming to see him through the lens of rose-coloured glasses. Over the years, she had created an idealised portrait of Mario, substituting it for the awful reality of living with, and ultimately being deserted by, a philandering and irresponsible husband. It seemed like those times were forgotten. Reggie knew that challenging her was a waste of time, but he couldn't help himself.

'I wish you would forget him, Mother.'

'You're so like him, Reggie. Sometimes I look at you and I see him again.'

'That's all we have in common. Our looks. Remember, I'm still here, and he's not.'

'Indeed, you are still here.' Her shoulders drooped. 'You missed your opportunity with Emma Hart. She inherited Mrs Darrow's estate in the end. Who was to know that her aunt would change her will? And now she's married and on her honeymoon.'

'As you say, Mother, who was to know? By the way, I received a postcard from her on Friday. She's enjoying Paris immensely. The art galleries. The salons.' He shook his head in wonder. 'But I could never have married her. She was a friend.'

'What are you saying?'

'That you should never marry a friend. A wife should be kept at a distance.'

Mavis tut-tutted. 'You're nearly forty and your waist is thickening. I'll have to let out the seams of your trousers soon.'

He scowled. 'No need to remind me, Mother. Besides, I'm thirty-six.'

Mavis carried the plates through to the little dining room, just off the parlour, while Reggie poured a glass of wine for his mother and another for himself.

'Tell me about your day,' he said as they sat down at the table.

'I was at Mildred Bardsley Smith's place. You remember my old school friend?' Her voice took on a hushed, reverential tone. 'You know that she lives in Grosvenor Street. In Brighton. Near the Bay.'

'Yes, yes. Go on.'

'It seems that her niece, Dotty Wright, has inherited the estate of a grocer.'

'A grocer?' Reggie chuckled with delight. 'Including tins of baked beans and jars of pickled onions?'

Mavis struggled to keep a straight face. 'Don't interrupt. It appears that the grocer shot himself, and now he's left all his money to Dotty. Quite extraordinary!'

Reggie raised an eyebrow. 'Was there something going on between Miss Wright and her grocer?'

'Don't be disgusting, Reggie. Of course not. Dotty was raised by Mildred and Alfred. She went to the best schools.'

'I've heard about this case. They said it was an accident.'

'Dotty doesn't think so. She thinks there was a reason he killed himself. I told Mildred that you would help her out.'

Reggie frowned. 'Why did you say that, Mother? I have better things to do than investigate grocers.'

'I promised her, and that's that. Besides, you might like Dotty.'

'Now you want me to marry Miss Wright? And help her spend her grocer's money? Really, Mother.'

'The funeral is on Friday at St Ignatius', on Richmond Hill,' continued Mavis, ignoring her son's look of displeasure. 'Ten o'clock. I said that you would meet Dotty there.'

There was nothing that Reggie could say to dissuade his mother from her promise to Mildred Bardsley Smith. Mavis da Costa's friendships were her lifeline to a past life, when money had been plentiful and life had been good. She was fortunate to be the grateful recipient of the largesse of a group of wealthy Brighton matrons, one of whom was Mildred, who included her in their social get-togethers, giving her a respectability that her husband had almost stolen. Each week, she braved the train trip from Richmond to Middle Brighton to maintain her contact with them. And, as she reminded him constantly, her friendship with these women gave Reggie access to the right social circles, and just might give him an introduction to a well-connected and wealthy wife-to-be.

To the funeral he must go.

Chapter Three

Floyd Kramer was a sub-editor with *The Argus*, Reggie's immediate boss in the chain of command. His languid, monotonous tone of voice belied a sharp, inquisitive mind.

'What do you want, Reggie?' Kramer asked, looking at him over the top of the newspaper. He chewed on the end of a pencil, looking intently at Reggie through horn-rimmed glasses. The lenses were so thick that his eyes were magnified, unsettling those who sat on the other side of his desk. One wag in the newsroom compared it to feeling like an insect under a microscope.

'I want to follow up the police investigation into The Basement Murder case.'

'That could take time,' replied his boss, tapping the newspaper article with his pencil. 'You already have this business with Angus Murray.'

'I have it under control.'

'Give me a rundown on where we're at with it.'

'Angus Murray has been remanded into custody. He's been charged with escaping from Geelong Jail, and for wounding Thomas Berriman in an armed robbery.'

'Berriman was—'

'The bank manager.'

'How did Murray escape?'

'Sawed through the bars and loosened a large stone with a poker. He worked at the hole in the wall while the other prisoners slept.'

Kramer whistled. 'The screws must have been asleep, too.'

Reggie chuckled. 'There's more. He'd tied together bits of blankets and threw them over the wall, then made his getaway. They caught up with him in St Kilda, along with our good mate, Squizzy Taylor.'

'And Squizzy?'

'He's out on bail. I saw him last week. He reckons that the coppers are victimising him.'

Kramer chewed away at the end of his pencil, considering his options. 'You're keen to follow up this Basement Murder case?'

'That's right. We're ahead of the pack with this one.'

Kramer pushed his glasses up and gave Reggie a mournful and magnified stare. 'Alright. But I want regular reports.' He tapped the desk with his pencil. 'And don't let go of Squizzy. I have a gut feeling there will be more happening with that young thug.'

Reggie nodded and went back to his desk in the newsroom. Even after all this time, Kramer still insisted that his staff check in with what they were working on. It was irksome that his boss could dictate priorities, irrespective of a reporter's seniority.

Reggie ran his fingers through his thick black hair, its dryness reminding him that he was almost out of Brilliantine. He sat back and propped his feet up on the edge of the desk, admiring his highly polished two-tone shoes, cream and tan. It had taken him ages to remove the mud from the basement, but it had been worth it. They were the same colour as his suit, and were irreplaceable.

'The autopsy should be through in a week,' he surmised. 'That gives me plenty of time to get this business of Dotty Wright and her grocer out of the way, before I get stuck into the East Melbourne murder.'

Chapter Four

Reggie stood on the steps outside the entrance to St Ignatius' Church, high on Richmond Hill, watching as the simple wooden coffin containing the remains of Eric Smith, grocer, was carried on the shoulders of pall-bearers and lowered into the shiny black hearse. He had dressed appropriately for a solemn occasion, wearing a subdued navy three-piece suit with a half belt across the back, the material draped to enhance his physical attributes. His striped shirt was in the American style, set off by a blue and gold striped tie, rolled gold collar pin, and Fedora hat.

The funeral service had been a morbid and dull affair, focusing on Smith's strong sense of community, his support of various charities, and his indefatigable work ethic. Reggie hoped that the speakers at his funeral would find more interesting things to say about him when he threw off this mortal coil: his good looks, his stylish taste in clothes, his raffish lifestyle, his dazzling command of the English language, and, of course, his dedication to his mother.

As the hearse began its slow journey towards Eric Smith's final resting place, a woman, wearing a simple black dress and large hat, stopped in front of him. She was in her early thirties, with red hair, green eyes, and pale skin.

'You must be Mr da Costa,' she said. 'I'm Miss Wright. I've read your articles in *The Argus*. You seem to be quite the reporter. I assume that my aunt spoke to your mother about my concerns? I was hoping that you might be able to help me.'

'That depends. I'm a busy man.'

'I understand that. If I must, I'll pay you. I'm going to the cemetery now for the burial, but perhaps you might like to join me afterwards? At Eric Smith's grocery shop. Swan Street, near the corner of Coppin Street. At noon.'

Reggie checked his watch. 'I can spare half an hour, Miss Wright.'

'You like mysteries, Mr da Costa? This is one.'

* * *

It was after twelve when Reggie met Dotty outside the grocer's, about half a mile from his home. The shop and its upstairs dwelling were made of red brick, with a parapet and a corrugated iron roof. Cheerful lettering on the window announced that it was the establishment of 'Eric the Grocer.' The narrow side path and backyard were overgrown with weeds.

Dotty had removed her hat. Her hair was straight and cut in a blunt fashion which, combined with the black dress, made her appear rather severe. Her skin was pale, with a few freckles dotted across her nose. She searched in her handbag for the key, then opened the door.

The air was musty. A thin layer of dust covered the counter, on which sat a set of scales and a large silver cash register. Built-in shelves were filled with jars of preserves and tinned goods. Shallow boxes, labelled as fruit and vegetables, were empty.

'I threw out the fresh food before it went mouldy,' she explained as they walked through into the hallway. 'The kitchen's out the back. That's where I found his body. Let's go upstairs.'

Reggie ducked his head as they took the narrow steps that led up to the first floor. Off the landing was the door to a small bedroom, containing a simple iron bedstead, bedside table, wardrobe, and a sink. Further on, the passage opened up to a little sitting room, which overlooked the street. The furnishings consisted of a two-seater sofa and easy chair, a bookcase, and a small dining table.

Reggie stood with his back to the window, facing Dotty. 'Tell me about Mr Smith.'

'I saw quite a bit of him, being neighbours. We talked a lot. He was a nice man, although he kept to himself. I hadn't seen him for a couple of days, and that was unusual. The shop was shut. The blinds drawn. On the isolated occasions when he went away, he would always let me know. I suppose I had a bad feeling.

'He'd left a spare key with me, so I let myself in.'

'You found him?'

Dotty paled. 'I did. He was downstairs, in the kitchen, on the floor. The gun was next to him.'

'And the police? What did they say?'

'That it was accidental. He must have been cleaning his gun and it went off.'

Reggie shrugged his shoulders. 'What's the problem then?'

'In my opinion, it wasn't an accident. He was driven to suicide.'

'How do you know that?'

'Mr Smith was different in those last few weeks,' she said, frowning. 'Always looking over his shoulder. Something was bothering him.'

'Perhaps he had financial problems? A bad investment.'

'Nothing like that has shown up since. The solicitor said his affairs were in order.'

'A love affair gone wrong?'

'Not Mr Smith. He was self-sufficient. Solitary. There was a lady who came in to clean, but it's been a while.'

She paused. 'I should explain that Mr Smith named me as his heir.' She shook her head in disbelief. 'Quite frankly, I was shocked. We weren't family. I wouldn't even call us close friends. Acquaintances, that's all. And yet, he left me everything: the shop, his savings, even his bicycle.'

'How much does that amount to?' asked Reggie.

'I'm not certain, perhaps about £400. I put advertisements in the Melbourne newspapers calling for any family of Mr Eric Smith to contact me. My search proved fruitless. The solicitor was blunt. If I refused the legacy, he said, the Crown would claim it. I'm going to inherit Mr Smith's estate even though I don't deserve it. It just doesn't seem right.'

'Why not?' asked Reggie. 'I'd take it.'

Dotty shrugged her shoulders. 'It doesn't sit well with me. I'm not well-off, but I make do. I had a hard life as a child, but it's made me tougher. My mother died when I was young. Dad handed me over to Aunt Mildred and Uncle Alfred. They raised me.'

Reggie's eyes narrowed. 'Your father deserted you? Where is he now?'

'He died about ten years ago. He was an alcoholic.'

'You've done well for yourself then. Why look a gift horse in the mouth?'

'I want to know about the man who left me this. Why did he die? Who was he?' Dotty walked over to the bookcase. 'Look at these authors. Dickens. Thoreau. Melville. Conrad. Austen. And dictionaries in Spanish, Italian, and German. More like the collection of a professor of English literature than a Richmond grocer. He was an enigma. I often wondered about him. He wasn't a man who shared himself with you.'

'What do you mean?' asked Reggie, his curiosity piqued.

'It's more than claiming his inheritance. Or finding his family. The fact is that I think he had a secret. He had opinions, that's for sure, but ask him about his life and he clammed up. Said "the past is the past," and that was the end of it.'

'I want to show you something.'

Reggie raised an eyebrow.

Dotty went into the bedroom and returned, carrying an ornate wooden box.

'I found this under the bed when I was tidying up.'

She emptied the contents onto the table and showed him a photograph. It was of two men standing on the deck of a barge called *The Gudrun*. 'I think that's a young Eric on the left.' She turned it over. On the back was written 'Lübeck 1900.'

'Sounds European, doesn't it?' said Reggie.

'Northern Germany,' said Dotty. 'It's a major port on the River Trave. Part of the Hanseatic League. They were a medieval trading guild. Eric told me once that he'd been a sailor. It came up when we were talking about the sinking of the *Lusitania*.'

'He was a sailor. And a grocer. I don't know what you want from me.'

'I'm not sure either. But I can only get so far with this. You're an investigator. You have contacts. Could you look through the rest of it? See what you can find out about him?' She noted the sour expression on his face. 'I'd pay you. Of course, if you'd rather not—'

Reggie hesitated. He foresaw the irritated look on his mother's face when she discovered that he had refused to assist Mildred's niece. 'Forget the money. What do you hope to gain from this?'

'I don't want to gain anything. It's quite simple. I want to know who Eric Smith was and where he came from. I want to know his secret. What he was afraid of. And, if you find a relative, then all this can be theirs.' Dotty waved her arm around the room. 'I don't want to benefit from his death.'

Reggie was shocked. 'Perhaps you're being naïve?'

'Perhaps I am, but I won't rest easy till I know. Will you help me?'

Reggie shrugged his shoulders. 'I'll do it, but I can't pretend to understand you. Now, you say his situation was financially sound and he had no romantic liaisons. What about his health?'

'I don't think he was ill, just anxious. Mr Smith was a loner. He didn't entertain. He was a man of simple tastes.'

Reggie glanced around the room. 'Obviously.' He put the photographs and papers back in the box, cradling it under his arm. 'I won't promise anything. I have a few contacts who might be able to help, but I'm very busy as you can understand. A man in my position. However, I'll look into this for you. It may take some weeks.'

Dotty smiled. 'Thanks, Mr da Costa. I appreciate this. When you look through his papers, you'll agree that they raise more questions than they answer.'

She touched his arm as he was about to descend the staircase. 'Before you go. The last time I saw Mr Smith, he said something that struck me as strange. He said, "People aren't always what they seem." I keep wondering if he was talking about himself.'

Chapter Five

A crime reporter's most important asset is his circle of contacts. Without them, he would never be able to function effectively. Information, particularly insider information, is vital. Over the years, Reggie da Costa had acquired informants and contacts, from Melbourne's underworld, the coroner's office, and the police force. Consequently, he was able to access information that was not publicly available, which kept him ahead of most other reporters.

On his desk were two files: the first contained information on Angus Murray, while the second included the autopsy and police reports on 'The Basement Murder,' as Reggie liked to characterise it.

He opened the Angus Murray file first. The armed robber had been remanded into custody, charged with wounding Thomas Berriman, a Hawthorn bank manager. The final charge against him depended on Berriman's fate: if the bank manager died, Murray would hang. And Squizzy Taylor, his associate in crime, had been arraigned on a raft of charges, including being idle and disorderly, being in a house frequented by thieves and vagrants, and aiding and abetting Angus Murray in the shooting of Berriman.

Reggie closed the file and chuckled, stroking his moustache. Naturally, Squizzy was out on bail, sidestepping the best efforts of the Victoria Police to lock him away. And Reggie would bet his last ten-shilling note that a jury would find Taylor not guilty. Jury-fixing was one of his strengths. Business as usual.

The second file was infinitely more interesting. It was thicker now, given that he had been provided with a copy of the autopsy report, courtesy of an obliging mortuary assistant, as well as the police report, supplied by Detective Sergeant Michael O'Flanagan, the lead investigator on the case.

O'Flanagan was one of the first graduates of the Detective Training School, and was now a member of the Criminal Investigation Branch. Reggie's previous contact, Detective Sergeant Clary Blain, had been demoted for drinking on duty. Was it any wonder, thought Reggie? He'd spent a small fortune on whisky loosening up Clary's tongue.

The Basement Murder case was no closer to being solved. The corpse had been identified as that of Cornelius Henry Stout, a wealthy widower who dabbled in property speculation. He was the father of twins: Lily and Henry. Aged fifty-two when he disappeared around June 1921, his last known address was in East Melbourne. The police had been unable to make any connection between Stout and the terrace house in Punt Road, where his remains had been found.

Stout's identification had been based on his inclusion in the missing persons file, dental records, and the fact that he had suffered a broken leg in his youth. The medical examiner confirmed that the fibula had been subject to a transverse fracture at some stage in the past.

From the landlord of the Punt Road terrace, the police learned that the basement had never been occupied, due to the lack of proper ventilation. As far as the landlord knew, no one by the name of Cornelius Stout had ever lived at 1039 Punt Road, East Melbourne.

The autopsy report offered little, except to confirm that death was caused by a blow from a blunt instrument to the back of the skull. The dead man had been small of frame, around five feet four. The proximal phalange of the right little finger had been nicked by a sharp instrument, most probably a knife, between the webbing and the knuckle, in an attempt to remove the signet ring. He had been deposited in the trunk fully clothed. The process of decomposition had been slow, given the dry and cool atmosphere of the basement, but the influx of flood water had accelerated the process. The medical examiner concluded that Cornelius Stout had been murdered sometime between June 1921 and July 1922.

The police report, on the other hand, offered little information on which Reggie could base an investigation. There was a handful of suspects, but no apparent motivation for Cornelius Stout's murder. There were no witness reports, apart from his own, and the occupants of the terrace appeared to have been ignorant of what lay in the basement beneath them. No one seemed sure when the basement door had been padlocked.

Reggie smiled to himself. There was nothing better than the thrill of the chase. What he wanted was another Death Mask Murders, the case that had made him a household name in Melbourne five long years ago. He had been in this game for over twenty years and he wasn't about to let this one go.

Chapter Six

Detective Sergeant Michael O'Flanagan, 'Mick' to his friends, was waiting for his breakfast in a small café not far from the Russell Street police headquarters. He was a thickset bulldog of a man, with a fearsome countenance, and pugilistic stance that had cowed many a petty crook in his time. A committed Roman Catholic, he brought an almost religious zeal to the task of putting offenders behind bars, in much the same way as he intended to tackle his breakfast.

He nodded appreciatively as the waitress put the plate down in front of him. Three poached eggs with lashings of bacon, two pieces of toast, and four sausages. Delicious. He picked up the salt cellar and sprinkled a liberal quantity over the eggs. Then he broke the yokes and watched as they soaked into the bread.

Lately, he'd been feeling that his time in the Force was coming to an end. So many changes. So much to get used to. And he didn't know if he had it in him. The new police commissioner, Mr Nicholson, had recently reorganised both the Criminal Investigation Branch and the plain-clothes branch. Wireless telephone sets had been installed in police motor patrols so that members could get to a crime scene quickly. Trained dogs were being used to track criminals at night. Dogs, for goodness' sake! And Nicholson had even appointed four women as 'police agents,' although they dealt primarily with young women on the streets and cases of neglected children. Next thing they'd be out catching criminals! It was true: time seemed to be catching up with him.

He stabbed at a piece of toast with his fork and slotted it into his mouth, his jaws rotating rhythmically as he chewed. At least there was breakfast to enjoy.

O'Flanagan heard the café door open and looked up. Reggie da Costa was coming his way, his eyes fixed on him. The detective smiled to himself. There was no other reporter who dressed like Reggie. In a smart grey pin-striped suit, with red and blue tie, and the collar nipped in by a silver pin, he looked more suited to The Hotel Windsor, than to a breakfast eatery.

'Pull up a chair, Reggie,' said O'Flanagan, speaking in his distinctive low growl. He caught the eye of the waitress. She nodded and headed over to their table.

'Tea and toast, thanks,' said Reggie.

The detective directed his attention back to his plate and attacked it with relish. He cut off a piece of sausage and dipped it into the watery yolk of his poached egg. He eyed the meat in much the same way as he eyed a suspect about to crack under interrogation, then he shoved it in his mouth, chewing slowly, savouring the flavour.

'What do you need?'

'Information, Mick.' Reggie leaned forward. 'Cornelius Stout. Any leads?'

O'Flanagan took a piece of paper from a folder in his bag and dangled it in front of the reporter.

'Police Widows and Orphans Fund?'

Reggie extracted a ten-shilling note from his wallet and pushed it across the table. 'Clary was cheaper.'

'You're contributing to a worthy cause.' He placed the list on the table and stabbed at it with a fat finger. 'The tenants at the Punt Road property, including Horace Striker.'

Reggie was shocked. 'The gangster? He lived there?'

'That's right.

'There are two apartments in number 1039,' O'Flanagan continued. 'We know that the basement has never been occupied, unlike the others in the terrace. There have been six tenants over the last four years. Some stayed for a few months, others a couple of years. That's our starting point. I've already eliminated a couple.' He took a pen out of his top pocket and drew a line through two names. 'Those ones don't fit the timeline for the murder. Of the four left, one is deceased.'

The waitress placed Reggie's breakfast in front of him. He nodded at her then lathered his toast with butter. 'That's it? What about suspects?'

'You're a dab hand at investigation. Do it yourself.' O'Flanagan cracked his knuckles and picked up his knife and fork. He devoured another mouthful of toast and egg.

'Not exactly ten shillings' worth of information.' Reggie bit into the buttered toast and chewed slowly, looking steadily at the detective.

'Alright, but nothing's conclusive,' conceded O'Flanagan. 'Let's see. Suspects? The tenants in the building. A few disgruntled business partners. Stout's daughter, who inherits everything. Then there's the son. They didn't get on.' O'Flanagan shrugged his shoulders. 'On the other hand, it could be a robbery gone wrong. Stout's wallet is missing. Apparently, he carried a wad of fifty-pound notes. But personally, I don't think the motive is robbery.'

'No wife?' Reggie finished off the toast and licked his fingers.

'Dead.'

'What was Stout worth?'

'Well over a million. A house in East Melbourne. Gold bullion. Stocks and shares. Property in Hawthorn.'

Reggie took out a pen and made some notes. 'It's lucky we had the flood. The killer would be getting away with murder otherwise.'

O'Flanagan pulled a face. 'He still might. There aren't a lot of leads to follow. The perpetrator had two years to cover his tracks.'

'Anyone you're focusing on?'

'The son, Henry. His relationship with his father was volatile. In fact, he was disinherited. We interviewed him early on. He's a bit of a hothead.'

'Was he familiar with the Punt Road apartment?'

'Not as far as we know.' O'Flanagan pushed away his plate and wiped his mouth with the back of his hand. He filled his pipe with tobacco and proceeded to tamp it down in the bowl. 'You found the body. You've seen the coroner's findings. Any thoughts?' He lit a match, then sucked on the pipe as the tobacco caught.

'As a matter of fact, I do,' said Reggie, wiping his moustache with a napkin. 'Whoever did this had to be familiar with the apartments. The layout of the terrace house. The fact that the basement was empty.'

'You have a point,' agreed O'Flanagan, puffing on his pipe. 'On the other hand, there may be a connection between Stout and the apartment, one we haven't found yet.'

'Any idea where Stout was murdered?'

The detective shook his head. 'Not at this stage. The flood washed away any evidence in the basement.'

'Try this, Mick,' offered Reggie. 'If Stout were killed somewhere away from the Punt Road terrace, the killer had to transport the body there, and bring it in from the street. That's risky. He might be noticed by a passer-by. He might meet someone on the staircase or in the foyer.

'But if Stout were murdered upstairs in one of the apartments, it would be easy to move him into the basement. If we assume that the killer knew the building, he'd know the routines of the other tenants. He'd know when he would have the place to himself, so that he could shift the corpse downstairs.'

'You're amazing,' said O'Flanagan, leaning forward and patting him on the arm. 'You should have been a copper.'

'Don't patronise me, Mick. Anyway, the pay's no good.'

'I agree with you there. But there's one flaw in your argument. In most cases, the victim knows his murderer. Look closer to home and you have the killer.'

'You're probably right. One thing's bothering me, though. What was the significance of the ring? Why cut off Stout's finger?'

'Perhaps to make identification of the corpse difficult. Perhaps attempted robbery.'

'Was there anything engraved inside the ring?'

'"Love Rita."'

'What was his wife's name?'

'Mary.'

Reggie poured himself a cup of tea. 'Anything else I should know?'

'Cornelius Stout went missing mid-1921. The odd thing is that his older brother is missing too. Disappeared around June 1919. Edmund Stout. Lived alone. Wealthy like his brother. Still hasn't turned up. Given what happened to Cornelius, we could have a murderer who killed both of them.' He studied his pipe then took another puff. 'Once I clear the decks of some of my cases, I'll take another look at that file.'

'If you examined both cases together, you might find a clue common to both.'

'That's true. Trouble is, we're short-staffed. Angus Murray and Squizzy Taylor take up most of my time.'

Reggie nodded. 'Understandable. How's the new boss going?'

O'Flanagan growled, his jaw jutting forward. 'Him? Chief Commissioner Nicholson? I tell you, Reggie, things are bad. He's appointed four "special supervisors"—essentially spies—to supervise the boys on the beat. It's causing a lot of resentment. If the Chief Commissioner doesn't call them off soon, there will be serious repercussions.'

'Can't say I blame them for getting upset. Being watched at work? Not good.'

'There's more. Every other state has a pension scheme, but not Victoria. We're paid less than the coppers in New South Wales and our hours are longer. The lads even have to buy their own uniforms. It's not right. But does Nicholson listen? No. I tell you, Reggie, our boys are at breaking point.'

Reggie pushed away his cup and saucer. 'Getting back to Cornelius Stout, I'd like to talk to the son. Got an address?'

O'Flanagan put down his pipe and picked at his teeth with a long fingernail. 'As long as you share everything with me.' He jotted the address on the back of the sheet listing the tenants. 'Henry Stout is clearing out his father's house. You'll probably find him there.' He put on his hat. 'Must go. Remember the rules. Share and share alike.'

'Thanks, mate.'

O'Flanagan stood. 'Good to see you, Reggie. By the way, you have a spot of butter on your tie.'

He walked off, chuckling to himself.

Chapter Seven

That night, after he had finished dinner and his mother had retired to her boudoir (as she characterised it), Reggie wrote up his notes from his meeting with Detective Sergeant O'Flanagan. That done, he turned his attention to the task entrusted to him by Dotty Wright. Life was a delicate juggling act, keeping both his boss and his mother happy.

Reggie poured himself a whisky. He pulled down the blinds in the parlour and turned his attention to the personal possessions of Eric Smith.

The box itself was a curiosity. It was carved from dark, almost black, wood with two brass hinges, and an elaborate lock and key. It was approximately twelve inches long, six inches high, and eight inches deep. Game birds had been carved in high relief on the top, while floral decorations adorned the four sides.

Reggie lifted the lid and carefully picked over the contents that lay within, studying each. The documents themselves were a hodgepodge: Smith's birth certificate, a receipt for a new suit and shoes, some newspaper clippings, a cargo inventory for the N.D.L. steamship *Lothringen*, and the title to the grocer's shop in Richmond.

At the bottom of the box were two photographs. The first one he'd seen. It was of Eric Smith, on the deck of *The Gudrun*. The second was presumably a family portrait. In the front row was a young Eric, in his teens, standing alongside what were most certainly his parents and two brothers, given the resemblance. Both photographs showed evidence of being handled regularly: they were creased and yellow.

Reggie took out a notepad and pen. He smoothed out the birth certificate and studied it. At the top of a blank page, he wrote:

- Eric Smith. Born June 4, 1873. Ballarat, Victoria.
- Died October 2, 1923. Aged 50 years.
- Photograph. Family group. c.1890.
- Photograph. *The Gudrun*. Barge. Lübeck, Germany. 1900. Smith aged about 27?
- *Lothingren*. Inventory. February 10, 1914. Sailor? Smith aged about 41?
- Title to grocer's shop Richmond. September 1917.

The newspaper clippings covered a period of years, including a couple of advertisements from the Classifieds and some newspaper reports.

Reggie put the documents back in the wooden box and placed it on the bookshelf. He took up his Waterman fountain pen and a piece of creamy cartridge paper, then wrote a quick letter to Theo Georgiou, his contact in the Registry for Births, Deaths, and Marriages. In it, he asked if the details on Smith's birth certificate could be authenticated. He sealed the envelope and put it in his jacket pocket. Tomorrow, the office boy could take the letter to the registry. If anyone could validate Eric Smith's birth certificate, it was Theo.

For now, he could put the matter of the grocer aside, having made a start on Miss Wright's 'mystery.' He doubted whether it was even worth pursuing, most probably a total waste of time, but placating his mother by pleasing Miss Wright was a necessary evil. Feeling satisfied with himself, he sat back in his chair and put his mind to solving a much more intriguing question: 'Who killed Cornelius Stout?'

Chapter Eight

If Reggie da Costa thought he'd have trouble organising a meeting with Henry Stout, Cornelius's son, he was in for a big surprise. There was a message on his desk from that very person inviting him to meet up on Wednesday at East Melbourne.

Two days later, Reggie stood outside the former home of Cornelius Stout, in Albert Street. The house was a double-fronted, brick Victorian residence, built in the 1880s, with an ornate iron gate leading onto a tiled front verandah fringed with lacework. A bay window and two highly decorative parapets announced that this was a home for the wealthy. But first impressions were misleading. Looking closer, Reggie noticed the cracks in the façade, the peeling paint, and the rusty guttering. The small front garden was overgrown and neglected.

Reggie stepped up onto the verandah. The large oak front door was wide open. From within he could hear someone whistling. He rapped on the door and waited.

'Come in,' called a voice from inside the house.

Reggie stood on the threshold, peering in. The wide hallway, with its original hardwood floorboards and fourteen-foot ceilings edged with elaborate cornices, had once been a feature of the house, but not now. It was in an advanced state of disrepair. He went inside.

It was the smell that struck him first. Not just musty. More that of damp, mould, and decay. Above him, the ceiling was stained and peeling from where the rain had come in. On each side of the hallway, old books and catalogues were stacked against the walls. Boxes full of junk were propped perilously on top of each other, threatening to spill their contents across the floor. A narrow twisting path, amongst the hodgepodge of miscellanea, snaked through to the back of the house. Reggie shook his head in disbelief.

He paused and studied the once formal drawing room to his right. The curtains were drawn, but even in the gloom, he could see that every inch of space was filled with junk. Bound stacks of newspapers were piled up against the windows, while clothing was heaped on the sideboard and on the occasional tables. A makeshift bed, almost invisible amongst the clutter, had been made up on the couch. In every nook and cranny were piles of odd shoes. It crossed Reggie's mind that finding a matching pair would be a trial.

He proceeded down the hallway, stepping gingerly over old biscuit tins, bottles, jars, and bags of refuse. On the left was the first of three large bedrooms, with a marble fireplace and large mahogany wardrobe. Bicycle parts and their rusted frames covered the threadbare Turkish carpet. A tired-looking, wooden rocking horse lay on its side, its right eye staring mournfully up at the ceiling.

He passed a central bathroom, its floor given over to piles of old newspapers and magazines, tied up with string. Incongruously, pots and pans and kitchen utensils spilled over the edge of the bath.

'I'm in the kitchen,' called the voice. 'Out the back.'

Reggie moved slowly down the hallway. A one-eyed teddy bear, propped up against a doorway, watched him pass. Within an adjacent room, old toys, broken and unloved, lay next to trunks filled with hats. Legless tables and chairs, treadle sewing machines, and a pile of dirty blankets filled the remaining space. He caught a whiff of cat piss as he entered the lean-to that was the kitchen.

A man was on his hands and knees, peering into a cupboard. A packet of Rough on Rats was on the counter. He looked over his shoulder at Reggie.

'Rats. I'm laying bait.'

'I don't doubt it. The place stinks.'

'It's the cats. I evicted them and now, the rats are back. I think Dad lost his sense of smell living here.'

The door leading to the backyard had been thrown open, allowing fresh air to dissipate some of the stench.

'You're Henry Stout?'

'You must be Reggie da Costa.'

The younger man wiped his hands on a towel and shook hands with him. It gave Reggie his first chance to take a good look at the deceased's son. Henry was in his mid-twenties, small of frame, and wiry. He had a jutting jaw and thick, dark eyebrows which were almost knitted together. He was wearing a pair of dirty overalls and a khaki shirt.

'I read that you found my father.'

'That's right. You wanted to see me?'

'I do. I want you to find out who killed him.'

Henry's forthrightness took him by surprise.

'He's been missing for a while,' Reggie commented.

'Over two years. It was such a shock when I heard you found him,' confessed Henry. 'Since June 1921, we've not had a letter, not a phone call. I thought he'd taken off. And this mausoleum he lived in, empty all that time. Well, not empty. Full of rubbish.'

'Who benefits from the will?'

'My sister, Lily. She inherits the house and most of the money. Nothing strange about that. She looked after him as best she could. He also left a small amount to the animal welfare people. Funny that! I saw him kick a dog once.'

'You miss out on the inheritance? Why was that?'

Henry frowned. 'I've always been a disappointment to him. Not cutthroat enough for Dad. I'm with the Railways. I never had the desire to follow in my father's footsteps. He never forgave me for that.' He shrugged his shoulders. 'The final straw for him was when we argued over his business dealings.'

'About what specifically?'

'I had a friend who went bankrupt,' Henry explained. 'Stanley Duggan. It was Dad's fault. He talked him into investing in a property deal that went bad. My friend was left with nothing. Dad didn't take well to criticism. Of

31

course, he got out before the sky fell, his money intact. That was my father for you.' He frowned. 'Look, I'm not proud of the way I acted towards him, but the fact was that he looked after himself, no one else. Selfish bastard.'

Reggie wiped down a chair with his handkerchief and sat down. 'I'm trying to build up a picture of your father. Did he have any enemies?'

'How many do you want? Failed business partners. Women he met.'

'What happened to your mother?'

'She died just after the War. Spanish flu. 1919.'

'I'm sorry.'

'She was lucky.'

Reggie was surprised by Henry's candour and his willingness to answer questions. It was a quality that he rarely met with in his role as crime reporter unless, of course, the interviewees were attention-seekers wanting publicity. He felt a glimmer of excitement. Along with the information provided by O'Flanagan, Henry might even provide him with some leads.

'Your sister was on good terms with your father?'

'She cared about Dad, despite his limitations. And she cared about me. Lily's my twin sister. She was very upset when he took me out of the will. She tried to talk him into taking me back, but he wouldn't have a bar of it. To be honest, I really couldn't be bothered. I didn't want his money, if I had to crawl for it.'

'You miss out completely?'

'No. Lily is sharing the proceeds of the estate with me. Twins, as I said. Dad would turn over in his grave if he knew.'

'You know the police will be taking a close look at you. Have you anything to say in your defence?'

'My life is an open book. I have nothing to hide. That's why I want you to look into it. To prove we have nothing to do with Dad's death.'

'Your sister. Can I meet her?'

Henry brightened visibly. 'Of course, you can, but she's away. She's a secretary. She's in Ballarat with her boss for a week.'

'Could you give her my card? Ask her to call me when she gets back?'

'Don't see why not.' Henry Stout took the reporter's card and put it on the

32

table. 'Is that all?'

'Did your father know someone called Rita?'

'Rita? She was his lady friend for a while.'

Reggie felt a quiver of excitement pass through him. 'Did you ever meet her?'

Henry shook his head. 'I heard through Lily that she was a pushy woman. Liked money. Dad was never keen on sharing. I think that's why they broke up.' He paused as a thought occurred to him. 'There might be something amongst Dad's papers that could help you.'

Reggie smiled. 'Do you mind if I take a look at them? There may be some clues as to the identity of the killer.'

'Help yourself. In fact, you can take them away, but don't throw them out. The police might want another look at them. There are three boxes. They're in the second bedroom. It's on the right. Lily and I have been through them already and picked out the important stuff. The police have already had a look, not that they spent much time on them. Dad never threw anything out.'

Reggie looked around him. 'What are you going to do with this place?'

'Neither of us wants it. We're putting it to auction once probate is finished. The second-hand dealers are coming in next week. There are a few decent pieces of furniture under all this rubbish. They can have that. The rest will be given to charity or taken away to the tip.'

Reggie shook his head as he surveyed the mess. 'I don't envy you.'

Henry shrugged again and turned his attention back to the inside of the cupboard.

Reggie found the second bedroom and forced the door back to clear a path. Suitcases filled with old clothes were stacked on top of each other. Three boxes full of miscellanea and documents were shoved against the wall. He sighed heavily and proceeded to carry them out to his car, then brushed the dust off his suit, and made his way back to the kitchen. Henry Stout was sitting at the kitchen table, drinking from a bottle of whisky.

'Can I pour you one?' he asked, offering a fresh glass. 'It's clean.'

Reggie laughed. 'Why not?'

'How he lived here, I'll never know,' said Henry. 'I always thought we'd find his body under a pile of garbage.' He laughed mirthlessly. 'Never thought he'd be murdered. He was an old bastard, to tell you the truth, but to die like that? It's wrong. He was still my flesh and blood. I'd like to help you, if I can.'

'I'll keep it in mind. Good luck.'

Reggie finished the whisky and took a couple of steps down the hallway. He turned back. 'Have you ever been to the Punt Road terrace?'

'Where Dad died?' Henry shook his head. 'Never been there.'

Reggie nodded. If he weren't mistaken, there had been a slight hesitation before Henry Stout had answered in the negative.

Chapter Nine

Reggie stood outside The Rose Hotel in Fitzroy, waiting for Theo Georgiou to arrive. He tapped his foot impatiently. It was past four and it would be impossible to find a quiet spot inside if he didn't come soon. Over the years, Theo, from the Department of Births, Deaths, and Marriages, had been invaluable in filling in the gaps of information Reggie needed when researching his cases.

At last, he saw the portly figure of his friend heading towards him.

'Sorry, I couldn't get away,' said Theo, mopping his brow. They shook hands and went inside.

'This hotel is a landmark,' said Theo. 'When I was young, I used to come here with my father and listen when he'd talk football. Look at all the memorabilia on the walls. The ghosts of football teams past. Not only that,' he added, 'the beer's cold.'

A few drinkers turned their heads to watch the arrival of the newcomers. The two men couldn't have been more dissimilar. Theo was short, solidly built, with dark, deep-set eyes, white thinning hair, and an untidy, thick moustache. He was conservatively dressed in a well-worn grey serge suit. Reggie, on the other hand, was stylish, with his shiny black hair immaculately coiffed, and his thin moustache trimmed in the style of Ronald Colman. His three-piece suit was light-blue and double-breasted. They walked past the horseshoe-shaped bar and found a table towards the back of the room.

'How about a beer? My shout,' said Reggie. He headed to the bar and returned shortly, holding two lagers.

'Thanks, mate,' Theo said, quaffing his beer. 'I needed that.' He smacked his lips with satisfaction.

'Well, what have you got for me?'

'Not a lot, I'm afraid. I knew it might be hard given the surname. Smith. There are hundreds of them out there. But giving me the place and date of birth certainly helped.'

'You found him?'

'I found an Eric Smith, born June 4, 1873, in Ballarat. My next step was to cross-check the death certificates and I found him there, too. He didn't live long. Died in 1881. Only eight years old.'

'But that suggests—'

'That your Eric Smith wasn't born in Ballarat at all.'

Reggie stroked his moustache. 'Dotty Wright won't be happy about this. A dead end.'

'Not so fast, old man. Births came up with two other Eric Smiths who were born on that day, but not in Ballarat. It's extremely unusual but I thought that there may have been a mistake recording the place of birth. The second Eric Smith, born on the 4th of June, 1873, came from Bendigo. I cross-checked Deaths. He never came back from the Great War. Missing in action. That left a third Eric Smith, born in Clifton Hill. I checked the electoral rolls and found him. He's alive and living in Kew. I can give you his address if you like, but don't say how you got it. I'd lose my job!'

Their conversation was halted by the angry comments of a man at the bar, who was pointing at Reggie.

'Bloody Italians! You can't get into America so you come here instead. Taking our jobs.' He spat on the floor. 'Peasants, that's what you are.'

Reggie stood; his fists clenched. 'A peasant? Me? Look at you! I wouldn't be seen dead in those trousers. If you must know, I was born here.'

The man took a step forward. 'We need British migrants, not you bloody Macaroni.' He caught sight of Theo and shook his fist. 'Bloody Greeks too. Go home. Sitting on the bloody fence in the bloody war.'

He moved threateningly towards them.

The bartender came out from behind the bar and laid a hand on the man's shoulder. 'I suggest you leave now before I call the coppers. It was nice and quiet here before you turned up. I don't want no trouble. Now, out you go.'

The man left reluctantly, swearing loudly.

'You see it all the time,' said Theo. 'Intolerant bastards. I've been here for years. What do you have to do to be accepted in this bloody country?' He shook his head in disgust. 'Now, where were we?'

'Eric Smith,' said Reggie. 'Is that all you can tell me?'

'Nearly there. Five other Eric Smiths were born on the 4th of June, 1873. They all had middle names, unlike your man. Not one of them was born in Ballarat.'

Reggie shook his head in disappointment. 'I told her it was a wild goose chase. Sorry to waste your time, Theo. How about another beer?'

'No, I'll have to get on. On second thought, you don't have the birth certificate here, do you?'

'As a matter of fact, I do.' Reggie took the document out of his bag.

'No doubt about it,' said Theo, rubbing his thumb against the paper and examining the typeface. 'It's a fake, and not a particularly convincing one at that. The paper isn't the type we use.' He pointed to a column. 'The date of birth is in the wrong place too. It looks legitimate to the untrained eye, but not to someone who handles birth certificates regularly. Unfortunately, your Eric Smith used an assumed name.'

'So how would he get this?' asked Reggie.

'There's a black market in identity documents, dating from the War. A good forger can make a lot of money. The man who made this would most likely have checked through death certificates to find someone with a birth-date to suit the purchaser. A common name makes it easier, as in this case. There are lots of Smiths around, so you'd be unlikely to come across a relative who might prove that you were a fake. The counterfeiter effectively rebirths the dead man, and no one is the wiser.'

'That means that Eric Smith was someone else.'

'In a sense, yes. Your Mr Smith is, but the real Eric Smith is buried in a graveyard somewhere.'

Reggie contemplated the bogus birth certificate and shook his head. 'I appreciate this, Theo. I owe you one.'

'Sorry I couldn't be of more help. And thanks for the beer.'

They shook hands and parted company.

Reggie took one more look at the birth certificate. 'How can I trace you, if I don't even know who you really were?'

Chapter Ten

It was just over a week since Eric Smith's funeral. On Saturday afternoon, armed with the information provided by Theo Georgiou, Reggie decided that it was time to pay Dotty Wright a visit.

She lived in a neat little worker's cottage, inherited from her parents, next door to the grocery shop. There were flowers growing in pots in the tiny front garden, and the tiled porch had been swept recently. Reggie knocked on the door, stood back, and waited.

Dotty Wright answered the front door and smiled at him. 'Mr da Costa, you must have some news.'

'Not what you're expecting, I'm afraid. And please, call me Reggie.'

'Reggie, it is. And you may call me Dotty.' She paused on the front porch. 'I'm going to the cinema. *The Glimpses of the Moon*. Bebe Daniels is in it. You could walk me to the bus stop, if you like.'

Reggie looked her up and down. The change in her appearance was startling. Gone was the black dress that had leached the colour from Dotty's cheeks, replaced by an emerald green satin dress with a dropped waist. Cream lace on the neckline and a wide-brimmed hat trimmed with green ribbon framed her face. Her short red hair had been crimped and just covered her ears. Miss Dotty Wright looked rather nice, even if she were too old for him.

With a green-checked overcoat slung over her arm, Dotty picked up her handbag from the hall table. 'Come on. If we hurry, I'll have time for a cuppa before it starts.'

Reggie raised an eyebrow. He wasn't used to being bossed around.

As they walked, he glanced her way. She was quite attractive really, not severe at all. Probably early thirties, slightly over five feet in height, with what one would describe as a 'womanly' figure.

'What do you do for a living? I assume you work?' he asked her.

'Teacher. Senior mistress at Richmond State School. Do you know it?'

'Vaguely. I'm not from around this area.'

'I thought you lived here.'

'Temporary. It's temporary.' He looked her up and down. 'You don't act like a senior mistress. Or dress like one.'

'I'll take that as a compliment. Did you find out anything about Eric?'

'I'm still not sure who he was.'

He explained how Theo Georgiou, at the Registry of Births, Deaths, and Marriages, had searched through the records and found that the birth certificate was a fake.

Dotty frowned. 'Are you saying that Eric took on an assumed identity? That muddies the waters.'

'I'm afraid so. Why he did that, I don't know yet. But I have a few other leads to follow.' He paused, considering his next words. 'Are you sure that you want me to continue with this? I mean, is there any point?'

She stopped and glared at him. 'What do you mean?'

Reggie studied her. There was a distinct edge to her voice. He found her reaction irritating. After all, he was a reporter for *The Argus*, not some silly lackey who had the time to run around on pointless errands, investigating a man who did not exist. And doing it for a woman who was stupid enough to refuse a nice little inheritance.

'Far be it from me to tell you what to do—'

She cut him off. 'Then don't,' she replied. 'I'll do it myself. You obviously have no understanding of the ethical issues involved.'

Reggie sniggered.

Dotty turned on him, her face red with anger. 'Why did you agree to help me? Were you forced into it?'

Reggie was silent.

'So that's it. Your mother told you to. How embarrassing for you.'

It was Reggie's turn to go red. Before he had a chance to reply, the bus rounded the corner and pulled into the curb, a few feet ahead of them.

'Here's my bus,' she said, rummaging in her handbag for her purse. 'I won't ask you to join me. Goodbye, Mr da Costa.'

Reggie watched grim-faced as the bus pulled away. Mother would not be amused when she heard what he had done. Feeling wretched, he headed home.

Chapter Eleven

Working through the boxes of documents from Stout's East Melbourne home took time. Reggie devoted most of Sunday to examining and considering their contents. He was constantly amazed at Cornelius Stout's capacity to retain records of insignificant transactions. There were receipts for purchases of grocery items, clothing, furniture, and accommodation going back over ten years. None of it was in any order. Reggie chuckled as he read the advertisement that Stout had posted in the local newspaper requesting the services of a housekeeper. Attached to it were the responses he had received from women who could have no idea of the mess that awaited them in the East Melbourne home.

Letters, from relatives, business acquaintances, and friends, were interspersed with quotations for maintenance work, information on bank interest rates, and newspaper articles on subjects as diverse as property auctions and wool prices. It was hard to see if any of this confusing mishmash of documentation bore any relevance to the man's death.

At the top of the third box were letters from Stout's son and daughter, bound in a blue ribbon. Reggie was surprised that Henry had allowed him to take them. Perhaps they had gone unnoticed? He rested them on the arm of his chair. After pouring himself a Scotch, Reggie read them carefully, trying to gain an insight into the relationship between Henry, Lily, and their father.

There were two letters from Henry to his father, angry letters that deplored Cornelius Stout's lack of morality in his business dealings, and his blatant disregard for the wellbeing of those he had damaged by his actions. They were blunt and to the point. Reading them, Reggie was not surprised that Stout had reacted badly. But then came a third letter, dated just before Cornelius's disappearance, in which Henry lamented the breakdown of their relationship and asked if they could be reconciled.

Given that there were no letters from Cornelius, he could only imagine the nature of his response to his son's criticism. Reggie sensed that Cornelius Stout was a harsh man who dwelled on the wrongs done to him. No doubt, he had believed himself unfairly judged by his son, and cut him off from his inheritance as a result. Yet, he had kept the letters and bound them in a blue ribbon, which seemed to indicate that they were precious to him. Had Henry's last letter pricked his conscience and made him reconsider restoring his son as heir alongside his daughter? The answer to that question would never be known.

Lily had also written to her father. The first was dated May 1921, a month or so before Cornelius had disappeared. She and her father had seen the stage production of *Cousin Kate* and had enjoyed it.

Reggie smiled. He had taken his mother to the same play for her birthday.

Lily went on to say that she lamented that her brother had not been invited. It was important to her that they become a proper family again. She believed that Henry had not intended to insult his father, but was moved by strong feelings of loyalty towards the friend who had been sent bankrupt.

In a second letter, written a week later, Lily pointed out that father and son tended to be headstrong and of similar temperament, although their choices of occupation could not have been more different. A speculator and a clerk. Surely it was possible to respect each other, even if there were disagreements between them? They were family, after all.

She referred to Stout's lady friend and how she had alienated him from his children. Now that the relationship was over, Lily wrote, could not the three of them rediscover the bond that once existed between them? But Reggie knew that her words had been in vain. Henry had been cut out of the will despite the erstwhile entreaties of his sister.

Reggie re-tied the blue ribbon and put the letters aside. Then he sorted through the rest of the documents, putting them into four different categories: business letters; personal communication from friends and family; newspaper articles and advertisements; quotations, receipts, and invoices.

There were also two photographs. One was of the family: Cornelius, his wife, and the twins, aged about three years. The second was of Cornelius, Henry, and Lily in happier times, about five years before. There was a family resemblance there; all were dark-haired, small of stature, and finely built. He put that photograph in his pocketbook. It might prove useful, he thought, in the future.

Satisfied that he had gained an insight into the lives of the Stout family, Reggie gulped down another glass of Scotch and headed to bed. As he folded the bedspread carefully and placed it on the chair, his mind returned to his spat with Dotty Wright. Within days, Mavis would meet up again with Mildred Bardsley Smith at some social get-together or other, where she would hear, to her great displeasure, that Reggie had insulted Dotty, Mildred's niece. Then there would be the often-repeated reminders that Mrs Bardsley Smith's social circle might give him access to a wife, one with money and social standing. Predictably, in a *coup de grâce*, his mother would remind him, in that irritating and mournful tone of voice, 'You're not getting any younger, Reggie.'

He gritted his teeth and climbed into bed.

Chapter Twelve

Detective Sergeant Michael O'Flanagan's prediction, that dissatisfaction in police ranks would erupt, came to pass. Just before ten o'clock on Friday night, the 31st of October 1923, the Victoria Police went on strike. And, it was the actions of a lowly police constable, William Brooks, that precipitated the refusal to go on duty. Outraged by the presence of Chief Commissioner Nicholson's 'Spooks,' a squad of twenty-four constables at the Russell Street Police Headquarters went on strike, calling for the withdrawal of the 'spies' within their ranks and the re-introduction of a pension plan. Within hours, hundreds more police had joined them, leaving Melbourne protected by only a skeleton police force.

First thing Saturday morning, Floyd Kramer, Reggie's boss, directed all available reporters to hit the streets. Reggie, accompanied by Sid, his photographer, positioned himself at the intersection of Bourke and Swanston Streets, which was soon packed with strikers, larrikins, and curious citizens. All traffic had been blocked from entering the centre of the city.

As the day wore on, the mood became ugly. Reggie and his colleague watched on, documenting the strike. Around them, the streets teemed with thousands of people. The word had spread that Melbourne was effectively unprotected. Reggie took notes which would form the basis of his report, while Sid recorded the mayhem with his camera.

At five o'clock in the evening, with the closure of the pubs imminent, the numbers swelled. Hundreds of drunken patrons, armed with beer bottles, arrived ready to join in the fun, their emotions spilling over.

'Watch out, Sid!' yelled Reggie as a bottle sailed past him, then exploded into fragments at the photographer's feet. Pieces of glass were hurled indiscriminately into the crowd. A woman ran past Reggie, her face streaming with blood.

'Get back. They're starting to riot.'

Sid and Reggie retreated to a safe distance. Elevated on the steps at the entrance to a large department store, they were in the perfect position to see all the action.

'Get a photograph of that!' Reggie pointed his finger as the mob moved in and derailed a tram.

'Bloody hell,' responded Sid. 'They're setting it on fire. This is out of control.'

Fights were breaking out. Two blokes were facing up to each other, fists raised. The smaller one was felled by a wild punch and lay screaming on the ground as the pack moved in, kicking him savagely. His cries for help were lost in the sounds of screams, chants, and foul language.

The mob turned their attention to the shops on Bourke Street. Yelling and gesticulating, they aimed bricks and stones at the large windows of The Leviathan men's clothing store. Glass was smashed, and the rioters burst in through the opening, grabbing the display items in the shopfront window.

From out of nowhere, three brave constables, brandishing batons, charged at the looters, attempting to drive them off. The chant went up: 'Scabs! Scabs!' The mob pushed back; the police drastically outnumbered were forced to retreat as the rioters yelled obscenities and hurled missiles at them. A cheer went up as the police sought shelter in a shop.

The mob erupted again. More store windows were smashed. Jewellery shops were targeted and ransacked. A man ran past Sid, clutching suits and shirts. A rough-looking fellow, wearing khaki army pants, stuck out his foot and tripped him up, then took off with a pair of trousers. Fights were breaking out as the looters fought each other for the spoils.

Reggie shook his head in disbelief. 'This beats the Red Flag riots in Brisbane. I thought they were bad! There's no purpose to this. It's violence for its own sake.' He grinned. 'But it makes for a good story!' A warning shot rang out. 'Here come the coppers.'

Reinforcements of police arrived at last. They waded into the middle of the drunken mob, oblivious to their own safety. They whirled around, cracking heads with their batons, making arrests, ignoring the cries of 'Bloody scabs' which were directed at them.

'Reggie,' called Sid, pointing into the crowd, 'look at that poor sheila.'

The reporter followed the line of his finger and saw a woman being pushed back and forth. Her emerald green dress was torn, strips of cream lace hanging from her bodice. Her red hair was a tangled mess; her make-up streaked with tears. A cold wave of recognition flooded over him. It was Dotty Wright.

'Bloody hell!' Reggie dropped his notebook, jumped down the steps, and waded into the crowd, using his elbows to gain traction and to push against the surging mass of people. The smell of body odour, foul breath, and stale beer was overwhelming. It was like being in a roiling tub of filthy, stinking water. Someone knocked Reggie's hat off and he saw, to his dismay, his expensive homburg trampled beneath people's feet. He swore and gritted his teeth.

Now that he was down with the masses, he had lost sight of Dotty. A brawl broke out next to him, a woman screamed, and punches were thrown. He dodged past, avoiding getting caught up in the mêlée. He took a deep breath and shoved hard, forcing his way through the crush. In front of him, a drunken man lay sprawled on a bench, snoring, an empty beer bottle pressed against his chest, oblivious to the cacophony of sound around him. Reggie jumped up next to him, searching the crowd for signs of Dotty's red hair. And then he saw her, about five yards away.

He jumped down into the seething mass of people, letting himself be dragged along in her direction, hoping that she wouldn't be driven even further from him.

A shot was fired. Someone screamed. The police were shooting over the heads of the mob. Men swore and shouted, showing their defiance. A man shoved Reggie hard, but he managed to stay upright, so tightly packed was the crowd. It was getting dangerous. If he didn't find Dotty soon, he risked being shot, arrested, or attacked. He ducked left then right, like a prizefighter, then pushed through, feeling the resistance against him dissipate.

And then he saw a flash of red hair in front of him, not two yards away.

'Dotty!' he yelled.

Her face turned towards him. He saw the spark of recognition in her eyes. 'Reggie, help me!'

Next to her was a weasel of a man, an evil grin on his face as he lunged towards her. But he didn't see Reggie's fist until it was too late. Next thing, he was sprawled on the ground, flat on his back. The crowd surged forward. His cries were lost in the uproar as he was trampled beneath their feet.

Reggie grabbed Dotty and pulled her to him. 'Come on, old girl. Let's get you out of here.'

He put a protective arm around her and, sheltering her with his own body, forced his way through the throng.

Another volley of shots rang out. The police were firing over the heads of the crowd again. It started a stampede. Reggie saw a break and made for open space, half-carrying Dotty. He was just in time.

Motor patrols, stacked with citizens sworn in to fulfil the role of constables in times of crisis, had arrived and were driving straight at the mob, scattering them in all directions. Some of the rioters panicked and ran off in the direction of Flinders Street station. The police leaped down from their vehicles and took off after them, arresting those who weren't fast enough to escape.

Safe on the other side of the intersection, Reggie gently lowered Dotty onto the step of a shopfront. He leaned against the wall, catching his breath, then took a good look at her. She was exhausted, her eyes closed, her face smudged with tears and makeup. Her dress was ruined, her shoes gone, and her stockings ripped.

'Take some deep breaths,' he said, taking off his jacket and putting it around her shoulders. 'Only a bit further and we'll be at the car.'

He glanced over his shoulder, watching the result of the police charge. The mob was dispersing, battered and bruised, but still showing signs of defiance. His report on the strike would make great copy in the next morning's *Argus*.

He hoped that Sid had captured some of the action on film.

Reggie turned his attention back to Dotty. She was breathing heavily, her head sunk on her chest. Reggie lifted her up and supported her around the waist. She was limping badly, favouring her right leg. Slowly, they made their way back to where Sid was waiting.

'I got some terrific pictures,' said the photographer, a huge smile on his face, ignoring Reggie's companion. 'Page one, for sure!'

'Leave it till later, will you?' Reggie snarled. 'Help me with Dotty.'

The two of them carried her to Reggie's automobile, which was parked well away from the riot.

Reggie opened the door and slid across the seat to the driver's side. Sid helped Dotty into the passenger seat and closed the door. He leaned in. 'I'll meet you back here tomorrow.'

Reggie nodded and started the car. 'Are you alright, Dotty?'

She grimaced. 'I think I've broken my ankle.'

'What on earth were you doing there?'

She flushed angrily and glared at him. 'Don't blame me. I didn't know about the strike. I was supposed to be meeting a friend in the city when I got caught up in the riot. I started back towards Flinders Street station, but it was too late by then. I couldn't get away.'

'Should I take you to hospital?'

'No, it will be bedlam there. Take me to Aunt Mildred's, please.'

'If that's what you want. She'll be horrified when she sees you.' He put the Citroen into first gear.

She put her hand on his arm. 'Reggie—'

'What is it?'

'If I'm honest, I never wanted to see you again. I thought you were superficial, selfish, and vain.'

Reggie raised his eyebrows. 'And I thought you were opinionated and unwomanly.'

'Perhaps I am, but I haven't finished.' She took her hand away. 'I admit I was wrong about you. You saved my life. I would have been trampled alive if you hadn't turned up. You were very brave.'

'Thank you.' He paused, considering his next words. 'I'll concede that we got off on the wrong foot with each other in the beginning. Let's put that behind us now.' Then he grinned at her. 'You cost me a hat, you know.'

Dotty chuckled, despite the pain. 'Send me the bill. Then again, I probably couldn't afford it. But there's one more thing.'

Reggie looked at her warily. 'And what would that be?'

'You've got a great left hook.'

Chapter Thirteen

MOB VIOLENCE IN CITY
RIOTING AND LOOTING
RESULT OF POLICE MUTINY
ORDER RESTORED

By REGGIE DA COSTA, Senior Crime Reporter

T he Premier has announced measures to restore law and order to Melbourne. State Cabinet is to introduce a Public Safety Bill into the State Parliament tomorrow, ensuring that firm action is taken against police mutineers.

The damage wrought by the police mutiny has been far-reaching. Approximately 100,000 people clogged the streets of Melbourne after the police went on strike. Casualties from the mob violence are estimated to be about 200, arrests are calculated to be in the hundreds, and looting and damage to shops amounts to thousands of pounds.

The Government has taken action to combat the violence. More than 8,000 men were enrolled as special constables at the Town Hall, while other men are still being accepted in the suburbs. More than 1,000 private motorcars have been offered for the use of the police during the mutiny. On Sunday, hotels were closed at two o'clock to prevent further instances of drunken mayhem.

Bayonets and ammunition at the ready!

All military leave has been cancelled. Soldiers and sailors have been directed to guard the banks, Treasury, Government House, and other public buildings. A detachment of 200 men from Queenscliff Garrison Artillery and Engineers has been sent to Victoria Barracks, each man supplied with a rifle fitted with a bayonet and 200 rounds of ammunition.

On Sunday night, a detachment of ex-Australian Light Horsemen, who fought at Gallipoli, Beersheba, and the Western Front, rode into the city to patrol the streets of Melbourne and keep the peace.

Many shopkeepers have erected barricades to guard their shop windows against a possible further outbreak of lawlessness. In spite of the request of the authorities, there were more than the usual crowds in the streets of Melbourne yesterday, but they were in the main, orderly.

The courage and determination shown by the loyal police and the special constables, as well as the untiring work of the ambulance men, are the only cheering features in this, the darkest page of Melbourne's history.

[*The Argus* November 6, 1923]

Reggie was putting the finishing touches to his report on the police strike when the telephone rang.

'A woman wants to speak to you, Reggie. Putting her through.'

'Hello. Reggie da Costa. Crime desk. Can I help you?'

A cool voice came down the line. 'It's Lily Stout here. I'm back from Ballarat.'

Chapter Fourteen

Reggie met Lily Stout outside the boarding house where she lived in East Melbourne, a half-mile from her father's house. She was small, like her brother, with grey eyes framed by long dark lashes, and lustrous, black hair cut into a fashionable bob. Her stylish dress, with its sash tied at the hip, was cobalt blue, which suited her colouring and accentuated her slim boyish frame. Her cloche hat was also trimmed with a touch of blue, tying in very nicely with her dress. Reggie's eyes moved down to her feet, noting her fashionable navy-blue shoes with their silver straps. He was impressed.

'Let's sit in the park,' she suggested.

They crossed the road and found a bench seat under a sprawling Moreton Bay fig.

'May I offer my commiserations?' said Reggie, edging closer. 'It's been very hard for you lately.'

'That's very kind of you, Mr da Costa.'

'Reggie. Call me Reggie.' He removed his fedora and stroked his moustache. He had dressed with care, as always, selecting a single-breasted brown herringbone-patterned suit, which coordinated with his bold striped tie and matching pocket square.

She smiled, showing perfect white teeth. 'Reggie, it is. I'm familiar with your reputation as a crusader when it comes to solving crime.'

'Without the chain mail and sword.'

Lily laughed. 'You're making fun of me.' She looked up at him through her thick dark lashes. 'Henry said you have some questions about our father.

I want to help you. Whatever you want to know.' Her voice was low and buzzy.

Reggie felt rather disconcerted. He reached for his notepad and pen. 'I've been told that your relationship with your father was, for want of a better word, complex. But you were on speaking terms, unlike your brother. Did your father ever mention anyone in particular who might have wanted him dead?'

Lily cocked her head, as if she were making a decision. 'Dad was ... difficult. He had a temper. His former business partner and he argued a lot. Joshua Bentwhistle. Then there was Henry's friend, Stanley Duggan. Dad ruined him. But I couldn't imagine either of them killing him.'

Reggie jotted down the names in his notebook. 'What about women?'

Lily raised her eyes to heaven. 'Dad was terrible with the ladies. The truth is that most of the women he associated with would not have been welcome in respectable society.'

'Did Mr Stout have a lady friend?'

'There was one. I turned up unexpectedly at his house and she opened the door. A big woman, too much make-up, bleached hair. She looked like one of those tarts from St Kilda. I remember staring at her in shock, then she backed off and went into another room. I could hear her talking to Dad, and then he came out and asked me what I wanted. It was clear that I wasn't welcome, so I left.'

'Did you ask your father about her?'

'Dad told me later that he was sick of her. She was hanging around, wanting him to marry her, but he wouldn't have a bar of that. He broke off the relationship with her just before he went missing. Dad was the sort of man who couldn't be talked into doing something that he didn't want to do. He was a hard man.'

'What was her name?'

'Rita.' She nodded slowly. 'That sounds right.'

'Your father was wearing a ring engraved with that name.'

'I noticed a ring the last time I saw him.'

'Did you find out where she lived?'

'Dad never shared that with me.'

'She must have been angry when their relationship ended.'

'I would expect so.'

'You were hoping that your father and Henry would reconcile.'

She cocked her head on the side. 'How did you know that?'

'It was in your letters. Henry let me take them.'

Lily nodded. 'I suppose they may help you.'

Reggie referred to his notes. 'Detective Sergeant O'Flanagan said that your uncle, Edmund Stout, went missing in mid-1919. Can you tell me anything about that?'

'You're very thorough, aren't you? I can see you've done your homework on our family.'

Reggie cleared his throat. 'Your uncle?'

Lily lit a cigarette. 'Dad and his brother were quite close. They both liked money. But Uncle Eddie never married. Unlike Dad, he wasn't good with women. Dad used to tease him about it.'

'Did you have any theories about why Edmund went missing?'

She shook her head. 'We thought it was out of character. We couldn't explain it.'

'Where did he live?'

'In East Melbourne, two miles from Dad's place. We found his house locked up, like he'd gone away for a holiday. But Uncle Eddie didn't believe in holidays. Or banks. He paid the price. Someone had cleaned out the safe.'

'One more thing. Did you ever visit the terrace house where your father was found dead?'

Lily Stout didn't blink. 'Never been there.'

'What are you going to do with your inheritance, Miss Stout?'

'Lily. Call me, Lily.' She studied her nails. 'Share it with Henry. Resign from my job. Buy myself a new wardrobe, not these cheap imitations of Paris fashions.' She glanced disparagingly at her dress and flipped the hem with her fingers. 'In short, live in style.' She stared at Reggie, as if she were challenging him. 'How does that sound to you?'

'Right up my alley.'

'That's convenient. Must go, Reggie. See you again soon.'

She stood and smoothed down her dress, then gave him one last lingering look. Slowly, she sauntered back towards the boarding house, Reggie's eyes upon her.

He smiled and stroked his moustache. 'Nice, very nice.'

Chapter Fifteen

Reggie was a creature of habit. On Friday nights, he would eat at a little Italian restaurant in Melbourne, after work.

Mamma Lombardi's reminded him of his last visit to Sicily, just after the War. He had travelled its length and breadth, taking in the culture which was his birthright, given that was where he'd been conceived. 'Beneath the shadow of Mt Etna,' his father had whispered to him, when he'd imbibed more than was good for him.

Surrounded by white table cloths and napkins, the glow of candlelight which lit the restaurant, and the chatter of patrons, Reggie felt quite mellow as he waited for his dinner. A bit of light-hearted banter with Mamma was followed by a steaming bowl of pasta with Napoli sauce and a plate of crusty homemade bread. Pappa Lombardi insisted that Reggie partake of a glass of grappa, made in an illegal still in the backyard of their establishment.

The week had gone well, Reggie reflected. His meeting with Lily Stout had been productive, and the following day he had returned to the Punt Road terrace to interview the present tenant of the upstairs apartment, Frank Feely.

It was fortunate that Feely remembered Reggie from the day of the flood. He had invited him into the flat, the atmosphere of which was hot and stuffy. There was a fire burning in the grate, despite the fact that it was a warm day in November.

Frank Feely bent over and stoked the fire, then settled into a comfortable armchair placed strategically beside the window. It offered a good view of the street.

'I spend most days sitting here,' he confided. 'I watch people going about their business. I like to imagine who they are and what they do.'

Reggie took a good look at his host. Feely was wearing the same worn dressing gown and striped pyjamas that he had been wearing on the day of the flood. He appeared to be in his fifties, but could have been younger. Pale and drawn, Feely wheezed as he spoke. Despite his ill health, he was a cheerful man who clearly enjoyed having company.

'You've lived here long?'

'Over two years. I moved here in October 1921, after I was released from hospital.'

'What was wrong with you?'

'I was gassed. The War, you know.'

'You were in the War? Weren't you too old to enlist?'

'How old do you think I am?'

Reggie thought it wise to lower his estimation. 'Late forties?'

'I'm thirty-five.'

'Younger than me?' Reggie was shocked. Frank Feely looked like an old man in comparison.

'I was at Passchendaele in August 1917. The Germans were trying out a new chemical weapon, mustard gas. I was exposed to it.'

'What happened to you?'

'I didn't get my gas mask on in time. Even if I had, the vapour penetrates clothing. Excruciating. Skin irritation. Large blisters filled with pus. I ended up with fluid in the lungs. They said I should have died.'

'But you didn't.'

'Look at me now, the picture of health.' He laughed then hunched forward, gripped by a hacking cough. 'I try to make the best of what I have, but I live my life through others.' He nodded at the window of his apartment. 'Enough about me. What brings you here?'

'Can you tell me about the people who lived here?'

Frank Feely took a sip of water and cleared his throat.

'How about a cuppa first?'

Once the tea was made, strong and sweet, and he'd settled back into his armchair, Feely recounted what he knew about the tenants who had occupied the Punt Road property over the previous two or three years.

His predecessor had been Clyde Bracegirdle, a widower. As far as Feely knew, Clyde had moved in before the War and had remarried shortly before his death in mid-1921.

'How did he die?' asked Reggie, jotting down notes as Feely spoke.

'Heart attack, I believe. I heard that his wife stayed on for a couple of months before finding other lodgings, then I moved in.'

'Do you know where she lives now?'

Feely shook his head. 'Only saw her briefly when she came back to pick up the last of her belongings.'

Downstairs, in Flat 1, were the Adlers, Frank told him. Their daughter was living with them. They were away at the moment, staying with friends in Sorrento. They had lived in the apartment for seven months.

Before them was Mr Lennox Lush, a pawnbroker. His business was in Sydney Road, near the Brunswick Town Hall.

'More like an undertaker. He didn't like to chat,' said Feely, disapprovingly. 'He was here for about eight months.'

The previous tenant was a young man called Micah Youngblood.

'Strange one, that. Very religious. He used to say that the end of the world was nigh. God was going to punish us for our sins. That sort of thing.' He paused. 'I didn't talk to him much. Too depressing.'

Reggie laughed. 'I know what you mean. Everything's black and white.' He leaned forward. 'How long did he live here?'

'He came a few months before me. Stayed till July last year.'

'Do you know where I might find him?'

'I don't have an address, but every Friday he preaches from a soapbox near Luna Park, in St Kilda.'

'The detective who's working this case mentioned a tenant called Horace Striker. Do you know anything about him?'

'He was here before Youngblood?'

'I believe so.'

'Can't help you there, Reggie. Never met him.'

'You've been very helpful.' He took out the photograph of Cornelius, Henry, and Lily. 'One last thing. You have a good view of the street from your window. Have you ever seen this man?' He pointed at Cornelius.

Frank Feely studied the photograph carefully. 'Only his picture in the paper. But I remember the one on the right.'

'Henry?'

'I saw him on the street months ago. He was leaning up against the lamp post, staring up at the window. I'm sure it was him.'

Mamma Lombardi interrupted Reggie's reverie. '*Mi scusi, signore.* You like gelati or an espresso?'

'Espresso, *per favore.*'

Reggie took out his notebook and checked his notes from the information that Frank Feely and Lily Stout had given him.

The tenants of Flat 1, 1039 Punt Road, East Melbourne were the Adlers, preceded by Mr Lush, Mr Youngblood, and Mr Horace Striker. If the murder of Cornelius Stout occurred sometime between June 1921 and July 1922, neither the Adlers nor Mr Lush could have committed the crime.

However, Micah Youngblood fitted the time frame for murder and, although Horace Striker had moved out earlier, Reggie had come into possession of a most interesting piece of information which might implicate him after all.

The tenants of Flat 2 included Frank Feely and the Bracegirdles. The former, who had lived there since October 1921, had the opportunity to commit the murder, but Reggie seriously doubted whether Frank Feely had the stamina to drag a body down two flights of stairs. Notwithstanding that, Reggie had learned that even the unlikeliest of people could be guilty of committing crimes. He couldn't afford to rule Feely out of contention completely.

Between 1914 and August 1921, the Bracegirdles had lived in Flat 2. It would be hard to implicate them in the murder, given that Mr Bracegirdle was now deceased and his widow's whereabouts unknown. That concluded what he knew about the tenants.

Reggie looked at the next name on his list: Stanley Duggan, Henry's friend and the man bankrupted by Cornelius Stout. He certainly had a motive for murder.

The only other suspects with a motive were Lily and Henry Stout, the heirs to the estate. Henry had been seen outside the Punt Road property prior to the discovery of his father's body. But was Frank Feely a reliable witness? And Henry had denied ever visiting the terrace in Punt Road. Why would he return to the scene of the crime if he had killed his father there? It made no sense.

O'Flanagan believed that Henry Stout was the most likely suspect. It was often true that there was a close connection between victim and murderer. Lily's letters proved that Henry had been estranged from his father and had a powerful motive for killing Cornelius. He loathed him and, despite being disinherited, would still profit from his death. However, Henry's candour had impressed Reggie. Why would a murderer be so open about his dislike for the victim?

Although he was not familiar with the people that Cornelius Stout had crossed in his business dealings, he had more than enough to go on with. For now, it was a case of narrowing down the investigation and closing in on suspects. What a coup it would be if he could find out who murdered Cornelius Stout.

Chapter Sixteen

Melbourne was awash with crime, and Reggie was in the thick of it. From the bluestone lanes of the city to the slums and alleyways of Fitzroy, Carlton, and Richmond, opium dealers and vendors of bootleg liquor, or 'sly-grog' as it was known, plied their trade. Earlier in the year, Reggie had scooped the other daily newspapers by revealing that a new drug, cocaine, had entered the illicit drug market. He had forced the police to acknowledge that the 'snow habit' had reached Melbourne.

Back in 1919, Reggie had witnessed the gang wars involving Henry Stokes, Leslie 'Squizzy' Taylor, and 'Long Harry' Slater. Stokes, the 'two-up king' of Melbourne's illegal gambling dens and Squizzy, who had branched out into illicit booze, gambling, and prostitution, had taken on Slater's Fitzroy gang. 'Long Harry' was six feet three inches and seventeen stone of solid brawn. The feud had come to a head when Stokes shot Slater five times, but was acquitted of attempted murder on the grounds of self-defence.

Those were the days, thought Reggie. There was nothing like a gang war to excite the public's interest and sell newspapers. Keeping his ear to the ground, Reggie had noted the emergence of a new player, an associate of Squizzy, who eschewed the spotlight of notoriety and inhabited the dim underworld of Richmond's seedy back alleys. Horace Striker was his name and, coincidentally, he had lived in the very same terrace where Cornelius Stout had met his end.

Reggie da Costa parked his car in Church Street, making sure that the Citroen was securely locked. He noticed a small group of street urchins lurking nearby, eyeing off his flashy, yellow automobile with its black mudguards. Reggie approached them and handed over threepence. There would be more, he promised them, if his precious car were in one piece by the time he returned.

Satisfied that his automobile was safe, Reggie plunged into the back streets of Richmond. The sounds and smells of the slums surrounded him. Mangy dogs and skinny cats slunk past. Dirty children, with impassive faces, bare feet, and filthy hair, sat in the gutters, playing games with sticks and stones. The smell of excrement and urine assailed his nostrils. He cast sidelong glances at the homes of the industrial working-classes—weatherboard houses with peeling paint, rusting corrugated iron roofs, and broken windows—and thanked his lucky stars that he didn't live there.

Horace Striker inhabited a nondescript brick terrace in Shamrock Street. From the front, it looked like any other house in the street, with its modest tiled porch and iron lacework. But there was no rust to be seen, and the paintwork was pristine. Before he had a chance to knock, Reggie was met at the door, and escorted into the inner sanctum, by a thin man with a bloodless face and red cropped hair.

Sumptuous, crimson velvet curtains hid the interior from curious eyes. Expensive Turkish rugs were strewn over highly polished floors. Reggie would guarantee that the only members of the Victoria Police to cross this threshold were those who were on the 'take.' Indeed, Reggie had heard that a highly ranked policeman had been seen in the company of Mr Horace Striker at one of his more salubrious establishments only a few weeks earlier. The tentacles of his influence were extending and closing in on the upper levels of Melbourne's legal and political classes.

Reggie's escort knocked on the door to Striker's office, then stepped back to let Reggie pass through. The crime reporter didn't like to admit it, but he felt nervous. Lining up this meeting had taken a lot of work, utilising his wide range of contacts in the underworld. Striker was unpredictable. 'Don't stay too long. Find out what you need to know and get out,' one 'snitch' had advised him. Reggie had determined that he should be upfront about his visit, knowing that Striker would see through any dissembling. For once, honesty was the best policy.

It took a few seconds for his eyes to adjust to the gloom of the office. He became aware that he was in the presence of the man himself, Horace Striker. Tall and lean, with a strong face, piercing brown eyes, and grey streaked hair, Striker was an arresting figure in a sharply cut suit. Reggie recognised the work of H. Huntsman & Sons, of Savile Row. Striker ignored the reporter's outstretched hand and beckoned to him to sit, while he remained standing.

'Mr Striker, I'm Reggie da Costa from *The Argus*.'

'I know who you are.'

'I'm investigating the murder of Cornelius Stout.'

'Tell me something I don't know.' Striker looked bored. He shifted from one foot to the other and stared down at him.

Reggie cleared his throat. 'You lived in the terrace where Cornelius Stout's body was found.'

Striker was silent.

'I was hoping that you could shed some light on the murder of Mr Stout.'

Striker's tone of voice was non-negotiable. 'No.'

Reggie looked up at the underworld figure and was palpably aware that he was the lesser of the two, in terms of influence and power.

'I understand your reluctance to cooperate with the authorities, Mr Striker, but if there's anything you can tell me that might contribute to the apprehension of a killer, I would appreciate it.'

The crime boss took three steps forward, and leaned down towards Reggie. 'Nice suit,' he commented, rubbing the material of Reggie's collar between his fingers, an action the reporter found acutely disconcerting. 'I like a man with style.' He grinned and stepped back.

Reggie ploughed on, trying to shake off his disquiet. 'Did you know Cornelius Stout?'

'No.'

'Can I show you a photograph of him?'

'No!'

Reggie paused, a trickle of sweat on his brow. 'Do you know who murdered him?'

The crime boss spoke slowly, enunciating his words. 'I don't deal in murder, Mr da Costa, not unless it's strictly necessary. I have better ways to occupy my time.'

'Stanley Duggan was bankrupted by Cornelius Stout.'

Horace Striker's eyes narrowed.

Reggie took a deep breath. Now or never. 'How is your nephew?'

The gangster took a step towards Reggie, his mouth contorted into a smile. 'I will offer you a piece of advice, Mr da Costa, because I'd hate to see a man of style have an unfortunate accident. Mind your own business. And now, it's time for you to leave.'

Chapter Seventeen

Reggie started up the Citroen and pulled away from the curb. He was aware that he'd been playing with fire implicating Striker and his nephew in the death of Cornelius Stout. But he'd wanted to see Striker's reaction. It was not definitive, one way or the other, which was disappointing. He knew that he'd been lucky to leave unscathed. He could still feel the impression of the bodyguard's firm grip on his arm as he was escorted from Striker's presence.

Family was important to those of the underworld. Relatives could be relied on: the ties of blood took priority over all other relationships. And if Stanley Duggan had been ruined financially by Cornelius Stout, it was quite feasible that Uncle Horace had decided to avenge his nephew and conceal Stout's body in the basement of the building where he used to live.

Reggie felt unnerved. Striker's threat hung in the air. He drove away from Richmond, putting distance between himself and the gangster. A bit of sea air would blow away the sense of menace and claustrophobia that had pervaded his visit to Striker. He put his foot on the throttle and the Citroen responded.

Port Phillip Bay came into view. The sight of a ship making its way to Station Pier reminded him of Captain Jack, who lived nearby. He had intended to catch up with his old friend in the near future, both to pick his brains and to see how he was, so to find himself in the neighbourhood seemed fortuitous. He turned the car towards Port Melbourne.

His ties to Captain Jack went back to the time when his father had run off with the maid. Reggie had been only thirteen years old. He and his mother had suffered the humiliation of loss of money and loss of face. Mavis refused to come out of the house, so afraid was she of being ridiculed. At night, through the wall, Reggie could hear her crying herself to sleep.

His school mates teased him mercilessly. He was sent home from school for fighting. Life became unbearable, given that there was no adult in whom he could confide. That is, until Captain Jack stepped in.

He had heard from his son that Reggie was not coping well with the ignominy resulting from his father's departure. A compassionate man, he offered Reggie a refuge from a cruel world. He spoke to Reggie's teachers, insisting that they protect the lad. His wife sought out Mavis and gave her a shoulder to cry on. And, when the boy expressed a wish to leave school and get a job, it was Captain Jack who secured a position for him at *The Argus*. In short, Captain Jack was instrumental in making life bearable again for Reggie and his mother.

Despite the passing of the years, Reggie never forgot the man who had been more of a father to him than his own.

* * *

Captain Jack was working in the garden when Reggie arrived. He was of indeterminate age, with a full beard and a froth of white hair. After his wife died, he had moved from Brighton to a simple weatherboard house near Station Pier, where he spent most of his time either feeding the seagulls or watching the ships come into port.

'Reggie, lad. Come inside,' he said when he noticed the crime reporter standing at the gate. He opened the door and beckoned for Reggie to follow.

The walls of the house were covered in paintings of seascapes and ships. Models of caravels, frigates, galleons, junks, paddle steamers, and windjammers filled every nook and cranny.

As a young boy, Reggie had been fascinated by Captain Jack's collection. Never had he met a true eccentric who was so willing to share his obsession with him. It made him forget his own problems, as he listened to tales of shipwrecks, pirates, and the exploration of unknown seas. And, what made it all the more intriguing was that Captain Jack, it was rumoured, was afraid of water.

'I've brought you something,' said Reggie. He had seen a French sailor's cap in a shop window some time before and had bought it on impulse, thinking that his old friend would enjoy wearing it. To his delight, Captain Jack balanced the cap on his head, the red pompom bobbing on top.

'Perfect,' said Reggie, watching as the old man looked at his reflection in the mirror.

'I like the cut of your jib too,' commented Captain Jack, admiring Reggie's smart attire.

They chatted about Mavis and her health, and then Captain Jack moved on to the topic that he found endlessly fascinating: ships. He explained that a new pier was being built at Station Pier to accommodate larger and more powerful steamships. The railway servicing the wharf was also being doubled in size.

After a respectful period of time, Reggie broached the subject that had brought him to Captain Jack's door.

'You used to collect the shipping news, didn't you?' he asked.

The old man nodded. 'Still do. I have newspaper clippings going back to the 1880s.'

Captain Jack unlocked a door leading to a store-room. Behind him, Reggie could see a bookcase full of scrapbooks, arranged in chronological order.

'I'm interested in a ship that docked in an Australian port in 1914,' said Reggie. 'The *Lothringen*. I'm not sure which port it arrived in or when exactly.'

Captain Jack laughed. 'There's no need to check the shipping news. The *Lothringen*? Now that was one for the books. The N.D.L. steamer, *Lothringen*, from Bremen, under the command of Captain Kohler, arrived at Portsea at 2:00 a.m. on the 15th of August, 1914.'

'What does "N.D.L." stand for?' asked Reggie.

'Norddeutscher Lloyd or North German Lloyd. It was a German shipping company.' He took off the French sailor's cap and put it on the table. 'When it docked, the ship was boarded by naval officers and an armed guard, and ordered to drop anchor.'

'Why was that?'

'The *Lothringen* was not fitted with wireless, so the captain was unaware that war had been declared. He entered port, only to discover that he and his crew were prisoners of war!' Captain Jack chuckled. 'Quite a story, don't you think?'

'That's incredible,' agreed Reggie. 'What happened then?'

'The *Lothringen* was placed under detention.'

'And the captain and crew?'

'Detained too.'

'Were any of them released?'

'That I don't know. But I seem to remember that a couple of crewmen escaped.'

'Interesting. You don't have a record of their names?'

'That's something I can't help you with. The maritime authorities should have records. Or the police. Now, tell me, what is this about?'

Reggie explained about Dotty Wright, her inheritance, and her curiosity regarding the man who had unexpectedly left her his estate.

'This Dotty of yours has scruples,' commented Captain Jack. 'You don't see enough of that these days.'

'Mmm,' said Reggie. 'I really must be off.' He shook the old man's hand. 'You've been invaluable, as always.'

Captain Jack grinned, showing a row of missing teeth. 'Don't leave it too long till your next visit, Reggie. I had a heart attack a month ago. The doctor says it was a warning shot across the bow.'

'Aren't you worried?'

'I'm not ready to abandon ship just yet. I'll change tack and make the best of whatever time I have left, whatever that will be.'

Reggie gave him a hug, then let himself out, leaving the old man to his maritime paraphernalia.

He was amazed by what he had learned. Fancy setting sail from Bremen in peacetime and arriving at port with the world at war? Feeling more optimistic about solving the Eric Smith conundrum, Reggie started the car and headed home to Richmond.

He was still pondering the vagaries of life when he let himself in the front door.

'Hello,' came a voice from the parlour.

Reggie stared at a sharply dressed man with thick, grey hair and a well-trimmed moustache, whose face bore an uncanny resemblance to his own. He realised, with horror, that he was looking at an older version of himself. It was Mario da Costa, his father, sitting in his armchair. *His* armchair! And drinking *his* fine Scotch. The nerve of him!

He ignored his father's greeting and stormed through to the kitchen, where his mother was preparing dinner for the man who had run off with the maid. Reggie was livid.

'What's he doing here?' he barked at her.

'He's not well,' Mavis replied, eyes downcast.

'What rubbish. How can you be so gullible?'

The tears began to flow. 'He's dying, Reggie. I can't put him out on the street.'

'He's run out of money. That's why he's back.'

Mavis shook her head, looking totally miserable.

'Where's he going to sleep, Mother? Not in your bed?'

She had enough spirit to look outraged. 'Don't be disgusting. And don't tell me how to live my life.'

'But everything you've strived for, all that effort that you put into restoring your reputation, and you're prepared to lose it all again. The sniggers. The gossip. And what about me?'

His mother lowered her eyes and said nothing.

And that said everything to Reggie. He went to bed, ignoring the meal that his mother had put on the table for him. How could he eat, with that man in his house?

Chapter Eighteen

Reggie parked his car along The Esplanade near Luna Park, the fun park situated opposite the St Kilda foreshore. He'd come in search of Micah Youngblood, relying on Frank Feely's advice that he'd find the preacher there on Friday nights. As one of the tenants in the apartment block where Cornelius Stout's body had been found, Reggie hoped that Youngblood could provide him with some useful information about the murder.

A bank of leaden clouds hung low across Port Phillip Bay, which aligned perfectly with Reggie's state of mind. He wrapped his coat around him and jammed his hat down on his head.

The last twenty-four hours had turned his life upside down. He had left the house that morning without saying a word to his mother, who had watched him nervously as he ate his breakfast.

'Reggie, dear, let me explain.'

But he had walked out, not wanting to hear again the rationalisation that she had offered him the night before. He just couldn't understand her reasoning. They had lived together, peacefully and agreeably, on their own for the last twenty-two years. And would the interloper still be there tonight, when Reggie came back from St Kilda? He knew the answer to that one.

* * *

The arrival of Micah Youngblood brought Reggie back to the present. The preacher was an extraordinary sight, with long flowing white robes and

71

white-blond hair, which reached to his shoulders. He looked like someone from the Old Testament which, given his occupation, was most probably his intention. At the foot of his soapbox was a bowl marked 'donations.'

Reggie lit a cigarette and waited patiently, watching a few hardy souls gather to listen to the street preacher.

'God is watching you!' He gestured towards Mr Moon, whose giant face and gaping mouth formed the entrance to Luna Park.

Reggie stifled a laugh.

A group of young men stopped to chat with a couple of prostitutes on a street corner.

'Resist your natural urges!' Micah Youngblood cried out. 'You are fine young men. These women are infecting you. They are full of pestilence. Resist them, I say!'

But his entreaties fell on deaf ears. The terms of transaction agreed to, the young men and the prostitutes headed towards the unlit parkland near the beach.

Youngblood embarked on a lengthy sermon regarding the perils of succumbing to temptation, but even he couldn't compete with the weather. The wind rose and the temperature dropped. His audience started to lose interest and drift away. The prostitutes followed, seeking more sheltered places to sell their wares. Soon the preacher was alone with Reggie da Costa.

'I'm saving souls in this den of iniquity,' he called out to the reporter. 'Have you come to be saved?'

'I'm Reggie da Costa from *The Argus*,' Reggie explained, approaching him. 'I'm investigating the murder that occurred at Punt Road, in the apartment house where you used to live. Can we go somewhere for a chat?'

The preacher nodded and beckoned for him to follow. They found a little café on The Esplanade and ordered two pots of tea.

'You certainly have a way with words,' said Reggie.

'In this business, it's a necessity.'

Youngblood paused while the waitress set the tea in front of them. As he heaped two spoonfuls of sugar into his cup, he seemed to shake off his spiritual persona. 'Excuse the robes. It's part of the act.'

'You're not religious?'

'Oh yes,' he replied. 'I'm more effective in bringing sinners to God this way.'

'Have you always been like this?' Reggie asked, unsure of how to describe Youngblood's appearance and calling.

Micah Youngblood stared off into the distance. 'I was sent to the Western Front. It was a vision of Hell. Mud, flooded trenches, barbed wire. Rats. Trees blasted to smithereens. The rat-tat-tat of machine guns and the whistle of shells. The screams of dying men. Feet and twisted hands sticking up out of the earth. The heavy, sweet stench of death.' He frowned. 'That smell: rotting bodies, gunpowder, human excrement, urine. It stays with you forever.

'I promised myself, that if I survived, I'd try to eliminate the evil in men's hearts. Do away with the suffering and destruction and wickedness. So that's why I'm here.' He shifted his gaze back to his companion. 'You never served?'

Reggie lit a cigarette and inhaled, then blew the smoke up towards the ceiling, watching it dissipate. 'I never believed that there was anything noble about that war. It was purely economic. British capitalist interests protecting their markets against the growth of Germany as a world power. No one would admit it at the time and I don't know if they ever will. But I was right, that's for sure.' He looked at Youngblood wistfully. 'I called myself a socialist once.'

'You don't look like a socialist to me.'

Reggie butted out his cigarette. 'Now Mr Youngblood, let's move on to the reason I'm here. You lived in Punt Road for about a year and a half.' He took a photograph from his coat pocket. 'Could you look at this, please? That's Cornelius Stout in the middle. His body was found in the basement below your flat last month. Do you recognise him?'

'He doesn't look familiar. As for the basement? I never went down there. From memory, it was always kept locked.'

Reggie took out his notebook and pen. 'I'll make notes if you don't mind?' Youngblood shrugged his shoulders. 'Did you know the Bracegirdles in the flat above?'

The preacher held up his Bible. '"For the love of money is the root of all evil." 1 Timothy 6:10.' His face softened. 'Mr Bracegirdle suffered badly. It was terrible what happened to him.'

'I heard he had a heart attack.'

'If only it had been that quick. It was as if the wrath of God were visited upon him. Within weeks of his marriage, he lost his hair, his eyesight, and the use of his limbs. Then he died. Natural causes, they called it.'

'But you don't agree?'

'I call it human intervention. There is a higher power that will judge those who do evil.'

'I'm confused. Are you implying that Mr Bracegirdle paid the price for his love of money?'

'Not Mr Bracegirdle. His wife. Mrs Bracegirdle. She will pay when Judgment Day comes.'

Although he questioned him further, Reggie was not able to elicit much more from the preacher. Youngblood had only known the Bracegirdles for two months and had been preoccupied with saving souls, not inquiring into the private lives of his neighbours. But, he added, he had had a conversation with Mr Bracegirdle on the staircase one day, shortly after his marriage, in which the man had complained that his new wife was spending money like water. She was even insisting that his will be rewritten, naming her as the main beneficiary. Whether he had submitted to her request, Youngblood did not know. As to a description of the wife, the preacher had been similarly unhelpful. She always wore a headscarf when going out and avoided conversation. He confirmed that she had stayed on for a month or so after her husband's death.

Youngblood finished his tea and was eager to be off. The sinners of St Kilda were waiting for his next performance. Reggie followed the preacher out onto The Esplanade and watched as he stepped up onto his soapbox outside Luna Park.

'Repent, ye sinners! The hour is nigh when you must meet your Maker!' he cried, shaking his Bible at a group of 'ladies of the night.'

Reggie strolled back to his automobile, turning up his collar against the chill wind. As he started up his car, Reggie wondered whether the 'sinner' who had killed Cornelius Stout would ever be held accountable in a court of law or if, as Micah Youngblood suggested, it would be before a higher authority.

Chapter Nineteen

Detective Sergeant O'Flanagan had a favourite 'watering hole,' a pub close to the docks in Port Melbourne. The Exchange Hotel reflected its working-class clientele, with its mismatched furniture, its walls decorated with sporting photographs, the dark patches of grog ingrained in the bare boards, and the whiff of urine emanating from the toilets.

Reggie found him sitting at the bar, contentedly sipping a beer. Nearby, a mix of seamen and wharfies clustered, tough, burly, and rowdy, fearing no one, but not one of them encroached on the invisible barrier that seemed to have been drawn around O'Flanagan. Whether his reputation had preceded him, as a fierce enforcer of the law, or because there was an aura about him that did not encourage familiarity, Reggie did not know. He often wondered why Mick liked to drink there, but drink there he did, despite the fact that he appeared to be the human equivalent of a square peg in a round hole.

Reggie slipped in next to O'Flanagan. 'Thought I'd find you here.'

The detective grunted as he slapped Reggie on the shoulder. 'What will you have?'

'A beer.'

O'Flanagan laughed. 'Good man.' He slammed his fist on the counter, immediately gaining the attention of the barman.

'Beer for my friend,' he growled.

The detective sergeant looked a little the worse for wear. His eyes were red-rimmed; his breath smelled of stale beer.

They chatted at first about the police strike and the fact that the government was not intending to reinstate the strikers.

'They've lost their jobs for good,' said O'Flanagan. 'It's ironic that the very things they complained about will be fixed. You watch. Pensions will be introduced, pay will increase, and working conditions will improve. The 'Spooks' have been stood down too, although nothing has been said publicly about that.'

Reggie nodded. 'The government won't let newsreel footage of the strike out of the country. They don't want the shame of it being seen overseas. They want the police strike forgotten. It's a blot on the country's reputation, they reckon.'

O'Flanagan nodded wistfully. 'Control. It's all about control.'

'On another subject, how's Squizzy treating you?'

'He's a slimy little creature,' slurred O'Flanagan. 'Every time we think we've got him, he slips out of our grasp. Like an eel he is.' He started to hiccup. 'Damn drink. What time is it? Should be on my way.'

Reggie touched his arm. 'Give me a minute, Mick. There's something I need to talk to you about.'

He told the detective about his interview with Youngblood, and the comments he had made about the Bracegirdles.

O'Flanagan seemed to sober up as he spoke. 'I think your man is exaggerating. One of my colleagues looked into it. Youngblood's been making extravagant claims, but the doctor's report was definitive. Mr Bracegirdle was in his sixties and in poor health. He died from natural causes. It's the word of a religious crackpot against that of a medical man. What's wrong with his missus wanting him to change his will? She needed some security when he died.'

'Have you located Mrs Bracegirdle?'

'Not yet.'

'What about Stanley Duggan, the bankrupt?'

'We interviewed him last week. It seems that he issued threats against Stout around May 1921. About a month before Stout disappeared. We haven't ruled him out.'

'And Joshua Bentwhistle, Stout's former partner?'

'Nothing to see there,' commented O'Flanagan. 'Bentwhistle moved to England just before war broke out. As far as we know, he's never returned to Australia.'

'Have you spoken to Lily Stout yet?'

'I have. She's going to inherit Stout's estate.'

'I met her recently. She's a good-looking woman. With all that money coming her way, she'll be a catch.'

O'Flanagan raised an eyebrow and smiled. 'Just right for a crime reporter who likes the good life.'

Reggie shrugged his shoulders. 'She could do a lot worse.'

O'Flanagan smiled. 'Who am I to argue, Reggie? Just keep your powder dry until the case is closed.'

Reggie guffawed. 'Miss Stout a killer? That little thing? She's sweet. You should have read the letter she wrote to her father before he disappeared. She was trying to make peace between him and her brother.'

'What letter?'

'From the boxes at Stout's house.'

O'Flanagan looked puzzled. 'I went through them. Must have missed that. Don't throw them out. I might take another look. Did she tell you anything of interest?'

'The "Rita" of the ring? She was Stout's lady friend. Lily's description of her was less than complimentary. She said that her father was wearing that signet ring the last time she saw him. Apparently, Stout was fed up with Rita. Broke it off with her. He wasn't interested in marriage.'

'You're suggesting that Rita was an aggrieved lover?'

'Possibly,' conceded Reggie. 'According to Henry, his father was a lady-killer. Reckons that there would be a lot of women out there who hated Cornelius Stout, Rita among them.'

'Last drinks!' called the bartender.

'Another?' asked Reggie.

O'Flanagan nodded. 'Thanks, mate.'

Reggie gestured to the bartender, then leaned in. 'By the way, Mick, I met up with Horace Striker earlier this week.'

'Stanley Duggan's uncle?' O'Flanagan chuckled as he saw the look of disappointment on Reggie's face. 'Sorry. I heard about that connection last week. I hope you didn't say that to his face?' Reggie smirked. The detective laughed out loud. 'I'm amazed you lived to tell the tale. Horace doesn't like a Smart Aleck showing him up.'

'I didn't get much out of him, despite pointing out the connection with Duggan. He told me to mind my own business.'

'Take his advice. He's a nasty bugger. You don't want to cross him.' The barman placed a beer in front of O'Flanagan. He took a swig and wiped his mouth with the back of his hand. 'The word is out that he's training up his nephew to take over his empire. Anyway, I have my doubts about Striker being involved. This isn't his *modus operandi*. If Horace did have a hand in Stout's death, he would have him thrown off a bridge, breaking his legs first. He'd be sending a message: don't mess with my family. A body in a basement?' He shook his head. 'Too subtle.

'Besides,' he added, 'the coroner's time frame for Stout's death means that Striker moved out before the murder. Stout was still alive then.'

'But Striker knew about the basement. He would have known it was empty. He might have been the one to put a lock on it.'

'Reggie, my friend. Leave it to the professionals. Like me. Keep your nose out of Horace's business or you might lose it, and a lot more.'

Reggie scowled. 'I can look after myself.' He threw back the last of his beer and set the glass on the counter.

'One more thing before I go. I'm investigating a private matter. It involves a sailor who was on the steamship *Lothringen*. It sailed from Bremen and arrived in Melbourne in August 1914, after war had been declared. The ship and crew were detained, but I heard that a couple of sailors jumped ship in port. Could you check if there's any record of who they were?'

O'Flanagan took down the details in his notebook. 'I'll see what I can do.'

The drinkers were moving reluctantly toward the exit. It was six o'clock and the pub was shutting up for the night. O'Flanagan stood and steadied himself against the bar then pushed off, weaving his way out through the door.

Reggie da Costa went outside and stared up at the darkening sky.

'Better get home.' He frowned. 'Home, where *he* is.'

Investigating the cases of Eric Smith and Cornelius Stout had distracted him from thoughts about his father. But that situation had to be faced, no matter how much he dreaded it. If Mario da Costa didn't leave home soon, then he would have to go. He couldn't abide sharing his house and his mother with that blackguard any longer. It had been five long days since he first saw his father sitting in his armchair. Not one word had they exchanged. But he would have it out with him, and soon.

Chapter Twenty

Dotty Wright was bored. After a week at the home of her uncle and aunt, she had insisted that it was time for her to go home to Richmond. And now, she found, that without the companionship of Aunt Mildred and Uncle Alfred, there was little to occupy her mind. She was propped up on the couch, her broken ankle in a cast, with strict instructions from the doctor to take six weeks off work. Besides, he had added, school was not the place for her, given her traumatic experience during the police strike.

Perhaps he was right about that. Newspaper reports would never convey the overwhelming terror that she had felt that day. Caught in the midst of a seething mass of people in Bourke Street, she had been shoved and jostled and groped, scrambling to stay on her feet, and then she felt a sudden pain in her ankle as she was pushed sideways. Her screams had been lost in the pandemonium as the mob clamoured and fought and shrieked. Her hat and her shoes had been lost beneath trampling feet; her handbag ripped from her grasp by an opportunistic thief who had quickly melted away into the crowd. Never had she felt so powerless in her life.

And then she heard Reggie's voice above the racket. And saw him pushing his way towards her, like a knight in shining armour.

'Hold on, Dotty,' she said out loud. 'Reggie da Costa will never be your knight in shining armour. That man is gone.'

Her mind travelled back to 1915. At the age of twenty-four, Dotty had come to believe that love had passed her by. War had been declared and the call to arms was growing louder. Male friends enlisted and were shipped off to foreign lands, ready to fight for the British Empire.

And then she met Teddy. A New Zealander, he was visiting relatives in South Yarra. She had been sitting on a bench, reading in the park. He stopped to chat to her, admiring her little corgi, Socks. Before she knew it, they were meeting the next day, and then the one after.

Things moved fast, when it became apparent that Teddy's time in Melbourne was limited. It was his intention to enlist in the New Zealand Mounted Rifles Brigade.

He left. Letters passed between them. Then came the news that his brigade was shipping out to Egypt.

Dotty never knew that Teddy died at Gallipoli. Her letters went unanswered until, finally, his father in Auckland wrote, informing her that his son had lost his life just weeks before the evacuation. She was devastated. She was left to rue what might have been.

Never one to pity herself and aware that others were suffering loss too, Dotty volunteered for the Red Cross while she continued to teach. It was the least she could do to support the boys so far from home. But she had driven herself hard and, ultimately, she fell ill, necessitating an enforced spell at the home of her Aunt Mildred and Uncle Alfred. At last, she rallied, but she promised herself that she would never commit herself to another relationship again. She would make a life for herself as best she could, doing what she loved: teaching. And now, she couldn't even do that, while she was confined to home.

She reached for the letter that Reggie had pushed under her door the night before. It said that he would visit her the next evening. She was keen to see him, not only to distract herself from her inactivity, but also to thank him again for his heroic act in rescuing her.

Was there a purpose to Reggie's visit? That she did not know. She was sure that he was not interested in her romantically and she, most definitely, was not interested in him. But she had tidied her hair and put on a nice dress, and she had to admit that she felt better for making the effort.

Certainly, their relationship had taken a turn for the better after his intervention at the police strike. She was determined to be more tolerant, and not so judgmental, when it came to Reggie. There was little doubt in her mind that he lacked depth of character when it came to his obsession with appearances but, on the other hand, he had shown considerable courage and a disregard for his own safety in saving her from the mob. We all have our faults, she reminded herself, recognising that she was quick to anger.

As the grandfather clock in the hallway struck seven, there came a knock on the front door.

'Come in!' she called. 'It's open.'

Reggie entered the sitting room, a bouquet of flowers in his hand. 'For the invalid,' he said. He lay them on the side table.

'Thank you.' Dotty beckoned for him to sit down.

She smiled to herself. Reggie's outfit—a soft cream shirt and brown trousers—was a study in relaxed sartorial elegance. His thick black hair and his moustache had been recently trimmed. She watched as he glanced around the room, taking in the furnishings and decoration. The room itself was cheerful, with an attractive floral lounge suite dominating the space and landscape paintings on the walls. Probably not to his taste, she thought. She checked herself. She was already breaking her resolution not to judge him.

'Cup of tea?'

Reggie eyed the pair of wooden crutches, propped up against the couch. 'I'll make it. I'd prefer something stronger, if you have it.'

'Sorry, but there's no alcohol in my house. I've taken the pledge.'

He looked shocked. 'You're teetotal?'

'I'm a member of the Australasian Women's Temperance Union.'

'You're one of those women who wanted six o'clock closing? You didn't do me any favours!'

The colour rose in her cheeks. 'My father spent every night after work at the pub, rather than coming home to his family.'

'My father is a shiftless, worthless sponger, but I still wouldn't pass laws to stop others living their lives like he does.'

He stood abruptly and went into the kitchen.

Dotty's eyes narrowed. Her resolution was faltering again. 'Why does he make it so hard?' she muttered. She could hear him putting the kettle on, and opening and closing cupboard doors.

Reggie returned with a tray. 'Milk and sugar?'

They sipped their tea in silence. Finally, Dotty asked, 'Does something bring you here, or is this a social visit?'

Reggie missed the sarcasm. He leaned forward, putting his cup down. 'I have some news for you. About Eric Smith.'

'Really? I thought that was resolved.'

'So did I, but there was one angle that I hadn't pursued, and that was the *Lothringen*. Everything pointed to Mr Smith being a man with a past, and I've proved it.'

He sipped his tea then continued. 'As you know, Mr Smith concealed his true identity. His birth certificate was a fake. I think I know why. He was a German sailor, on the run from the authorities.'

He described how the steamer, *Lothringen*, en route from Bremen, had arrived in port just as war was declared.

'The captain and crew were detained.'

Dotty shook her head in disbelief. 'The inventory from the *Lothringen*. It was in the box. Are you saying that Eric was on board that ship?'

'That appears to be the case. I have a friend, an expert on ships and shipping. He told me that a couple of crew members escaped detention. It seemed too much of a coincidence to ignore. Think about it. The inventory. The photographs from Northern Germany. And the fact that you said that Mr Smith didn't like to talk about himself. It all fits. He had something to hide.' He paused, taking a notebook from his jacket pocket. 'I contacted a detective from the Criminal Investigation Branch. I asked him to track down the names of the absconding seamen. He did just that.'

'And—'

Reggie thumbed through his notebook. 'Two sailors jumped ship at Portsea in August 1914. Their names were Harald Goldwasser and Erik Schmidt. That's E-r-i-k.'

Dotty was quick to make the connection. 'Erik Schmidt. Eric Smith. He anglicised his name.'

'It's an amazing story. When he left Germany, he was a sailor in peacetime.

When he arrived in Australia, he was destined to be a prisoner of war.'

Dotty shook her head. 'Incredible.'

Reggie continued. 'Remember the photograph from Lübeck? Of Mr Smith standing on the deck of *The Gudrun*? And then those newspaper clippings? I went back into our archives and read the reports in full. In 1917, the people in the German Baltic ports of Stettin and Lübeck were starving. They waited on the wharves for ships from neutral countries to bring food. Some supply ships were stormed. It was chaotic. I suspect that Lübeck was Eric's home town. He kept those newspaper clippings to connect him to his homeland. No doubt he was worried about the family he left behind.'

Dotty put down her cup. She shook her head. 'What happened to Harald Goldwasser?'

Reggie shrugged his shoulders. 'Went his own way, I suppose. It would maximise their chances of not being caught if they split up. At some stage, Eric bought fake identity papers, and when the time was right and he thought he would fit in, he bought the grocery shop. You never noticed that he had an accent?'

'Eric had a gift for languages,' replied Dotty. 'Those dictionaries in the bookcase. I remember one day he rattled something off in Spanish.' She paused and leaned forward. 'But now I think of it, there was that incident about a year ago. I was chatting to him one day when he dropped a glass jar. Smashed it to pieces. He said something that sounded like "Mein Gott" and then went very pale. Then he said that his mother had lived in Germany for a time and that he'd picked up some of her expressions. I didn't think too much about it. I put it out of my mind.' She frowned. 'I don't understand. The War's over. Why would he go to all that trouble to hide being German?'

'He's an illegal immigrant,' said Reggie. 'On the run from the authorities. Likely to be locked up.

'I'm half-Italian, Sicilian actually,' he added, 'which is neither here nor there, but I still get comments thrown at me. Australians don't trust foreigners. During the war, people were nervous, suspicious of the threat from within. Enemy aliens. They thought their neighbours might be plotting to overthrow the Government. Innocent people were accused of being spies.'

'I didn't realise how bad it was.'

'And still can be. Take it from me. As for the Germans living in Australia during the war? They became pariahs, particularly when the German navy sank HMAS *Sydney*. They lost their jobs. Their schools and churches were closed. Businesses were destroyed. The Government set up internment camps. The propaganda against them was rampant.' Reggie frowned. 'Think about it, Dotty. German immigration to Australia is still banned.'

'So that's why Eric hid his true identity,' concluded Dotty. 'You really couldn't tell he was German.'

'Someone did,' said Reggie. 'That's what I think happened.'

'But who did this to him? Who made him kill himself? If you could have seen his body—' Dotty choked back a sob. 'It was horrible.'

Reggie shrugged and picked up his hat. 'We'll never know the answer to that. He's dead and that's that. Take the money, Dotty. There's no reason to feel guilty anymore.'

He stood in the hallway. 'Goodnight. I'll return Mr Smith's box to you tomorrow.'

Dotty looked resigned. 'At least I know the truth now. I suppose that's the end of it. Thank you, Reggie.'

He doffed his hat and left.

Dotty fluffed up the cushions and leaned back on them. What a revelation! Reggie had made short work of tracking down Eric Smith's true identity. But there was something about Reggie's manner that night that was different. Instead of being his usual brash and confident self, he had seemed uncharacteristically subdued at times, and then very touchy at others. The reference to being part-Italian. The lack of bravado about the discoveries he had made about Eric Smith. The irritability about hotels closing at six o'clock.

She had heard through her aunt that Reggie's father had returned to the family home after living a hedonistic lifestyle on the continent, his re-appearance causing ructions in the da Costa household. The word was that Mario da Costa was dying, but Aunt Mildred was sceptical. Money, she said. It was always about the money. And then she had recounted to Dotty the story of how Reggie's mother had met her future husband, piecing their history together from Mavis's own recollections, as well as comments that Mr Morgan, Mavis's father, had made to Mildred before he died.

Mavis had been the only child of Edward Morgan, a wealthy investor whose wife had died in childbirth. He raised her with the help of a nanny, and lavished every indulgence on her. She attended a good grammar school, where Mildred and she had become friends. Although Mavis was not of an academic bent, she was a sweet girl, and a loyal and generous friend.

After finishing school, Mavis acted as an assistant to her father, organising his appointments; accompanying him on business trips; taking notes of his meetings. But he was not in the best of health and the doctors recommended that he take a break from his work. His investments were going well, and he decided that he could afford to travel to the continent for a few months, in the company of his daughter. He thought it would expand her view of the world, as well as giving him a much-needed rest.

They sailed on the R.M.S. *Iberia* in April of 1886, travelling via Adelaide, Suez, and Naples, to Plymouth. At their first stop, a new passenger alighted, Mario da Costa. He was an Italian, who had spent a few dissolute months travelling around the south-eastern states of Australia looking for 'opportunities' to support his gambling and wild wanton ways. However, he'd grown tired of Australian life and determined that he should go back to London where, if he must, he would earn a living as a musician. Unexpectedly, his two talents—playing the violin and being in possession of a smooth tongue—were put to good use much earlier than on his arrival in England's capital. Over the six weeks of the voyage, he employed both to ensnare the gullible Mavis, convincing her of his love and his determination to make her his wife. Despite the misgivings of her father, Mavis fell deeply in love with him. By the time the *Iberia* docked in Plymouth, they were engaged.

In the presence of Mr Morgan and a fellow passenger whose cabin he had shared, Mario da Costa married Mavis. She was just twenty. While her father holidayed in England, the newlyweds sailed to Italy and spent their honeymoon in Taormina, on the eastern coast of Sicily. Nine months later, back in Melbourne, Mavis gave birth to Reginald da Costa, his Christian name a tribute to his mother's English heritage.

Mario showed a reluctance to earn a living. Although his wife received an allowance from her father, it was Mario who spent it, enjoying the high life. He gambled, he drank, he played the violin for the entertainment of friends, and he dabbled in adulterous affairs.

Following hard on the land boom of the 1880s, the next decade brought depression. Edward Morgan's investments became worthless as the banks closed and the economy contracted. Ultimately, Mavis's father was unable to pay his debts, and he could no longer fund Mario da Costa's lifestyle. He gave his son-in-law an ultimatum, that he should support his wife and child through his own labours. Instead of buckling down, Mario packed up and left, in the company of the maid. His son was just thirteen years old. In the absence of a breadwinner, Mavis and Reggie struggled to survive, dealing also with the scandal of Mario's departure. Shortly after, Edward Morgan died.

* * *

Aunt Mildred's account went some way to explaining Reggie's mood that night, now that his father had returned. Dotty had to admit that she felt sorry for him. An upbringing like that would scar anyone, giving a reason for his insecurities and obsessions. And yet, when she considered her own early life, it too had been difficult, what with her mother's death and her father's alcoholism. But, in her case, Aunt Mildred and Uncle Alfred's kindness in taking her in had dulled much of her early memories, and given her a sense of security and a moral compass which had laid the foundation of what she had become in adulthood.

Dotty considered what a strange relationship she had with the crime reporter, alternating between finding him amusing, and being irritated by him. Knowing his background made her determined to be tolerant, but the simple fact was that she spent more time being provoked, annoyed, and exasperated by Reggie da Costa, than she did enjoying his company. She shook her head in dismay and, leaning heavily on her crutch, hobbled off to bed.

Chapter Twenty-One

On arriving home, Reggie found his mother sitting alone in the parlour.

'Where is he?'

'He's gone out. He said he was bored.'

Reggie took a deep breath and sat down opposite her.

'You know he'll leave. If it's not today, it will be in a week or month. Leopards don't change their spots.'

'He's not well, Reggie.' She lapsed into silence and stared at the fire which was smouldering in the hearth. She shivered and wrapped her shawl around her.

Reggie stared at Mavis. For once, no argument came to mind that might convince her to rid their house of his parasite of a father. He knew she was a hopeless case. Only Mario's departure could return their home to the comfortable sanctuary that it had once been. In truth, he loved his mother dearly and hated to see her being taken advantage of, but, at the same time, her inability to see her husband for what he really was, rankled him, and made him irritable and fractious.

The clock struck ten and, as if on cue, the front door slammed shut. Mario da Costa stood in the doorway to the parlour, smelling of whisky and cigars. His eyes were not quite focused. Reggie's hackles rose at the sight of him.

'Keeping your mother company?' said Mario, a glimmer of a smirk on his lips. 'Good boy.'

'More than you ever did for her,' replied Reggie. He stood, his fists clenched. 'I see that you've been out spending Mother's money on drink.

And probably loose women. As if she can afford it.'

'Your mother knows who I am,' he slurred. 'I've never misled her about my preferences in life.'

'Your preferences, never hers. You walked out on us when I was thirteen. You left Mother with nothing. You made us the laughing stock of Brighton. Nobody was in any doubt about your disgusting behaviour. You made sure of that. I had to claw my way up from being a pariah to being someone of substance.'

Mario poked his finger in Reggie's chest. 'You're not someone of substance. You're a newspaper reporter, that's all. From what your mother tells me, you want some rich *signorina* to support you; keep you in the style to which you'd like to become accustomed.'

'I want to marry, not be a parasite like you.'

'The distinction is a fine one.'

Reggie scowled. 'I'm the man of the house now. And I tell you to get out.'

'The man of the house? Ha. What's a thirty-six-year-old man doing living with his mamma?'

'What's a sixty-five-year-old bloodsucking leech doing coming back to the woman he deserted years ago? Oh, that's right, you're *dying*.' An ugly smile contorted Reggie's handsome face.

Mavis had gone white. She stood up suddenly and glared at Reggie. 'Stop this! This is my house. He is my husband. I have the right to decide who lives here. If you don't like it, you can leave.'

Reggie was shocked. He stared at his mother, saw the tautness in her face, heard the strain in her voice. He took one last look at his father and stormed out of the room.

He slammed the bedroom door behind him and sank onto the mattress. All the hurt, all the resentment he had harboured against his father, rose to the surface. But he was floored by his mother's reaction. She, whom he had loved above anyone else, had not supported him. Was this how she repaid him for his years of devotion? But there was no mistaking the import of her words. His father should stay. He should go. It beggared belief.

He took down his suitcase from the top of the wardrobe, then opened the chest of drawers, staring at the clothes neatly folded within. It was time. He took each article of clothing out separately, packing them into the case carefully, then he took his suits and his dinner jacket from the wardrobe and hung them in a storage bag. The silver box, with his cufflinks, collar pins, and fob watch, was next, then his prized set of silver embossed hair brushes. Finally, he filled his wash bag with toiletries and put it in his Gladstone bag.

Apart from his personal possessions, there was little else to take. The boxes from Cornelius Stout's East Melbourne mansion could be stored in the boot of the Citroen for now, in case O'Flanagan might decide to go through them again. And the carved box, belonging to Eric Smith, could be returned to Dotty in the morning.

Reggie sat on the bed and stared at the door, waiting. Perhaps Mother might come in and apologise? Perhaps she'd tell Mario to leave? He knew the answer to that one. She was still the hopeless romantic, blinded by his charm and good looks.

He sighed. Tomorrow he would find a rooming house, closer to work. Any landlady would be pleased to welcome a man of his status and appearance into her establishment.

He lay on the bed and closed his eyes, letting his thoughts drift. Eric Smith. The name popped into his mind, unbidden. Despite his comments to the contrary, Mr Smith's demise came under the category of unfinished business. Did he commit suicide because he was being blackmailed? Was there something that he, Reggie da Costa, crime reporter for *The Argus*, had overlooked?

He took down the wooden box and lay the contents on the bed. Photographs. The *Lothringen* inventory. Newspaper clippings. A couple of advertisements from the Classified section of *The Argus*. It occurred to him that he had given the latter scant attention before, but now he took them up and read them carefully.

BUSINESS FOR SALE. Grocer's shop and dwelling. Price negotiable. Contact Eric Smith. Cnr Coppin and Swan Streets, Richmond.

The clipping was dated about a month before his death. Was he under pressure to sell up?

CHAPTER TWENTY-ONE

The second clipping had been published a few months earlier.

HOUSEKEEPER. Female. Cleaning and preparation of meals. Experience preferred. Twice a week. Good wages. Apply to Eric the Grocer. Cnr Coppin and Swan Streets, Richmond.

A housekeeper. Dotty had mentioned that Eric had one. Reggie scratched his head. It reminded him of something else, but what was it?

On an impulse, Reggie went out into the hallway. All was silent. His parents had gone to bed. In a corner of the dining room was the box containing the newspaper articles and advertisements that had made up part of Cornelius Stout's papers. He carried it back to his room and emptied it onto the bed. He searched through the pile, looking for an advertisement that Cornelius had posted in the local newspapers. And then he found it.

HOUSEKEEPER. Over 40. Experience preferred. Cleaning and most meals for respectable gentleman. Must be hard-working. Good wages and conditions. No Sundays. East Melbourne. Apply to Cornelius Stout Tel JL1141.

He had laughed when he had first read it, given the condition of the East Melbourne house, but he had not examined the letters from applicants for the position. Attached to the advertisement were five responses. He scanned each one, looking for something, anything. It was the fifth that made him sit up straight. Not only was the address familiar, but so was the surname.

'Bloody oath!'

Flat 2, 1039 Punt Rd
East Melbourne
March 4, 1921

Dear Mr Stout,

I wish to apply for the position of housekeeper. I am a good cook and will make meals that will please you. Nothing will be too much trouble. Your bathroom will be shining like a new pin. Your breakfasts will be rich and tasty. You will appreciate my delicious cooking. My previous employers have spoken of my kindness and pampering. I will wait on

you hand and foot.
    Regards,
    Rita Bracegirdle.

The 'Rita' of the ring and lover of Cornelius Stout was the wife of Clyde Bracegirdle. Reggie sat down and read it again. She had been under his nose all along. He sat in silence digesting the significance of what he'd just learned. The letter was the link he'd been seeking between Stout and the terrace house where he had found the corpse.

Reggie took out his notebook and checked some dates. In March of 1921, Rita's husband was still alive. And, in June of 1921, Cornelius Stout had gone missing, his body ultimately found in the basement beneath Mr Bracegirdle's flat.

He re-read the notes that he had made in his interviews with the tenants. What struck him was the insight shown by none other than Micah Youngblood:

'After marriage, Mr Bracegirdle lost his hair, eyesight, use of limbs. Died. Natural causes? Human intervention. Mrs Bracegirdle responsible.'

'Mr Bracegirdle said wife was spending money. Wanted to be beneficiary of will. Mrs Bracegirdle stayed on after husband's death.'

O'Flanagan had pooh-poohed the idea that Mrs Bracegirdle might have something to do with her husband's death. The detective hadn't even known that Mrs Bracegirdle's Christian name was Rita. But if she were implicated in the Stout case, did that not beg the question that she might have been responsible for the death of her husband, too? Micah Youngblood had thought so.

Even Reggie could see that the evidence was thin, although there were signs of her involvement. Rita, whose name was engraved on Stout's signet ring, had applied for a position as housekeeper at the East Melbourne mansion while she was still married to Mr Bracegirdle. What if she had dispatched her husband to the next world, so that she could move on to her next meal ticket, Cornelius Stout?

What did he know about her? He turned to the notes from his interview with Lily Stout. She had described Rita as 'a big woman, too much make-up, bleached hair. Like one of those tarts from St Kilda. Rita gave Stout a signet ring. Father was sick of her. Wouldn't marry her. Ended relationship. Father went missing. No address for Rita known.'

It appeared that Rita Bracegirdle had come to work for Cornelius Stout and had tried to inveigle him into marrying her. Their relationship must have changed rapidly, from that of an employer-employee to an intimate one, given that he wore the ring that she gave him, inscribed with the words 'love Rita.' Angry that she had been unable to secure another husband who would provide for her, she had killed Stout, leaving him in the basement after she had vacated the apartment. There had been nothing to link her with Stout until now.

Reggie was sure that he was onto something. If he could find out more about Rita Bracegirdle, he could uncover the evidence to put her away. Perhaps stop another murder. He'd wrap up the case in a red ribbon and present it, *fait accompli*, to Detective Sergeant Mick O'Flanagan.

The clock on his dresser ticked over to midnight. He packed up the box and listed the lines of enquiry to follow up the next week. What he needed was a good night's sleep. The excitement of his discovery had only added to the exhaustion he was feeling when he considered his personal circumstances. It was going to be a big week. Tomorrow, he would need to find lodgings. Then, he would go in to *The Argus* to tie up some loose ends on Angus Murray's involvement in the Berriman robbery and murder. On Monday, he would familiarise his editor with the developments in the Cornelius Stout case. No doubt Kramer would heap praise upon him, perhaps even give him a pay rise. But the priority for him would be researching the murderer who was just out of his reach: Rita Bracegirdle. There was nothing like a female killer to get his gastric juices flowing. But enough of that. It was time to rest.

Reggie undressed and climbed into bed. The light from the moon had found a gap in the curtains. He closed his eyes and dropped into a troubled sleep, inhabited by big, buxom women with blood-red lips and bleached hair, who were being chased by a man bearing an uncanny resemblance to his father.

Chapter Twenty-Two

It was Saturday morning. The Citroen was packed and Reggie was ready to leave. All that he had to do was say farewell to his mother and shut the door on the life that he had known. It was to be much harder than he thought.

Mavis da Costa protested when she realised that her beloved son was about to leave. It had not been her intention to drive him away. Her motivation, she claimed, had been to tamp down the argument that was brewing between father and son, but it had backfired and she had forced Reggie into making a choice. She wrung her hands in agony, and her big blue innocent eyes had filled with tears when he said goodbye. He gave her a quick hug, ignored the presence of his father standing behind her, and left the key on the hall table.

He sat in the automobile, the engine idling. He looked back at the house, feeling deep regret that it had ended this way. If he were honest, however, he wanted to get away from his father. That man would affect his mother's reputation and send her catapulting down the social ladder once again. And he might suffer the same fate by association.

Inside, he felt a curious excitement now that he was travelling into parts unknown; change was on the horizon and perhaps it had come at the right time. Inadvertently, his father had hit the nail on the head: what was a mature-aged man doing, living with his mother? It was time to go. It was time to find a wife, although there were few women out there with the prerequisites that he required: money and beauty. If the opportunity arose in the near future, he would not hesitate. Reggie released the brake and put the car into gear, driving away from the only stable relationship he had had in thirty-six years.

He had intended to stop briefly at Dotty Wright's house, in order to drop off Eric Smith's wooden box. However, he was drawn into conversation with Dotty, who had noticed the suitcase on the passenger seat of the car. A short time later, Reggie was unpacking his belongings in the dwelling above Eric Smith's grocery shop. It didn't take much to convince him. The house was vacant. There was a laneway behind, where he could park his car safely. He would be responsible for any costs incurred in maintaining the home and would pay the utilities but, other than that, the accommodation would be gratis. Reggie would be doing her a favour, Dotty insisted. The previous Thursday night someone had broken into the shop, although nothing appeared to have been taken. Reggie's presence would discourage thieves. She was certain that the solicitor would agree, given that it would make the place secure until the will was finalised and the title transferred to her.

* * *

A few hours later, Reggie was at his desk at *The Argus*, feeling in a much better frame of mind now that his accommodation was sorted. The jacket of his suit hung from the coat stand behind him, his homburg propped jauntily on one of the hooks.

The telephone rang. 'Crime desk. Reggie da Costa speaking.'

'I have Miss Stout on the line.'

'Put her through.' Reggie took his feet off the desk and sat upright.

The low and melodious voice came down the line. 'It's Lily Stout here. I've found her. I've found Rita. I saw her at Leggett's Ballroom.'

Reggie clutched the handset, feeling a tremor of excitement go through him. 'Rita?'

'That's right. I asked the girl at the cloakroom and she says that Rita comes there every Friday night.'

'That's wonderful, Lily. Did she recognise you?'

'No. I've only met her once before, although Dad had some photographs of me on his mantelpiece. To be on the safe side, I stayed out of her line of sight.'

An unpleasant thought entered Reggie's mind. 'Who were you with?'

'Henry, of course. Why? Are you jealous?' She laughed, a deep throaty laugh.

He jiggled his foot. 'I've made some progress in investigating Rita.' He paused for effect. 'Her full name is Rita Bracegirdle. She lived at 1039 Punt Road, East Melbourne.'

There was silence at the other end of the telephone. 'She's still there?'

'No. She's moved. But now we have the crucial link between your father and the Punt Road property. She worked for Mr Stout as a housekeeper, then they became more than friends. She's the "Rita" of the ring.'

'You're amazing, Reggie. You'll contact the police now, won't you?' she asked. 'Insist that they investigate and charge her with Dad's murder?'

Reggie sat back, resting his feet on the edge of the desk. 'Not so hasty, Lily. All we have is circumstantial evidence. We need real proof that she was involved. You'll have to trust me on this. It's my area of expertise.'

Lily sounded irritated. 'She's a murderer. She wanted his money and when he wouldn't marry her, she killed him out of revenge. What more do you want?'

'Now, now, calm down,' he said. 'I have a plan. I'll go to Leggett's and observe her. I want to get a feel for the type of person we're dealing with. The more I can give the police, the better the case against her. I promise you, Lily, that I'll do my best to bring Rita Bracegirdle to justice.'

'Will you go this Friday?'

'That's my intention.'

'I'll come too. Henry can drive me and wait outside. Once I point her out to you, I'll go home.'

'That would be helpful. What time will I meet you?'

'Half-past eight. That's when the dancing starts. I'm relying on you, Reggie,' said Lily. 'My brother is in the crosshairs of a police investigation and I don't like it one bit. You have to help us. I'm beside myself with worry.'

'The police don't have a case against Henry. Leave it with me. I'll fix everything.'

Reggie hung up the phone. His investigation into The Basement Murder was progressing nicely. He would prove the case against Rita and, in the process, secure the innocence of Henry Stout. But first he would take a good look at the woman he suspected of murder. Friday could not come soon enough, particularly if it meant seeing Lily again.

He packed up his desk and drove to his new home, the dwelling above the grocer's shop in Swan Street, Richmond. It would be a temporary measure until he could find lodgings that were more suited to his social status, he thought. But the extra money, to spend on clothes and entertainment, would be welcome. And there was room for more wardrobe space to hang his extensive collection of suits and shirts, if he decided to stay. The grocer's home would do for now.

Chapter Twenty-Three

That first night in his new abode, Reggie accepted an invitation to dine with Dotty Wright. He felt buoyed by his conversation with Lily and so was at his entertaining best, sharing with Dotty his investigation into the case he referred to as The Basement Murder. Her admiration for his investigative powers was most gratifying, and he was pleased to have such an enthusiastic audience. However, he warned her that it would require all of his vast experience and analytical skills to track down this elusive perpetrator.

'Let me help you,' Dotty insisted. 'Here I am, stuck at home, and here you have a mystery that needs to be solved. Let me be Dr Watson to your Sherlock Holmes. I'm so bored and I need a distraction. Let me help you find this Rita Bracegirdle.'

Reggie was amused and, if he were honest, rather delighted at being compared to the Great Detective. Dotty had, he admitted, a good head on her shoulders, and it might be helpful to be able to bounce some ideas off her. However, she was a woman and lacked the experience with the criminal classes which was his domain. But, given that she had just allowed him to move in to the house next door, free of charge, he was prepared to indulge her somewhat.

'Perhaps you can help,' he conceded, 'but my first step is to contact my friend in Births, Deaths, and Marriages. Rita Bracegirdle's maiden name will be on file, which should give me another avenue to investigate.'

'Is there a process you follow for exposing a killer?'

Reggie puffed out his chest. 'When you are an investigator, you need to look into the victim's background. From there you develop a list of suspects. Then, you look for motive and opportunity.'

'It's very complicated.'

'Indeed, it is. Dealing with a crime that took place some time ago, as in the case of Cornelius Stout, creates problems. The crime scene may have been tampered with, perhaps inadvertently. Clues have been lost or destroyed. The evidence trail has become obscured over time. Suspects have moved away, died, or developed alibis. Witnesses forget important information. The more time between the execution of a crime and the discovery of the body, the harder it is to get a conviction.

'Cornelius Stout's murder took place around two years ago, but I have identified a very real suspect in the person of Rita Bracegirdle. I know that she had motive and opportunity to commit the crime.'

'How exciting,' said Dotty, her eyes shining.

'Just another day in the life of a crime reporter,' Reggie replied, yawning. He looked at the clock on the mantelpiece. 'It's nine o'clock. If you don't mind, I'll settle in next door. It's been a trying day.'

'Forgive my directness, Reggie, but I heard that your father's back. Is he staying long?'

Reggie scowled. 'Just till the money runs out.'

He wished her goodnight and went next door, to his new home, feeling deflated. Dotty's comments had made it clear that the Brighton social set, notably Dotty's Aunt Mildred and her friends, knew all about his father's return and were gossiping about them. Mario da Costa's sordid reputation as a philanderer and hedonist would, no doubt, have ramifications for the social standing of both him and his mother.

The truth was that he missed Mavis. She was the only one who truly cared for him and appreciated his talents and abilities. He hated the thought that she was back in the grip of a blackguard who would take advantage of her generosity and good nature. But there was nothing he could do to remedy the situation at home.

Reggie looked at himself in the mirror. His black hair was peppered with grey and there were lines around his eyes and mouth. He turned side on and noted with displeasure that his waist really was thickening. His mother was right: he was getting older.

Reggie undressed and switched off the light. As he lay waiting for sleep to come, he remembered the words of Captain Jack.

'I'm not ready to abandon ship just yet. I'll change tack and make the best of whatever time I have left, whatever that will be.'

Reggie couldn't change the fact that he was ageing. Or that his father had returned. But he needed to make the best of what he could control. And his new home was a good start. Tomorrow he would advertise for a housekeeper to cook and clean for him. A couple of shopping expeditions over the next few weeks would make his new abode more to his liking. He'd decorate it with those little touches that defined his sophistication and gentility. He smiled and closed his eyes. Sleep settled over him, like a warm blanket.

Chapter Twenty-Four

Detective Sergeant O'Flanagan stared moodily at the pile of dirt that lay next to the shallow grave. The remains had been removed and had been taken away to the coroner's office. The hole was around six feet long, three feet wide, and two feet deep. Just enough to conceal a body. O'Flanagan absent-mindedly raked the dirt with the toe of his shoe.

He had already been inside and interrogated the occupants of the house, in whose garden the body had been buried. The place had been empty when two vagrants had made it their home about six months before. The police had chased them off, but they kept coming back. One of them, John Black, had decided to plant some vegetables that Sunday morning. He started digging. The shovel hit bone and he stopped. He called the police.

'Didn't want no trouble,' he told O'Flanagan. 'I know a human bone when I see one.'

Afterwards, the detective had interviewed the neighbours on each side of the property. Apparently, the owner had gone missing eighteen months before. Just packed up and left, they said, in the dead of the night. Didn't tell anyone. Armitage Flagg, he was. A widower. Wealthy. This made O'Flanagan feel distinctly out of sorts. Flagg's story contained overtones of the Cornelius and Edmund Stout cases.

'Bugger. Another one.'

O'Flanagan entered the house and walked around, trying to get a feel for whom Armitage Flagg was and how he lived his life. But it was difficult. A year and a half had passed, and there were few reminders of the man. The vagrants had made themselves at home. They had helped themselves to his possessions and sold off portable property, availing themselves of the beds, couches, and armchairs that remained. Understandably, the house was filthy and the kitchen stank.

The neighbours were useless. They didn't want to get involved in a murder investigation and told O'Flanagan in no uncertain tones. The body in the backyard was an aberration, one neighbour insisted. Nothing like that had ever happened in their neighbourhood before. People were law-abiding around here. Nice people. Not like those suburbs—Fitzroy and Collingwood and Richmond—where Squizzy Taylor and his gang ruled the streets. South Yarra was different. Could the detective sergeant please hurry up and evict those vagrants? It was most probably their doing. Property values would fall if the press got wind of a murder happening in the street.

With little to go on, O'Flanagan left the house and drove back to his office, where he wrote a preliminary report for his superiors. Then he went into the file room, which contained information on missing persons. He had a hunch and he needed to follow it up. It was going to be a long afternoon.

Slowly and methodically, he pulled the files on missing persons from 1916-1923. He was looking for a pattern. Three disappearances, with two found dead, had landed on his patch, all involving wealthy, unmarried gents around fifty to sixty years of age, who lived in the suburbs close to Melbourne proper.

- Cornelius Stout. Fifty-two years old. Disappeared June 1921. East Melbourne.
- Edmund Stout. Fifty-four years old. Disappeared June 1919. East Melbourne.
- Armitage Flagg. Sixty-one years old. Disappeared May 1922. South Yarra.

It didn't take long to find another suspicious disappearance. Julius Mathieson had gone missing in 1916. Separated from his wife, he was rich and living alone on Richmond Hill. He had cashed in some of his bonds in the weeks before his disappearance but, other than that, his bank accounts remained untouched. The police had made preliminary enquiries, but had not noticed any suspicious behaviour on the part of his relatives.

By late afternoon, O'Flanagan had the names of three other men whose circumstances fitted the criteria. It was a long shot to suggest that they were all linked, but he couldn't ignore the facts. More than seven men, all wealthy and living in suburbs close to Melbourne, had disappeared off the face of the earth in the last seven years. Either it was a coincidence, or there was a killer on the loose, picking off men of a particular age group and class. And, what made it worse was that the suspects in the Cornelius Stout murder most probably had no links with five of the other cases. How could Henry Stout or Horace Striker or Stanley Duggan have had anything to do with Armitage Flagg, Julius Mathieson or the three others he had just found in the files? O'Flanagan shook his head as he considered the amount of work that this case would generate. The pressure would be on again, once Reggie da Costa sniffed the air and caught a whiff of multiple murders.

'Is every bloody missing person going to end up dead?' he growled.

It was getting late. He stared at his notes. As if he needed this. He had so much on his plate. Tomorrow, he would have to make enquiries about Flagg's financial and marital status, the extent of his assets, and who would benefit from his death. It was going to take a lot of desk time and that was something he loathed.

As he walked along the corridor, he saw that the door to the police commissioner's office was wide open. He groaned inwardly. There was no avoiding Chief Commissioner Nicholson. The familiar voice stopped him in his tracks.

'Working on a Sunday? What have you got, O'Flanagan?'

'Murder in South Yarra.'

'I'll have a report on my desk tomorrow morning, Detective Sergeant.'

'Yes, sir.'

As he went down the stairs towards the exit, he considered what he would have liked to have said in reply to Nicholson's question.

'What have I got, sir? I'll tell you what I've got. A headache. There's a murderer on the loose, and I haven't got a clue who it is.'

Chapter Twenty-Five

Reggie da Costa stood outside Leggett's Ballroom, watching a stream of well-dressed men and women cross the road from Prahran railway station. The ladies were wearing a confection of evening dresses, while the men wore everything from lounge to dinner suits. Reggie, of course, was wearing the latter, and was feeling rather vexed that his jacket felt a tad tighter. However, he had taken particular care with his personal grooming—thin moustache neatly trimmed, hair flat and slicked with Brilliantine—given that Lily Stout would soon be standing alongside him. To be honest, he had never thought about patronising Leggett's, regarding it as a venue for the masses. However, the fact that Lily had been amongst their number made him consider whether he had been wrong about Leggett's clientele.

An automobile pulled up alongside him. It was Henry in an Australian Six motorcar, with tan paintwork and upholstery. No doubt he'd be upgrading to a newer model, once the inheritance came through. Reggie opened the passenger door and took Lily's hand, as she stepped out onto the footpath. Even in the half light of the street, she put all the other women in the shade. Quite frankly, she was stunning. Her frock was exquisite, a stylish dress in ivory lace with an elaborately embroidered bodice. Her hair was bobbed, framing an immaculately made-up face. A shawl was draped around her pretty little shoulders.

She smiled winningly and pecked him on the cheek. 'Reggie. So good to see you again.'

Reggie was captivated.

After paying the entry fee of three shillings and checking Lily's shawl into the cloakroom, Reggie escorted her into the ballroom, which was bubbling with people. He was shocked. There had to be around four hundred inside. A sign on the wall indicated that a motorcar would be awarded to the winners of the Amateur Championship of Victoria.

'They're giving away an automobile? At a dance venue? What sort of event is this?'

Lily checked her lipstick in a mirror. 'I can't believe you've never come here. It's great fun. There are competitions, fancy dress, theme nights, and tuition, if you want it. The place is usually more crowded than this. It's very popular.'

'I had no idea,' he confessed. 'How will we find Rita in this crowd?'

'We'll find her. Can you dance, Reggie?'

He was appalled at the question. 'I could dance before I could walk. Foxtrot. Waltz. One-step. Tango. Mother said I was a natural.'

'Then show me.'

He took her hand and led her out onto the dance floor, where they waited for the band to begin. It was a waltz. Smoothly and expertly, Reggie took her in his arms and they began, their bodies rising and falling in time to the music, as they glided effortlessly around the hall. She was so petite, so graceful, and so accomplished as a dancer, that he wished the music would never stop.

'We make a good couple,' he whispered in her ear.

She smiled enigmatically. 'I've never met anyone like you. Perhaps we can come back here again when this terrible business is over. But our purpose tonight is to find Rita. And don't forget that my brother is waiting outside for me. Come, Reggie, let's work our way around the dance floor.'

The band was playing a foxtrot, which allowed them to progress around the auditorium. Lily looked around Reggie's shoulder, searching for Rita Bracegirdle. It was like finding a needle in a haystack, such was the crush of people on the dance floor. They steadily worked their way up towards the bandstand, where the conductor turned side-on to beam down at the dancers going past. Catching sight of Lily, he winked at her then turned back towards the orchestra.

Reggie felt Lily stiffen. 'There she is,' she whispered. 'In pink. Blonde.'

Reggie swung Lily around so that he could see whom she was talking about. Rita stood out from the crowd, unlike any other woman in the room. She was about five feet eight inches in height, a big woman with strong arms and large breasts that were barely contained by a satin dress at least two sizes too small for her. Her long blonde hair was scraped back into a bun at the nape of her neck, a tawdry flower behind one ear. She was heavily made-up: her cheeks smeared with pink rouge and her mouth a slash of deep red. A little wizened man with a bald head was trying to lead her, but it was an impossible task, given that he barely came up to her shoulder.

'I should get out of here,' said Lily, 'before she recognises me. Besides, Henry will be wondering where I've got to.'

Reluctantly, Reggie escorted her back to the lobby, where she retrieved her shawl from the cloakroom. She gave him a peck on the cheek, which went some way to assuaging his feelings.

'We're depending on you.' She took his hand and held it for a moment. 'You know where I live.'

He watched her go out into the street, to be met by Henry. Then he turned and went back into the auditorium, where he found a seat along the side, close to where Rita was dancing. A couple of women strolled past him, slowing down in case he should ask them to dance. He ignored them and they walked away, looking disappointed.

Without the company of Lily Stout to distract him, Reggie was able to settle into a close scrutiny of Rita Bracegirdle's behaviour. He was interested to see how she interacted with the men around her. If it were true that she had been involved in the murder of Cornelius Stout and Clyde Bracegirdle, then he surmised that she would be the type of woman who used her feminine wiles in the pursuit of men. He watched her as she thrust her body up against that of her dancing partner. His cheeks went pink and he started to sweat. Poor devil, thought Reggie, he doesn't stand a chance. Rita resembled a mongoose sizing up a mouse.

Although the little man was her focus of attention, Rita was aware of those around her, greeting friends, laughing at their comments, waving to those she knew across the room. Her smile never faltered. Not once did her energy levels drag. She was on show and she played up to it.

After watching her for over half an hour, Reggie felt confident to draw some conclusions about Rita Bracegirdle: she liked attention, she liked men, she was an accomplished dancer, and she knew how to use her body to seduce the opposite sex. From the number of men and women who greeted her, it was obvious that Rita was a regular at Leggett's.

He felt a tap on his shoulder. A man sat down next to him.

'You're intrigued with Rita. I can tell,' he said.

Reggie raised his eyebrows. 'Perhaps.'

'Run a mile. She's poison.'

'Sorry, I missed your name.'

'That doesn't matter, mate. Just think of me as a friend.'

'Why is she poison?'

'I met up with her last September. Here, at Leggett's. Rita has a way about her. No doubt you noticed that. She makes you think that you're the most important person in her world. Everything you say, everything you do, she compliments you. Admire her and she glows. She loves it.

'She can pick the ones who need her. Lonely men. Those who are never very good with women. Widowers. Men with money. When you're with her, she presses up against you. Dresses like a tart and reeks of cheap perfume. Leaves nothing to the imagination, if you know what I mean. She wants you to beg for it.

'Don't be fooled. It's an act. You think she's easy, but there's strings attached. You only get the full treatment if you give her what she wants. Presents, flowers, attention, and, ultimately, money. I fell for it and she took me home. There's this daughter there, watching you, offering you drinks and food. Like a maid, but creepy. To be honest, I couldn't get out of there fast enough. It was bizarre.'

'Is that right?'

'It was for me. Maybe you're different. You don't look her type, to be honest, but I saw the way you were looking at her.' He leaned in. 'Look, mate, I'm not telling you what to do, just to be careful.'

He got up, turned on his heel, and made his way down the side of the hall, Reggie staring after him. He'd seen and heard enough. It was time to go. He knew that he was right to pursue Rita Bracegirdle. She was firming up nicely as the premier suspect in the Cornelius Stout murder.

Chapter Twenty-Six

'I thought I'd find you here.'

Reggie stood next to the table at which O'Flanagan was eating his breakfast. The detective sergeant looked up and motioned for Reggie to sit. He cut off a big piece of sausage and slotted it into his mouth, chewing slowly.

The waitress came towards him, but Reggie waved her away. 'I'm following up the discovery of Armitage Flagg's body, Mick. I thought I would have heard from you, but not a word. We had an arrangement to share information.'

O'Flanagan pointed his fork at the crime reporter. 'I was meaning to contact you.'

Reggie waited but the detective remained silent, concentrating on his breakfast. 'It's been a week since Flagg was found,' he continued. 'I've spoken to the neighbours and they say he disappeared eighteen months ago.'

'So?'

'Rich. Alone. Missing. Remind you of anyone?'

O'Flanagan put down his fork. 'You're not suggesting that there's a connection with the Cornelius Stout murder? Really, Reggie, you have an overactive imagination.'

'Perhaps, but have you checked whether any other older, lonely, wealthy men have gone missing?'

'You think I have nothing better to do? The bank manager died, so Angus Murray has been charged with murder. Squizzy's been remanded for the Berriman robbery and murder, too. I'm trying to put him away, once and for all. Why should I go on a wild goose chase like you suggest?'

'Because there may be a connection between Stout, his brother, and Flagg.'

'Don't be ridiculous.' He dropped a piece of bacon into the egg yolk and skewered it with his fork, then popped it into his mouth. 'Can't you see I'm busy?' He ran his tongue over his lips to capture any leftover bits of yolk.

Reggie da Costa stared hard at the detective. 'You're not playing fair. We had an agreement.'

'You're a reporter. I'm a detective. We're not a team.' O'Flanagan's expression was distinctly chilly.

Reggie let out a breath. If that was the way Mick was going to play it, Reggie thought, then the police could find out for themselves who 'Rita' really was. That she was the wife of Clyde Bracegirdle and had become housekeeper for Cornelius Stout. And then his lover. It would be O'Flanagan's loss, not Reggie's.

But he needed any information that the police could give him, if he were to break the case. He tried one more time. 'You think that Horace Striker and his nephew are behind Stout's murder? Or are you still looking at Henry Stout? Come on, Mick, give me something.'

O'Flanagan put down his knife and fork, and looked at Reggie steadily, his bulldog face blank. 'Our investigation is proceeding as normal. We are following certain leads that will be revealed in the course of time.' He tore off a piece of toast and stuffed it in his mouth.

Reggie was livid. 'Good luck, O'Flanagan. You're going to need it. But don't come looking for me when you need some help with this. I'll solve it without you.'

The detective ignored him. Reggie turned on his heel and stalked out the door. It had been so different with Clary Blain, O'Flanagan's predecessor, he thought. The information had flowed between the two of them, back and forth, as smoothly as the whisky that Blain had poured down his throat. Those were the days.

* * *

Back at the office and devoid of any extra information from his usual sources, Reggie had to dig deep to put a new slant on the Cornelius Stout story. Kramer was expecting a follow-up article on the progress of the investigation, and he couldn't disappoint him.

He re-read the report, which he would send down soon to the typesetter.

POLICE BAFFLED
THE BASEMENT MURDER CASE

By REGGIE DA COSTA, Senior Crime Reporter

The Criminal Investigation Branch is following up links between the murders of three men who went missing between 1919 and 1922. At this stage, it is apparent that the police have no answers.

Rich, alone, and missing!

The body of Cornelius Stout, a wealthy widower, was found in October. Edmund Stout, his brother, disappeared in June 1919. The body of Armitage Flagg was recovered from his South Yarra backyard late last month. All three men were wealthy and living alone, and were aged in their fifties or sixties when they went missing.

Are there more bodies out there?

Police refuse to reveal whether other missing persons may be involved, but we have it on good authority that a fourth person, Mr Julius Mathieson, disappeared from his Richmond Hill home in 1916. He fits the description of rich, lonely, and missing.

Police have turned their attention to Melbourne's underworld in an attempt to solve the murder of Cornelius Stout. Of particular interest is Mr Horace Striker, a well-known gang leader, whose expertise lies in the murky fields of illegal gambling, prostitution, and sly-grog. Coincidentally, Mr Striker was a tenant at the East Melbourne terrace where Stout's body was found. His nephew, Mr Stanley Duggan, was bankrupted after investing in a property deal proposed by Mr Stout. This gives Mr Striker and Mr Duggan both motive and opportunity

in relation to the death.

At this stage, there are no definitive answers to the question: Who killed Cornelius Stout?

Members of the public are asked to contact *The Argus* or Detective Sergeant Michael O'Flanagan, of the Criminal Investigation Branch, Victoria Police, if they have any information that might help in the investigation.

[*The Argus* October 15, 1923]

Admittedly, his assertion that the police were investigating an underworld figure was fanciful, but it was Reggie's job to stretch the truth in pursuit of a good story. His readers loved anything to do with the gangs of Melbourne, and mention of Squizzy Taylor and his ilk would sell papers. Besides, he rather liked putting pressure on O'Flanagan, given his cavalier treatment of the press. And, by now, Horace Striker's threats against him would have lost their sting. Or so Reggie thought.

Chapter Twenty-Seven

Theo Georgiadis was waiting outside the front entrance to the Department of Births, Deaths, and Marriages. He smiled as he saw the familiar yellow Citroen, with its flashy black mudguards and boat-tail, pull into the curb in front of him. Reggie da Costa stepped out of the automobile and shook his hand.

'Lunch, Theo?'

'Not today. I have an appointment with the Registrar, so I can only spare a moment.' He handed him a piece of paper. 'It's all there. Rita Bracegirdle has been very busy. I traced her back from her last marriage and was able to find out where she came from. She covers the gamut of births, deaths, marriages, and annulments. Amazing! Unfortunately, I don't have a current address.'

Reggie raised his eyebrows. 'Not under Bracegirdle?'

'Your lady, to put it mildly, isn't interested in keeping her married name. Or her husbands, for that matter. They have an unfortunate tendency to die. I'm surprised that the police don't know about her. She's either very unlucky or—'

'Or what?'

He shrugged his shoulders. 'I'll leave that in your capable hands.'

He doffed his hat and went back into the building.

Reggie stared down at the lengthy record of Rita Bracegirdle's marital history. It would take more than a couple of minutes on a windy Melbourne street to come to terms with her conjugal activities. He started the Citroen and headed to the offices of *The Argus*.

117

Back in the newsroom, Reggie settled into his chair and read through Theo's notes. Rita Bracegirdle had fitted much into her life. By the age of fifty-three, she had had four husbands and apparently innumerable lovers, and was not finished yet. His typewriter sat waiting, a fresh piece of paper on the roller. Slowly, he transcribed Theo's notes into something that approximated a chronological biography of Rita Bracegirdle:

- Rita June SAVAGE Born May 4, 1870. Castlemaine.
- Birth of Dolores May SAVAGE. June 17, 1886. Queen Victoria Hospital, Melbourne. Rita aged 16. Unmarried. No record of adoption.
- Rita SAVAGE married Sylvester STURGESS. January 3, 1893.
- Marriage annulled 1895.
- Rita STURGESS married James HARDCASTLE. February 7, 1901.
- Death of husband December 31, 1903 from natural causes.
- Rita HARDCASTLE married Alexander ROPER. December 6, 1915.
- Husband missing in action July 1, 1916. France.
- Rita ROPER married Clyde BRACEGIRDLE. February 28, 1921.
- Death of husband May 14, 1921. Natural causes.

A mother at sixteen. A baby borne out of wedlock. Four marriages. Two deaths from natural causes. Sylvester Sturgess had miraculously survived. Reggie made a note to interview him, if he could be found.

Incredibly, Rita had applied for the position of housekeeper to Cornelius Stout before her husband, Clyde Bracegirdle, was in his grave. She had subsequently worked for Cornelius Stout, become his lover, and then had been dumped unceremoniously after pestering him to marry. What was her motive in committing murder? Money? Revenge? Was she involved in the disappearance of Edmund Stout? They were brothers, so it couldn't be ruled out.

He poured himself a Scotch from the bottle in his desk drawer, and pondered what his next step should be. He knew from experience that a criminal's early life gave an indication of what they would become in adulthood. Poverty, abuse, and deprivation could all have deleterious effects on personality, and could create a breeding ground for criminal tendencies. Perhaps Rita's family still lived in Castlemaine. It wouldn't be hard to locate them because Savage was not a common name, and Castlemaine was a typical country town where everyone would know everyone else. A former colleague, who now worked for *The Castlemaine Mail*, might be able to help him with that.

Gaining some background information on Rita Bracegirdle was a necessary first step, before he started digging deeper into the likelihood that she was involved in murder. It was all speculation at this stage, with no hard evidence. But Reggie da Costa was determined to change all that. If he could solve the Death Mask Murders case, he could solve anything.

Chapter Twenty-Eight

The ringing of the telephone interrupted Reggie's little snooze at his desk.

'Call for you, Mr da Costa.'

'Put it through,' Reggie answered groggily.

He had been out late the previous evening, and was finding that his capacity to bounce back was reducing as his years increased. The rather attractive lady that he had met at The Hotel Windsor had been quite beguiling. She had helped while away the hours in a most satisfactory fashion. In fact, he had been daydreaming about her when the phone rang.

Lily Stout's dulcet tones came down the phone line. 'Reggie, is that you? It's Lily Stout.'

That got his attention. He sat up straight and adjusted his tie.

'Miss Stout.'

'Lily, call me Lily. Could we meet? Would this evening be convenient?'

Despite his yearning to retire early to recoup lost sleep, Reggie replied in the affirmative. Who was he to pass up an heiress, if she were keen enough to seek him out? He suggested dinner at the Café Latin.

Now, fully awake, he felt that life was taking a turn for the better. He propped his feet up on the edge of his desk and leaned back, his hands behind his head. He had been thinking of an excuse to meet Lily Stout again, and she had solved his problem. That tantalising, soon-to-be wealthy, young woman wanted to see him. God knew he wanted to see her. She fitted his exacting pre-requisites for a wife. And, she had seemed particularly interested in him when he first met her. Why wouldn't she be? He was a worldly, well-dressed man-about-town who was on the way up in his chosen profession. No doubt, she'd be impressed even further when he picked her up in his Citroen 5CV 'Torpedo' tourer, with its yellow boat-tail and black mudguards.

Things were definitely going his way, in spite of his father's return to Melbourne. Earlier that morning, he had met with Floyd Kramer, presenting him with evidence of Rita Bracegirdle's involvement in Cornelius Stout's murder. Admittedly, it had been touch and go at first, Kramer resisting Reggie's reasoning that a woman could be behind Stout's death.

'He was in a trunk in a basement,' said the editor, tapping his pencil on the desk to emphasise his point. 'How would this Rita Bracegirdle manage that? She'd be on her own. It defies belief.'

'She's a big woman, Floyd. Not some shrinking violet.'

Slowly and methodically, Reggie built up the case against her. Stout's advertisement for a housekeeper. Her letter in return. Soliciting a job before her husband was dead. Moving quickly from being housekeeper to having a personal relationship with her employer. Residing in the terrace where Stout's body was found. The signet ring with her name inscribed on it. The resentment that he would not marry her eventually exploding into anger and violence. The attempt to remove the ring and thus hide her involvement. Her departure from the Punt Road terrace without leaving a forwarding address.

To this, he added the character analysis of Rita Bracegirdle, provided by Lily Stout and Micah Youngblood. According to them, Rita was mercenary, loved spending money, and was a blowsy, bleached blonde tart with few scruples.

Kramer had sat back in his chair. 'Does this say more about Miss Stout and Youngblood than Rita?' he had asked.

That had pulled Reggie up short. 'Possibly,' he had admitted. 'A religious pedant on one hand and a jealous daughter on the other.'

'At least you acknowledge the problems.'

'The case will be stronger if I can look into her past. She was raised in Castlemaine. I'd like to go there and talk to the family. My source at *The*

Castlemaine Mail tells me that Rita's sister still lives in the town.'

Kramer chewed the end of his pencil then pushed his glasses up the bridge of his nose, giving Reggie the full effect of two magnified eyes. 'I'll give you a week. If nothing comes of your Castlemaine visit, you drop the Rita Bracegirdle angle. Understood?'

'Of course, boss.'

'But if this comes to something, there might be a promotion in it for you.'

* * *

It was half-past six. Nearly time to meet Lily Stout. Reggie went into the staffroom and opened the wardrobe that he had appropriated when he became a senior crime reporter. He had planned ahead for times like this, fitting a mirror to the inside door. He noted, with satisfaction, that the shirt he was wearing still looked sufficiently fresh. He changed into his navy-checked suit. Thank goodness he'd had it pressed recently. He sensed that Lily would notice if it were creased. He changed his socks and buffed up his spare pair of black shoes.

On the top shelf, he kept a clothes brush and a small toiletry bag. He poured a liberal quantity of hair oil onto his upraised palm and rubbed it between his hands, then smoothed it over his thick mane of hair. He combed it carefully, capturing the right fashionable style. Finally, he took a small pair of scissors from the toiletry bag and trimmed his moustache. He stood back and surveyed himself in the mirror. He smiled.

What a lady-killer. Lily wouldn't be able to resist him.

Half an hour later, he pulled up outside the boarding house in East Melbourne. Lily was waiting on the front verandah. She ran her eyes over the highly polished yellow and black automobile that was Reggie's pride and joy. He, in turn, ran his eyes over her. She was wearing a sumptuous, black velvet coat with a thick fur collar, and carried a small, beaded evening bag in her gloved hands. He slid across the bench seat, pushed open the door for her, then shifted back into the driver's seat as she came up beside him.

'Reggie. It's nice to see you.'

'You look breathtaking,' he replied. He took her hand and kissed it.

She smiled. 'How European of you.'

He started the Citroen, then pulled out from the curb. Conversation was difficult over the roar of the engine, but Lily seemed content to sit in silence. Reggie alternated between watching the road and casting admiring glances in the direction of his passenger.

Shortly after, they parked near the entrance to the restaurant. Reggie leaned across in front of Lily, surreptitiously enjoying the fragrance of her perfume—tuberoses—and opened the car door for her.

The Café Latin was situated above a wine shop in Exhibition Street. Recently opened, it had a Bohemian edge to it, which he thought would appeal to Lily. In the short time of its existence, it had quickly established itself as one of Melbourne's finest Italian restaurants.

Once inside, Reggie helped Lily out of her coat. Beneath it, she was wearing a deep crimson dress in the finest silk, with a dropped waist. It was clear that she was no longer wearing imitation Paris fashions.

They were shown to a table in the corner of the restaurant, which gave them a bird's eye view of the other diners. Menus presented and orders taken, they sipped their wine and made casual conversation. Reggie had noticed, with some consternation, that the prices had gone up appreciably since his first visit. But one look at Lily, and the possibility that her future wealth would soon be his, calmed his fears regarding the bill.

Once the waiter had removed their plates, Lily placed a cigarette in a slender silver holder. Reggie immediately bent forward to light it.

Lily exhaled; her grey eyes fastened on Reggie's face.

'That was a delicious dinner, Reggie.' She looked at him coquettishly. 'Why haven't you contacted me? I thought you liked me.'

Reggie shrugged his shoulders, the epitome of self-possession. 'I've been busy. So much has happened. The police strike. The investigation into your father's death. Angus Murray. Squizzy Taylor's antics. It's not that I didn't want to, it's that I'm very much in demand.'

Lily cocked her head, her lips pouted. 'But you do like me?'

'Of course. Is this why you wanted to see me? To assure yourself of my interest?'

'Partly. Let's come back to that later. You must know that I'm eager to hear what you've found out about my father's murder. My brother and I are very concerned that the killer will get away with it.'

Reggie smiled and stroked his moustache. 'Have no fear, I'm on the case. It's my belief, no, conviction, that Rita Bracegirdle murdered your father. So far, I've compiled a veritable arsenal of evidence against her.'

Lily smiled and tapped the ash off her cigarette. 'Do tell.'

Reggie outlined the case against Stout's former housekeeper, as he had done with his editor only hours earlier, and then repeated his intention to dig further into her background before he presented his findings to the police.

'Why are you waiting?' cried Lily. 'I can't believe that you'd let my brother be interrogated by the police, when it's clear he didn't do it.'

Reggie reached across and took her hand. 'Don't worry. Once I have all the evidence, I'll be contacting O'Flanagan. Rita's guilty, I know it. They haven't got a case against your brother. It's all circumstantial.' He paused. 'There is one thing. I interviewed one of the tenants in the Punt Road property. He said that he saw Henry lurking outside on the street months ago. Why would that be?'

Lily took another drag of her cigarette, then butted it out.

'For your information, Henry doesn't "lurk." He didn't tell you because he thought you might misconstrue his motivation. The fact is that we knew where Rita lived. You see, Henry followed her home one night because we wanted to know who she really was. When Dad disappeared, we thought she was behind it. Henry decided to confront her. What we didn't know was that she'd moved out and someone else was living there. I know it doesn't look good, but that's the truth.'

'Did he find out where she'd moved to?'

'No. We were convinced that she killed Dad because he broke off the relationship. It's so frustrating that the police don't even appear interested in her. I can't understand it. It's so wrong.'

She reached into her bag and took out a lace handkerchief, dabbing at the tears which had formed in her eyes.

Reggie squeezed her hand. 'Don't worry. It's ridiculous to even suggest that Henry was behind this. Even if he hoped to inherit from your father, it would take seven years before he could, if the body couldn't be found. There has to be a declaration of death.'

'It's unfair, don't you think? Seven long years. That's an eternity to claim what's rightfully yours. But I'm so glad that you believe in his innocence. You can understand why I'm worried. Henry's my twin and we're very close. Family is so important, don't you think?'

Reggie didn't answer at first. Her comment about family conjured up visions of his mother and *that* man, his father. He smiled wanly and nodded his head.

'Yes, family is important.'

Lily picked up her handbag. 'This has been lovely, but I must be going. My landlady doesn't like her residents to be out too late. I will be so relieved when I move from there. I'll be able to entertain visitors in my new home.' Her eyes locked with his. 'You'd like that, wouldn't you?'

Reggie didn't trust himself to answer, but he felt a sense of delicious anticipation at the prospect of visiting Miss Lily Stout in the privacy of her 'villa.'

'When will you take possession of the estate?' he asked, returning to more practical matters.

'The wheels move slowly, but I'm hoping that it will be early next year. The will's been read, and the death notice has been issued. Then it's just a case of probate being approved.'

'Who's the executor of the estate?'

'My father's solicitor. He's one of those who does things by the book. I'll probably be old and grey before I see any money.'

'I can't imagine that you'll ever be old and grey.'

'You're so sweet, Reggie.'

He called for the bill, and was relieved to see that he had enough in his wallet to cover it. Fortunately, his new accommodation was costing him almost nothing, but if he wanted to pursue Miss Stout, he would need serious money. He would have to hold back on some of his more outrageous expenditure in order to win her.

As he took her arm, he thought what a good couple they would make. His excellent taste and her money would be a winning combination. Under his breath he whispered, *'Sei la donna dei miei sogni!'* You are the woman of my dreams! His Italian blood was most definitely coming to the fore.

* * *

Half an hour later, still basking in the rosy glow of a night out with Lily, Reggie drove the Citroen into the alley at the back of the grocer's shop. As he locked the car, he heard a voice call his name, a familiar voice that sent a chill down his spine. He spun around. It was Horace Striker. And, worse still, he was not alone, but was accompanied by two of his henchmen.

'Good evening, Mr da Costa. Don't say I didn't warn you.'

Chapter Twenty-Nine

Earlier that evening, Dotty had packed her bag and left it next to the front door, ready for the train trip to Castlemaine in the morning. She had felt quite excited when Reggie had come in a few nights before, and asked her if she were well enough to accompany him. Now that the cast on her ankle had been removed, she couldn't see why not. The doctor had given her a medical certificate till the end of the school year, which was only a couple of weeks away and, quite frankly, she was bored. A trip up the country would be a tonic for her.

'Why do you want me to come?' she had asked Reggie.

'You'll be a reassuring presence when I interview Rita's sister. She might not like a strange man in the house.'

Aunt Mildred had not been keen. She was concerned that her niece, an unmarried, respectable, young woman, would be travelling with an unattached man, but Dotty had assured her in no uncertain terms that there was nothing to worry about.

'I'm not young anymore. I'm thirty-two. Besides, I'm absolutely sure that Reggie has no improper thoughts about me. He's more interested in himself than in anyone else. But it will be fun, and I'd like something to occupy my mind while I'm on leave. My ankle is almost right now. A change of scene and a mystery to solve sound right up my alley!'

Aunt Mildred had acquiesced in the end, but had warned her niece to lock her hotel door.

After drinking a steaming cup of cocoa, Dotty went to bed early, in preparation for a big day ahead. Her travelling clothes were laid out in the spare room and she'd put aside a good book to while away the hours on the train. She read for half an hour, then fell into a deep sleep.

It was sometime later when she was awoken by the sound of raised voices coming from the back laneway. She switched on the bedside lamp and checked the clock. It was after ten. She sat up in bed and listened. Someone cried out. Then she heard doors slamming and a motorcar taking off at speed. Pulling on her dressing gown and leaning on her walking stick, Dotty made her way down into the kitchen. She paused at the back door then opened it, gazing out into the night.

The moon was high, illuminating the yard. It was empty. There was a knothole in the back fence, through which she could get a view of the lane. She ventured across the cobblestones and peered through it, but could see nothing of note. Tentatively, she opened the gate. Reggie's Citroen was parked next to the fence, but otherwise the lane appeared deserted. She sighed. False alarm. If there had been an argument, the men had left.

She turned to go inside, but froze as she heard an indefinable sound coming from close by. She paused, her ears pricked, her senses on alert. She raised her walking stick and approached the Citroen. A dark mass was lying in the shadows. She drew back, then, gathering her courage, edged forward. In the darkness, she could just make out the shiny, black hair and handsome face of her neighbour, Reggie da Costa.

She dropped the walking stick and bent down at his side. 'Reggie. Are you alive?'

He groaned, then slowly opened his eyes. 'Barely.'

'What happened?' she said, shocked at the sight of blood streaming down his face.

'I was bashed.' His face twisted in pain.

'I'll get an ambulance and the police.'

He raised his head. 'Don't, please. Get me inside. I'll be alright.'

She frowned, but helped him to his feet. Together they made their slow way back to the house, Dotty leaning heavily on her walking stick while she tried to take some of Reggie's weight. By the time they reached the kitchen, both were out of breath.

Reggie grimaced as Dotty lowered him into a chair. The kitchen light lay bare the extent of his injuries: face bruised and swollen; eyes like slits; blood streaming from his nose; his hand clutching his ribs.

'Who did this to you?'

'Horace Striker.'

'You need to tell the police.'

'Definitely not. It would be worse next time, if I did.'

Dotty held a glass of water to his lips. 'Drink this.'

He sipped it tentatively, then winced. 'Nothing stronger?'

She shook her head. 'I'm afraid not. Why would Striker do this?'

Reggie let out a strangled laugh. 'Horace values his privacy.'

'All because of your article about him?'

'And his nephew. Can you clean me up a bit?'

Dotty put the kettle on the hob and warmed some water, then gently bathed his face, washing away the blood. 'That's better. You look more like you now.'

He touched his face hesitantly. 'Give me a mirror.'

'No, Reggie. Not yet. Wait till the swelling goes down. Time to get you home.'

Chapter Thirty

It was a few days before Reggie and Dotty undertook the journey to Castlemaine, after waiting for the worst of his injuries to heal. On Dotty's insistence, he had visited a doctor, who had assured him that he had basically escaped unscathed, apart from sore ribs, a cut lip, and some bruising to his face, which was now fading.

The morning was bright and sunny when Reggie and Dotty caught the electric train from Richmond into the city. The steam locomotive, that was to carry them from the outskirts of Melbourne to the town of Castlemaine, was waiting at Spencer Street station. A porter carried their bags and showed them to their carriage, depositing the luggage in the overhead racks.

Dotty took her seat opposite Reggie. She opened the window and leaned out to take in the scene. The station was a hive of activity. Porters ran down the platform, pushing trolleys laden with luggage, while the station master strutted around importantly, watching the clock tick around towards departure time. Passengers climbed aboard and waved to loved ones. Doors slammed shut. Clouds of steam rose from the smokestack of the locomotive and blanketed the sky. She could smell the soot and feel the grit in the air, which added to her excitement. The station master, a little man with a thick moustache, waved his flag.

'All aboard!'

The whistle blew, and the locomotive slowly chugged out of the station, its wheels grinding against the metal of the rails. Dotty pushed the window up till it was shut.

'Filthy machine,' muttered Reggie, brushing invisible particles of dirt from his sleeve.

'It's rather magical actually,' said Dotty. 'Quite atmospheric.'

'If you say so.'

Dotty took a book from her bag and tried to read it, but her eyes were drawn to the scenes outside the window. At first, they passed the little brick terrace houses and modest weatherboard cottages of inner suburban Melbourne. Bluestone alleyways snaked off main streets, giving access to tiny backyards bordered by corrugated iron fences. There were no gardens or public parks to relieve the monotony of stone and metal; nowhere for children to play except on the streets.

Further out, the inner-city slums gave way to a wasteland of industrial debris, dotted with ramshackle housing. Sheets of iron and discarded timber made for temporary shelters. There was no future for the children that lived here, she thought. Born in a shanty and destined to die in a shanty. Here were the dregs of society, forgotten and abandoned. It was confronting. Her mood shifted to despondency as she faced the sobering reality of extreme poverty.

Dotty looked over at Reggie but he was taking no notice, more interested in examining the pages of the latest mail order catalogue from Sears and Roebuck. She sighed heavily and turned back to her book.

The locomotive chugged on, passing through open country, the hypnotic clickety-clack of the wheels a comforting sound. The landscape changed again, for the better. They were now about twenty miles out of Melbourne, pulling into the station at Diggers Rest, a pretty little town which had once been a stopping point on the road to the goldfields of Castlemaine and Bendigo. A few passengers boarded the train, and they were soon on their way again.

Dotty was enjoying herself. The train meandered past open fields, where sheep grazed on lush grass. Flocks of galahs and brightly coloured parrots perched on the boughs of gum trees, whilst sulphur-crested cockatoos squawked and screeched as they flew overhead. Crops were being sown in the fields, farmers still relying on horse-drawn ploughs and seed drills, rather than the new-fangled machinery that Dotty had read about in magazines. It

131

was an invigorating and pleasurable experience, taking in scenes of rural life that were so foreign to her.

'Reggie, come and look. It's beautiful.'

'There's nothing to see. Just grass and hills.'

But Dotty was not to be put off. She didn't want to sit in silence the whole morning.

'Why don't you tell me about Rita? What do you know about her?'

Reggie sighed and put the catalogue on the seat next to him.

'What do I know about Rita Bracegirdle? She's fifty-three years old. Her maiden name was Savage and she was born in Castlemaine. She came to Melbourne and had an illegitimate daughter when she was sixteen. She's been married four times. Two of her husbands died of natural causes, one went missing in action in the War. She was the housekeeper and lover of Cornelius Stout. She likes money and men.'

'What do we hope to find out in Castlemaine?'

'We look for background information that will explain her behaviour. A sweet and gentle church-goer who loves her mother, and does charity work, will not usually become a murderer. What I'm looking for is proof that she had criminal tendencies from the beginning.'

'In other words,' suggested Dotty, 'you want a selfish, immoral woman who steals from the poor box.'

Reggie chuckled. He looked at her properly for the first time that morning. 'You are a surprise, Dotty Wright. You're not at all what I thought you were. How is your ankle, by the way?'

'I can put weight on it now. But school has to wait till next year.'

'Those children better watch out.'

Dotty laughed. 'You're looking better too.' Then her face grew thoughtful. 'Do you think Rita's dangerous?'

'That's what I hope to find out later today.'

Chapter Thirty-One

Castlemaine was a country town about eighty miles north-east of Melbourne, with a population of approximately 5,000 people. It was nestled in a valley, with wide streets and fine Georgian buildings, which had been financed by the gold that had been discovered there in 1851. Indeed, at one point the Castlemaine diggings had been the richest goldfield in the world, the population ballooning to 30,000. Once the gold was exhausted, the miners departed, but what they left behind was the solid foundation for a town.

Reggie carried their bags as they made their way from the railway station to the Castlemaine Coffee Palace, on the corner of Templeton and Kennedy Streets. The landlady, dressed in black woollen serge and a high lace collar, greeted them.

'I have two nice rooms set aside for you. May I remind you that this establishment was associated with the Temperance movement,' she explained, as she led them up the stairs. 'We do not serve alcohol nor do we sanction drinking within these walls.'

Reggie pulled a face, which did not escape the attention of the landlady. She addressed herself to Dotty.

'A respectable lady such as yourself, Miss Wright, can stay here without sustaining a blemish on your character.' She handed over the keys to their rooms. 'I hope you'll be comfortable. Dinner is served at six o'clock sharp.'

'Thank you, but we won't be dining here tonight,' said Reggie. 'We're meeting a friend.'

The landlady looked him up and down. 'I have high standards, and I expect the same from my guests. I hope you understand that.'

She stalked off.

'What a self-righteous prig. I don't think she approves of me,' said Reggie, handing Dotty her bag.

'She's obviously a good judge of character. Who's this friend that we're meeting for dinner?'

'No one. I'd prefer to dine elsewhere.'

Dotty raised an eyebrow. 'What are we doing this afternoon?'

'We visit Rita's sister. She lives in town.'

'I need to freshen up first. It's been a long trip.'

'Of course. We'll meet downstairs in half an hour. Does that suit you?'

Dotty nodded. 'By the way, what time is she expecting us?'

'She isn't. I plan on turning up unannounced.'

'Is that wise?'

'There's more chance that she'll speak to us if we're standing on her doorstep.'

'What's her name?'

'Alma. Alma Savage.'

* * *

Rita's sister lived in a miner's cottage in Hargraves Street, about two blocks away from the Coffee Palace. It was a pretty little weatherboard place, built in the 1850s, with a small garden rimmed with roses and a wooden bench on the front porch. Reggie knocked on the door and waited. Presently he heard footsteps coming down the hall. The front door opened a few inches.

'Miss Savage. We've come from Melbourne to speak to you.'

'What about?'

'Your sister, Rita.'

'I haven't seen her for years. Please go away.' The woman went to shut the door.

Reggie put his foot in the gap. 'We think she's involved in the deaths of two men.'

There was a long silence, then Alma sighed heavily. 'You'd better come in.'

Dotty and Reggie followed Alma into the kitchen.

'I'll put on the kettle.'

She was a big woman, a shade under six feet, with strong arms, man-sized hands, and grizzled hair. A pair of light brown eyes were framed by thick dark brows, reminding Reggie of the peasant women he had seen in remote villages in Italy. Her body was bulky, hidden by a sack-like dress and a striped pinafore.

Alma took tea and cake into the backyard, where they sat in the shade of a large oak tree.

'Now, who are you and what's this all about?'

Reggie introduced himself, explaining that he was investigating a murder that had occurred some two years earlier.

The woman turned to Dotty. 'And you are—?'

'Miss Wright. I'm a teacher, here to support Mr da Costa. He's helped me with a personal matter, and I know that he wants to do the same for the family of the murdered man.'

Reggie glanced briefly at Dotty, the semblance of a smile on his lips.

Alma sighed heavily and leaned back in her chair. 'What's Rita been up to?' she asked, directing her question to Reggie. 'I knew she'd turn out bad.'

'I believe that she's been involved in the murder of Cornelius Stout. You may have read about him in the papers?'

Alma shook her head. 'I live a quiet life. I don't read newspapers.'

Reggie was not to be deterred. 'We believe that Rita worked as a housekeeper for Mr Stout. Their relationship became close.'

Alma laughed. 'Why am I not surprised?'

He went on to explain the links between Rita and the deaths of Cornelius Stout and Clyde Bracegirdle, as well as the disappearance of Edmund Stout.

'An innocent man is suspected of murder. I think it was actually your sister who killed Cornelius Stout. Money was a powerful motivator in Mrs Bracegirdle's life. If the victim didn't give her what she wanted, then he became expendable. She's been married four times, that we know of, and widowed three; two of those deaths suspicious.'

Alma shook her head in disgust. 'I always knew that it would come to this. That she'd turn out rotten. It was just a matter of time.'

'Be that as it may, Miss Savage, I was hoping that you could enlighten us about Rita's early life.'

Alma sighed and poured them all a second cup of tea. 'If I weren't a Methodist, I'd have something stronger in the house. I reckon we'll need it after you hear my sister's story.

'I'm ten years older than Rita so I watched her grow up. You need to understand that my sister saw herself always as the underdog, trying to survive against an unkind world. Dog eat dog; survival of the fittest. She was born that way. The last of five children.'

'Did you ever see any signs that she might become violent?' asked Reggie.

She frowned, her thick brows knitting as she considered the question. 'There was that incident with the cat. I'll never forget the look on her face when Mother confronted her. Rita said, cool as you like, "He asked for it." It was chilling. Mother gave her a good thrashing.'

Reggie nodded. 'What was your upbringing like?'

'A strict Methodist household. No creature comforts. No dancing. No drinking. Church on Sundays. You didn't argue with Mother. She was a big woman, like me. If you didn't do what you were told, then you'd be disciplined. Severely. Each of us was assigned duties: washing, cleaning, preparing meals, chopping wood, that sort of thing. Rita was always getting into trouble. She didn't want to be told what to do. She liked the easy life.

'As she grew, she learned how to manipulate men. Sweet talking. Calling them "princes." Making them feel like she was doing them a favour when all she wanted was flattery and "things." If you had something, she wanted it too. It got worse as she got older. She even took to stealing other girls' young men. Then she'd drop them, just like that. It was like a game to her.

'There was one person she couldn't wrap around her little finger and that was Mother. Mother saw through her and tried to break her. The trouble was that they were like two peas in a pod, both strong-willed, both not prepared to compromise. Mother had the advantage physically for a while, keeping Rita in check as far as possible. But then disaster struck.'

CHAPTER THIRTY-ONE

'What happened?' asked Dotty.

'Mother had a bad turn. She became dependent on others. Rita took full advantage of that. When she was alone with Mother, she'd say terrible things to her. She wouldn't take her to the toilet or change her. Kept what she needed just out of reach, so that Mother had to beg for it. It was only after Rita left that we found out what she'd been up to. Mother was too afraid of what might happen if she complained.'

'Your father let this happen?'

'She was the apple of his eye. She could wrap men around her little finger.'

'Rita left Castlemaine?'

'Not then. She focused all her attention on one of the young men at the church. I think she saw him as a way out. Arthur Bakewell would have married her even though his parents opposed it. They knew what she was doing. Dressed up to the nines. Turning on the charm. Using up what little money he'd saved. But she was pregnant so they had no choice. She was nearly sixteen.'

'She didn't want to marry him?'

Alma looked at Dotty. 'Most girls would have. But not Rita. No sense of what's decent.' She sighed. 'The wedding was planned. Just a simple church service, with none of the trimmings. I even made Rita a dress. But the night before the ceremony, she took off, no one knew where. She didn't even tell Arthur. She didn't tell anyone.'

'Why did she leave, do you think?'

'She was desperate to get out of Castlemaine. She wanted to go to the city. Arthur had a job here. He refused to go.'

'What happened to her?' asked Dotty.

'She wrote to my father about six months later, begging to come home. By that stage, Mother had died. Heart attack. Awful. He refused to have her back. Father had found out what Rita was really like by then; the way she'd treated Mother. He said that Rita had brought humiliation and shame on the family. He never wanted to see her face again. I often wonder what happened to the baby. Poor lamb.'

Reggie leaned forward. 'Rita gave birth to a daughter, Dolores. She kept her.'

'That would be right. Brazen hussy.'

'Is your father still alive?'

'He died ten years ago.'

'You never married?'

Alma frowned. 'I was Rita's sister. Tarred with the same brush. No man would look at me, thinking I might have a bit of Rita in me. My brothers married and moved away. My father needed looking after. It was left up to me,' she spat out bitterly. 'Rita wrecked more than one life while she lived here. People felt sorry for Arthur, but what about me?' Her eyes filled with tears.

'Does he still live around here?' asked Reggie.

'Not far from the Botanical Gardens, which is where he works. If I didn't know better, I'd say that he found solace in gardening. I wish I'd found something like that.'

'Do you think he'll talk to us?'

'That's up to him. She scarred him good and proper.'

Dotty shook her head. 'Was she really that bad? I find it hard to believe.'

Alma scowled. 'Then you never met Rita. She was evil, that's what she was. All she wanted was money and to be the centre of attention. The universe revolved around her. Men were weak, in her view. She ingratiated herself with them to get what she could. And, if she thought she'd been wronged, she'd go in for the kill. She won't have changed.'

'I intend to bring her to justice,' Reggie said.

'Be careful,' Alma warned. 'But, whatever you do, don't mention that you've spoken to me. I live a peaceful life now and, up until today, I've managed to put her out of my mind. I don't ever want to see Rita again. She's dead to me.'

Chapter Thirty-Two

Dotty and Reggie dined at the Railway Hotel, where they were served an ample meal of roast beef and vegetables. Conversation between the two was constrained, and it struck Dotty that Reggie seemed preoccupied.

'Is everything alright?' she asked him.

'Why shouldn't it be?' he said.

Reggie had ordered a bottle of Portuguese wine and poured himself a liberal glass. Dotty watched uneasily as he drained the first, then poured himself a second, barely pausing for breath in-between. By the time the homemade apple pie was placed in front of them, he had ordered a second bottle.

'Don't you think you've had enough?' she asked him.

He ignored her and poured himself a fresh glass, gulping it down as if daring her to object. She ate in silence, sipping her apple cider, looking anywhere but at her companion. She'd never seen Reggie like this before. In hindsight, she wished that they'd dined at the Coffee Palace, where alcohol was prohibited.

Reggie paid the bill. She watched in dismay as he tucked the bottle under his jacket.

'You're not taking that with you?'

'I paid for it. Why shouldn't I drink it?'

It was useless trying to talk him out of it. Dotty got up and, leaning heavily on her stick, walked out of the hotel dining room, ignoring Reggie, who trailed behind. Back at the Coffee Palace, she climbed the stairs and shut the door to her room, not bothering to say goodnight. She heard him swearing as he tried to open his door, then it slammed shut.

'Good riddance,' she said.

Half an hour later, Dotty was awoken by a knock at the door. She wrapped a shawl around her and opened it. Reggie was leaning unsteadily against the wall. He was dressed in a crimson silk robe, tied loosely at the waist.

'Can I come in?' he slurred.

'No.' She went to close the door but he stuck a slippered foot in the gap.

'You look quite fetching tonight, Dotty. Surely you'd like some company?' He moved in closer. She could smell the alcohol on his breath.

'Go to bed, Reggie. It's late, and you're drunk.'

'I'm lonely. And you're lonely too. Let's be lonely together.'

'No, thank you. I'm not interested. You should know that by now.'

The silence stretched between them, as Dotty glared at him. Reggie removed his foot from the gap in the door.

'Sorry, Dotty,' he muttered. 'It's just—' He took one last long look at her, then pulled his robe tighter and walked away.

Dotty waited till she heard him go inside. She locked her door, and leaned up against it, breathing hard. How dare he do that to her? She must have been naïve to think he wouldn't try something. Aunt Mildred had been right about him: he couldn't be trusted. Reggie was a selfish, immoral, opportunistic snake in the grass. She calmed herself and went over to the sink, splashing her face with water. Tomorrow would be intolerable. How could she face him after this? Perhaps she should catch the train home first thing in the morning? Unresolved, she climbed into bed and tried to put the whole unpleasant episode out of her mind.

* * *

It was nine o'clock the next morning. Dotty came down to the dining room. There were three or four other guests, but no sign of Reggie. She ordered breakfast and poured herself a cup of tea. She still hadn't decided what to do.

By half-past nine, he hadn't appeared, so she went back up to her room and sat, reading her book. It wasn't easy to concentrate. Her mind kept flipping back to the night before. The more she relived it, the angrier she became.

There was a knock on the door. She got up and opened it. Standing on the threshold was Reggie. His face was flushed, and his eyes were bloodshot. He looked at her sheepishly.

'Are you ready to go, Dotty?'

She stared at him coldly, then gathered her handbag, walking stick, and shawl. She walked straight past him into the corridor and down the stairs.

* * *

The entry to the Castlemaine Botanical Gardens was through an impressive set of cast iron gates. They took the path that led towards the ornamental lake and were advised by one of the staff that Arthur Bakewell was working near the rotunda.

Rita's former beau was a thin, muscly man, in his fifties, bronzed by the sun. He wore a battered hat, and khaki-coloured shorts and shirt, reminiscent of army garb. His face was lined and weathered, but his eyes were bright and alert as he took in his visitors.

'You want to see me?' he asked, straightening up and wiping the dirt off his hands.

Reggie introduced them both, and explained the purpose of their visit.

Arthur's expression hardened. 'I can't help you.'

Reggie ignored him. 'Alma told us that Rita tried to use you to get out of Castlemaine.'

'Go away. I mean it.' Arthur turned his back on them and took up his shovel.

Dotty stepped forward. 'The Gardens are a credit to you, Mr Bakewell. You've created a place of great beauty, a haven for people who need somewhere to find quiet and contentment.'

He turned around and appraised her. 'You see that, don't you? The wonder of this place?'

Reggie went to speak but was silenced by a look from Dotty.

'Indeed, I do. Perhaps you could show us around?'

'Please take my arm, Miss Wright.'

Leaning on her walking stick, with Arthur supporting her on the other side, Dotty listened as he explained the history of the Gardens, Reggie trailing behind them. Slowly, the gardener opened up, encouraged by her obvious interest and admiration. He told them of the Gardens' beginnings in the 1860s and how Ferdinand Mueller, the Government Botanist, had provided hundreds of plants. He showed them the ancient oaks and elms, the fine collection of conifers, and the recent addition of glasshouses. They came a full circle, arriving back at the rotunda.

'I hope I haven't worn you out, miss.'

'It's been wonderful seeing this place through your eyes, Mr Bakewell. Perhaps we can thank you by buying you a pot of tea. If that doesn't get in the way of your work?'

'No reason why not. I'm a volunteer so I can do what I like.'

Sitting at a table in the tearoom five minutes later, Arthur rolled himself a cigarette. 'I've been thinking about why you're here. I confess I promised myself I'd never speak her name again. But you've been so kind, so ask away.'

Reggie lit a cigarette and nodded imperceptibly at Dotty, as he watched their companion closely.

'Thank you, Mr Bakewell,' she replied. 'Could you tell us what Miss Savage was like?'

'Where to begin?' He took a deep drag of his cigarette. 'There was no one else like Rita. She was so pretty and she knew it. She could charm the birds from the trees. I thought she was a delicate flower, but she was more like a Venus Flytrap.' He laughed mordantly. 'I didn't realise at first that she was using me. It wasn't me she wanted, just what I could give her.'

'And what was that?'

'Alma was right about Rita. She wanted to escape. From Castlemaine. She played up to me, complimented me. I was a young fool and fell for it.

142

In hindsight, it was as much my fault as hers. I should have shown more restraint. You know, about the baby.'

Arthur reddened. Then he gazed into the distance, as if he were conjuring up the past. 'She lied a lot. I knew she went out with other boys, but she'd deny everything. Make out that I was imagining things. She'd blame me, claiming that I was jealous and possessive. It was my fault, always. Never hers.'

'But she left Castlemaine on her own,' said Dotty. 'Why didn't you go, too?'

'I loved it here, you see. My family, my friends, my work at the Gardens. She thought that if she got in the family way, she could talk me into leaving, but I said no. She had this idea that life would be more exciting in the city. I was ready to marry her but, instead of offering her escape, it looked like I was trapping her here for good. So, she went.'

'What did your parents think of her?'

He sighed. 'Mum and Dad didn't like her, but I wanted to do the right thing by her. Marry her even though I knew deep down that she didn't love me. It took me a while to realise that Rita loved herself more than anyone else. Even her relationship with her family was poisonous. In the end, she left and I never heard from her again. I still wonder whether the baby was mine.'

'Have you ever married, Mr Bakewell?'

'When I was in my forties. My wife died last year. I'd retired but I stayed on here as a volunteer. The Gardens have been the saviour of me. You can forget a lot of what happens to you when you see a tree grow from a seedling.' He looked down. 'You probably think I'm weak.'

'Not at all,' she assured him. 'I lost my fiancé in the War. Work made life bearable for me. The children I teach have always been important to me. They saved me from my grief.'

Reggie was looking distinctly uncomfortable at this turn in the conversation.

'Do you believe that Rita is capable of murder?' he asked, breaking in.

That stopped Arthur in his tracks. 'I don't know.' He shook his head, deep in thought. 'Me and her was nearly forty years ago. She was young, you see. But she was hard. She took no notice of her parents' opinions. She showed no respect for her elders. Only her feelings mattered. It was always about her. I know that she broke her mother's heart. But was she capable of murder? I don't know.'

Chapter Thirty-Three

The train journey home saw a thawing in the relationship between Reggie and Dotty, particularly after Reggie offered an apology of sorts.

'I was drunk. I don't remember what I said to you.'

'I'm not going to repeat it. You should take the pledge, Mr da Costa. You obviously can't hold your drink.'

'I have a lot on my mind. Family problems.'

Dotty stared at him. He looked down, unable to meet her gaze.

'No excuse, I suppose,' he muttered.

The train blew its whistle as it pulled into a siding, to take on water. Reggie sighed heavily then broke the silence.

'Mr Bakewell and Miss Savage gave us a good idea about Rita's personality. I think there were indications from the beginning that she could become a cold-blooded murderer. Then there's the fact that she's been widowed three times.'

'But one of them was a soldier. He died in the War,' countered Dotty. 'You can't include that.'

'I'll agree with you there,' conceded Reggie, warming to his theme. 'But consider the facts. James Hardcastle. Her second husband. Dies from natural causes. Clyde Bracegirdle. Her fourth husband. Natural causes again. What a coincidence. Don't you see that she selects a particular type? Wealthy. Older. On their own. She inveigles herself into their lives as a housekeeper or cook, and then turns on the charm. They either share their money with her or die. Cornelius Stout. His brother Edmund. Armitage Flagg.'

But Dotty was not easily convinced. 'This is all supposition. You don't even know if Rita knew Mr Flagg or Edmund Stout. She's a woman. How does she kill them? How does she do away with the bodies? That takes strength. She marries older men, men who may not live for much longer. As I said, you have no proof.'

'We need to interview her first husband, Sylvester Sturgess.'

'Why?'

'For the same reason we met up with her sister and Bakewell. Gather evidence. Learn more about her. Build up a case. Perhaps we'll stumble over something that's been missed. Once I know enough, I'll go back to Leggett's and contrive a meeting with Rita.'

'How do you intend to do that?'

'At the moment, I have no idea, but I'll think of something.'

'She's twenty years older than you. Why would she want to meet you?'

'I'll give her a reason. She won't be able to resist.'

Dotty pulled a wry face. 'It's been done before.'

Reggie smirked. 'I made a mistake. Admittedly it's rare. Anyway, I'm already taken.'

'You surprise me. You don't act like you are.' She looked at him archly. 'Who is the lucky woman?'

'It's in the planning stage. She's rich; very stylish. And she's very keen on me.' He stroked his moustache. 'You might be lucky too one day.'

'I'm perfectly content,' she said. 'However, I have to say that I've found this whole experience quite illuminating. It's been an education. Not necessarily what I expected. Or wanted.'

'I'm glad you came along. In fact, I meant to commend you on your handling of Bakewell yesterday. You played him so perfectly that he cooperated with us.'

'I wasn't *playing* him at all. I felt sorry for him. I was genuinely interested in the Gardens. There was nothing fake about that.' She frowned. 'Honestly, Reggie. You infuriate me sometimes. You have no empathy for others. You judge people according to a very narrow set of values, which are often questionable.'

Reggie flushed with anger. 'All that *namby pamby* about watching a tree grow from a seed. Really? Understanding and sensitivity are overrated. Give me good old-fashioned self-interest any day. At least it's easier to deal with.'

Dotty shook her head in dismay. 'I feel sorry for you. You'll find yourself drawn to a woman who is exactly that, and it will end badly.'

Reggie stood abruptly and took down a copy of the *Victoria Police Gazette* from the luggage rack. He moved to a seat in the corner and buried his face in it, ignoring her.

Dotty stared out the window, although she hardly noticed what she was seeing. Reggie da Costa was incorrigible, she decided. And now they were next door neighbours!

Chapter Thirty-Four

Reggie woke up on Christmas morning, aware that this year's celebration would be a gloomy affair for him. He dressed and had a light breakfast downstairs, then tidied up the kitchen and returned upstairs to the little sitting room. On the table was a letter. It was from his mother. It had arrived some days earlier, asking him to join his father and her for luncheon. He had put it aside, unsure what his reply should be. He missed his mother dearly, now that he was no longer seeing her. He had taken for granted her interest in his work, her support, the compliments about his appearance, and her firm belief that he had what it took to marry well. Without her approval, life felt meaningless.

He felt strangely emotional at the thought that this would be one Christmas that he could not share with her. Unbidden, a sob rose in his throat. But to visit her would give legitimacy to Mario's return to Richmond. How could he sit across the table from the father who had deserted them, and had returned to suck the last of Mavis's savings from her? The reply to her letter was written, thanking her for the invitation, but regretting that he would be unable to attend. He would be dining elsewhere.

He walked over to the window which overlooked the street. Down below, little children played, trying out the cricket set that Father Christmas had given them. Dressed in their Sunday best, families passed by on their way to church. It had been Reggie's duty and pleasure to do the same with his mother in the past, but today he felt disinclined to attend the service. He would look so alone. People would ask why he wasn't with Mavis. It would be humiliating.

The door to the next house slammed shut. Dotty Wright emerged onto the street. She was wearing a floral dress with a broad brimmed hat, which shielded her eyes from the sun. The day would be a hot one. Her white gloves and handbag looked fresh and smart. She looked up at his window, and he stepped back, hoping that she had not seen him. They had not spoken since their return from Castlemaine, and he didn't know how to deal with it. And now it was Christmas, and the last thing he wanted was for her to pity him, being alone on Christmas Day.

Two minutes later there was a knock on the door. Reggie went downstairs and opened it. It was Dotty. She must have seen him at the window.

'Reggie. Merry Christmas.' She smiled at him as if the argument at Castlemaine had never happened. 'These are for you.' She handed him two jars of preserves, decorated with a red ribbon. 'Homemade,' she added.

'Thank you,' he mumbled, feeling ill at ease.

'I'm dining at Aunt Mildred's house today. She specifically asked if you would like to come. She says it's been a long time since she saw you last.'

She paused, waiting for his reply. Then she reached out a hand and patted him on the arm. 'I'd like you to come.'

Reggie was torn between his pride and his fear of being alone at Christmas.

'Please, Reggie. I couldn't bear to think of you spending Christmas on your own.'

He stood in the doorway, undecided, then finally nodded his head. 'I'd love to. Perhaps I could drive you? The Citroen hasn't had much of a run lately.'

Dotty smiled broadly. 'Lovely. I'm off to church. I'll be back by half-past eleven. Aunt Mildred will be so pleased.'

Reggie closed the door and stood in the hallway. That was a surprise. An invitation to Christmas dinner. Despite himself, he felt relieved that he was not going to be alone. He went upstairs and laid his clothes out on the bed. The light-weight cream-checked suit would be perfect. But which tie? The gold one or the green?

* * *

Mildred and Alfred Bardsley Smith lived in an impressive home in Grosvenor Street, Brighton, not far from the beach. It was the sort of house that Reggie would have loved to call his own. 'Glenrothes' was named for the town in Fife, the ancestral home of the Bardsley Smith family. It was a beautiful 1890s Italianate Victorian mansion, surrounded by meticulously maintained gardens.

Reggie drove up the circular driveway and parked near the old stables. Dotty led the way, carrying a basketful of presents for her aunt and uncle, and her cousins. Reggie, not wanting to arrive empty-handed, had extracted two bottles of fine French wine that he'd been keeping for special occasions.

They were shown into a large drawing room, to be greeted by the host and hostess themselves. Mildred Bardsley Smith was a petite woman, dressed in what would have been the fashion in Queen Victoria's time. Beneath a dress in thick black satin, embellished with a lace collar, she was undoubtedly wearing a whale-bone corset, given that her silhouette could only be described as a 'wasp waist.' A long string of pearls was wound around her neck, while her wispy white hair was pulled back into a chignon. Alfred Bardsley Smith was an imposing gent, Mildred's physical opposite, being around six feet tall and almost as wide, with grey hair parted down the middle. His luxuriant side whiskers hung below his jawline, the two joined together by a well-waxed moustache. He wore a cream waistcoat and a suit in a sober dark-grey stripe. Reggie was familiar with the Bardsley Smiths, but he had seen little of them in the past few years.

As they gathered around the Christmas tree, decorated with glass baubles, stars, sprigs of holly, and wooden ornaments, they opened their presents. There was much hugging and kissing and laughing. Even Reggie was included, receiving a fine bottle of port from the host and hostess. Sherries were passed around, and a delicious selection of hors d'oeuvres tickled the appetites of the dozen or so relatives who were dining together that day. Reggie was made to feel most welcome, with the delicate subject of Mario da Costa assiduously avoided for the bulk of the day. It was as if the whole company had been forewarned about Reggie's 'situation.'

Soon they moved into the dining room, where a magnificent mahogany table had been decorated accordingly, the ends flanked by two splendid candelabra. Gold-leaf cornices, a large ornate ceiling rose from which hung a Murano glass chandelier, and a grand marble fireplace were the outstanding features of the room. They took their seats and were rewarded with a delicious three course meal, of pumpkin soup, roast turkey with all the trimmings, and plum pudding with lashings of cream.

Reggie sat back in his chair, as the maid took away his dessert bowl, and thought how much tighter his trousers had become, in the space of two hours. The wine had been good and his hosts had been most solicitous in ensuring that he was enjoying himself. Across from him sat Dotty. Her eyes were shining and her cheeks were a pretty pink colour, the freckles on her nose slightly enhanced by the summer sun. Her floral dress suited her colouring and, he decided, full as he was of Christmas cheer, that she looked quite becoming.

One of the cousins was an accomplished pianist. The guests moved back into the drawing room once the meal was over. They took seats around a highly polished baby grand piano and waited while the young woman shuffled through the sheet music.

Next to Reggie was Dotty's Aunt Mildred. She leaned over towards him and whispered, 'Please forgive me for mentioning it, Reggie, but I must tell you that your dear mother is suffering in your absence. She tells me that you haven't spoken since you moved out. Can't you find it in your heart to forgive her? It is Christmas, as you well know. She's torn between her spousal duty and her love for you.'

Reggie paused and ran his hand through his hair. He was torn too, torn between telling Mrs Bardsley Smith to mind her own business and the need to be polite, given that she had invited him into her home.

'It's difficult, Mrs Bardsley Smith. My father ruined my mother and left us penniless. I find it hard to understand how she could take him back.'

'She loves you dearly.'

'Yes, yes. I love her too.' Reggie looked at her directly. 'I appreciate your concern, Mrs Bardsley Smith, I really do. Let us leave it at that.'

'As you wish.' She turned her attention to her niece who was now poised to play. 'Come, Caroline. A Christmas Carol, if you please.'

The rest of the afternoon went quickly, as everyone joined in the singing. It was a convivial group, apart from Reggie, who struggled to hide the irritation he felt after his conversation with Mildred Bardsley Smith. He felt somewhat insulted that he, a thirty-six-year-old man, should be lectured to by his mother's friend.

As the party broke up, Reggie took Dotty's arm and escorted her to his car. She stopped him in the driveway.

'What's wrong? Something has upset you.'

Reggie refused to look her in the eyes.

'Is it about your mother? Did Aunt Mildred say something? I told her not to.'

'No one understands what it's like,' he hissed. 'I can't go back home, not while he's there. I just wish people would leave me alone.'

Dotty waited till Reggie started the car. 'Please don't think too badly of my aunt. She means well.'

'Doesn't everybody?' He raised his eyes and saw the look of concern on her face. 'I suppose you're right,' he conceded. 'She was very kind, asking me to dinner. It's just—'

'I understand, Reggie.' She touched his arm. 'Time to go home.'

Chapter Thirty-Five

I t was Saturday, the 29th of December. While everyone else was at home, Detective Sergeant O'Flanagan was sitting at his desk in the offices of the Criminal Investigation Branch, the day's newspaper spread out before him. There was a report on the improved conditions for the police force. Changes were being introduced by the Victorian Government, delivering the much sought-after pensions and pay rises demanded by those who had participated in the 'Police Mutiny.' But the irony was that those who had participated in the strike, or the 'mutiny' as the Government preferred to call it, would never see the reforms that they had requested, given that they had not been re-employed. They had paid the ultimate price for defying their masters.

He put the paper down for a moment and considered his own personal circumstances. When he had been a young constable, he had envisaged a future that included a wife and kids. The 'little woman' would be waiting at home for him to walk through the door, after a hard day's work on the beat. She would have dinner on the table, the children bathed and ready for bed, and later he would relax into his favourite armchair to chat contentedly about his day and hers, a beer in his hand. He sighed. That scenario had grown stale, as the years had passed.

With 1924 just around the corner, there was little chance that he would ever be a father or a husband. He was in his mid-fifties now and married to the job. He spent more time at his desk than he did at home sitting in his favourite armchair. His relationships were with his colleagues and the scum of Melbourne society: snitches, thieves, murderers, petty criminals, thugs, and reporters.

If it weren't for his religion, he would have thrown it in years ago, but somewhere along the way he had dedicated himself to rooting out evil and sending sinners to rot in prison. Within the criminal classes O'Flanagan was regarded with dread and trepidation, for he was considered to be incorruptible, impervious to threats and bribery. He was, it seemed, the transgressor's worst nightmare.

One of the few who had escaped O'Flanagan's clutches was Leslie 'Squizzy' Taylor. No matter how much evidence was gathered against the little gangster, he always managed to slip through the nets set to trap him. The detective picked up the paper again and read the latest report on the attempt to keep Squizzy behind bars. O'Flanagan shook his head and slammed his fist down on the desk. It was frustrating.

He put the newspaper aside and took out the file on the Cornelius Stout murder. That gave him no joy either. His enquiries into the circumstances of the case were failing to bear fruit. And, trying to tie Stout to the Armitage Flagg murder was an impossible task. There didn't appear to be any common links between the two men. Flagg's nephew, the person most likely to benefit from his death, had been living interstate since 1919 and had had only written contact with his uncle. He was not regarded as a suspect.

O'Flanagan had put an extra couple of investigators to the task of checking the financial dealings of both Stout and Flagg, but apart from a few shady deals on the part of the former, there appeared to be no links with organised crime for either of them. The only suspect from that world who might be involved in Stout's murder was Horace Striker, but O'Flanagan kept coming back to the premise that the nature of the killing didn't fit with Striker's *modus operandi*. Further enquiries had revealed that Stanley Duggan, Striker's nephew, had recovered financially through the intervention of his uncle. If Duggan or Striker were involved, the evidence against them was purely circumstantial.

His list of missing persons and murders had been systematically reduced. Three in the former category had been located. But the whereabouts of Edmund Stout, Cornelius's brother, and Julius Mathieson were still unknown. Without a body, their estates would be in limbo until they were declared dead. It stretched the bounds of credibility that Henry Stout would have been involved in the murder of both uncle and father. He did not benefit from Edmund's death, given that the estate was to be sold up and the proceeds go to charity. Mathieson's wife had been living apart from her husband for some years and was now in a relationship with a wealthy businessman. She seemed disinterested in Mathieson's whereabouts or the fate of his estate. In O'Flanagan's experience, murderers were usually very keen to get their hands on the proceeds of crime.

O'Flanagan cracked his knuckles. Something had to give. Someone had to break. But the interviews with witnesses and family had turned up no concrete evidence against any suspect that would be acceptable in a court of law. The tenants at the Punt Road property appeared to have neither motive nor opportunity to kill Stout. Micah Youngblood had not been acquainted with the dead man. Clyde Bracegirdle had been very ill, having passed away about one month before Stout was killed. As such, he sat slightly outside the murder window. Anyway, it was inconceivable that such an ill man could have dragged Stout down into the basement. Furthermore, Frank Feely was another unlikely suspect, suffering from all sorts of ills brought on by his exposure to mustard gas. The man most likely, Henry Stout, had been seen outside the Punt Road property. However, the evidence against him was still regrettably thin. Yet, he was the most logical suspect, given that he would benefit from his father's death. The fact was that O'Flanagan wanted someone, anyone, in the frame for the murder.

It was not looking good for the Criminal Investigation Branch. And now O'Flanagan was doubting the wisdom of his decision to keep Reggie in the dark about Mathieson and Flagg, as well as refusing to share his thoughts on the Cornelius Stout case. It occurred to him, as he contemplated the sparsity of suspects, that the crime reporter might think twice before sharing information with him. To add to the pressure, Chief Commissioner Nicholson was breathing down his neck.

He shook his head in dismay and packed up the files on his desk. Maybe it was time to call it quits and take up fishing. O'Flanagan groaned. Bloody fishing. Fancy waiting for a fish to take the bait.

He sat back in his chair. Perhaps that principle could be applied to the case of Cornelius Stout? Put some bait on a hook and see what rose to take it. He reached for the telephone and asked the exchange to put him through to *The Argus*.

'This is Detective Sergeant O'Flanagan. I'd like to leave a message for Reggie da Costa.'

Chapter Thirty-Six

Dotty Wright was surprised to see Reggie at her door. He was holding a bunch of flowers. 'Happy New Year's Eve. Sorry about Christmas Day. I was rude to you.'

Dotty took the flowers and invited Reggie inside. She went into the kitchen, Reggie following her. She opened a cupboard and took down a vase.

'I've been thinking about you,' he said, looking distinctly uncomfortable. 'I seem to be in the habit of provoking you. It's not intentional. I do like your company, and I value your opinion. In fact, I regard you as a friend.'

Dotty held her tongue. She filled the vase with water and started to arrange the flowers.

'I'm sorry, too, for the way I acted at Castlemaine. I hope that you can forgive me.' He paused. 'Dotty?'

She faced him. 'Apology accepted. Is there another reason why you've come here today?'

Reggie visibly relaxed. 'There is. On a practical level, I need you to help me catch a killer.'

'You need *me*?'

'You have better skills at drawing out a person than I have, as you showed with Arthur Bakewell.'

'Thank you,' said Dotty. She leaned over and patted his arm. 'There, there. It wasn't that hard complimenting me, was it?'

Reggie frowned, then took a deep breath. 'I'm hoping that you could help me with Sylvester Sturgess today. He's Rita's only surviving husband.'

Dotty performed a mock bow. 'I would be honoured.'

The crime reporter smiled, then grew serious. 'There's something else you could help me with. I need to meet Rita. But first, how's your ankle?'

'I can put weight on it now. No walking stick anymore. Why do you ask?'

'Can you dance?'

Dotty laughed. 'Dance lessons were part of my education. Aunt Mildred insisted that I should be accomplished in the arts of drawing, music, and dance. She's rather old-fashioned. I don't think she approved of my becoming a teacher, but there's only so long that you can take advantage of someone's generosity.' Then she smiled. 'So that's it. You want me to go to Leggett's with you?'

'In good time. First we talk to Sylvester Sturgess.'

'Where do we find him?'

'He lives in Hawthorn.'

Dotty carried the vase of flowers into the sitting room and put them on the mantelpiece.

She turned and faced Reggie. 'You said before that you value my opinion. If you ever want to talk to someone, I'm a good listener.'

Reggie stroked his moustache. 'You know my family situation. What would you do if you were me?'

Dotty considered the question. 'You love your mother. Why don't you try to talk to her when your father isn't around? Without getting angry. It might be that she has reservations about him now, and has no one to confide in. Except you. And you're not there for her.'

'Isn't that showing weakness? I said that I wouldn't go home while he was there.'

'It's showing that you love your mother. That's not weakness.'

Reggie nodded slowly. 'I'll think about it. Now, are you free to visit Mr Sturgess?'

'I'll get my hat.'

* * *

158

Rita Bracegirdle's first husband was a strange one. He was in his seventies, with long bony fingers, and scared eyes.

'You want to know about Rita?' he asked, scrutinising his visitors. 'She doesn't know you're visiting me?' His eyes darted past Dotty's shoulder, checking the front path behind them.

'No, Mr Sturgess,' Reggie reassured him, 'and we won't be telling her. We're here to gather information, that's all.'

Sylvester Sturgess breathed a sigh of relief. 'Follow me.' He took them into the front parlour and beckoned for them to sit. 'Now, how can I help you?'

'We have reason to believe that Rita may be responsible for the deaths of two of her husbands, amongst others.'

The old man nodded. 'It doesn't surprise me.'

'Tell us about Rita,' said Dotty.

'Where do I begin?' His eyes drifted to an old photograph on the mantelpiece, of a man and woman in their Sunday best.

'I was over forty, hopelessly naïve when it came to women. I met Rita at Flinders Street station in May 1892. She walked straight up to me and started to talk. Bold as you like. She must have been in her early twenties. I'd made some money in the boom times and I had this nice house in Hawthorn. Just the thing for someone like Rita.'

He looked at Dotty. 'Please excuse what I'm about to say, Miss Wright, but there's no other way to put it. Rita seduced me. She knew how to please a man and make him beg for more. She was like no one I'd ever met. Blonde hair. Voluptuous figure. Her face all made up. She was quite beautiful on the surface, but underneath she was tough. She knew what she wanted, and it was me. I fell for her good and hard.' He looked back at the photograph. 'I actually thought she felt the same way. It was just before the wedding that she told me she had a child. She'd kept that little piece of information to herself. Dolores was a shy little thing, and I was so in love with Rita that I took her story at face value. She told me that her husband had died, leaving her to raise Dolores on her own. All lies.' He shook his head, his hands trembling in his lap.

'It was a few months later that the truth came out. I found Dolores's birth certificate. No father was listed. Rita had been sixteen when she gave birth. Unmarried. I began to look deeper and questioned her about it.

'I accused her of deceiving me. She didn't like that. She said that it was my fault that she'd had to lie, because I was so stuck in my ways. She said that she'd treated me like a prince, and that it was wrong for me to talk to her like that. You couldn't argue with her. I got angry and told her that I'd leave her, and then she backed down. That's when things started to happen.'

Reggie leaned forward. 'What things?'

'I got sick. My mother came around. She was terribly concerned and tried to intervene. She wanted me to go to a doctor, but Rita didn't want that. Mother insisted. I was suffering from giddy spells and stomach cramps. The doctor didn't know what it was.

'You see, when we first got married, I'd changed my will in her favour. When I got sick, I got this idea in my head that Rita was poisoning me. It was all too much for me. I've always been a nervous, sensitive type. I refused to eat anything that Rita cooked. Mother was concerned. I was losing weight. My parents insisted that I come home, and then they contacted the police. When the police visited the house, they didn't find anything incriminating. Of course, they didn't. Rita was too smart to get caught.'

'What happened then?'

'I had it out with her. I accused her and she didn't deny it. She actually said that I didn't deserve to live. That I was weak. Maybe she was right. Anyway, I made a deal with Rita. I gave her some money and a place to live and, in return, she promised that she would never contact me again.'

'Where was this place?'

'By the Yarra River. A little weatherboard house in Mary Street, Cremorne. At the corner where it meets the river bank.'

'Did you transfer it to her?'

Sturgess shook his head. 'I pay the rates. She looks after the rest. I haven't gone there in nearly thirty years. It's still in my name but, to all intents and purposes, it's hers.'

'Does she still live there?'

CHAPTER THIRTY-SIX

'I believe so.'

'This is quite an accusation, Mr Sturgess,' said Dotty. 'How do you know that she was trying to poison you?'

'As soon as I moved home, the cramps stopped. I put on weight. There wasn't any pain or headaches.'

'Why don't you reclaim the house?'

'The truth is that I couldn't bear to have it out with Rita again. And now I've only a few months to live, you see. Then it will be over for Rita. She probably thinks that she'll still inherit, but I changed my will. The proceeds from the sale of my home and the Mary Street house will go to charity. The will is ironclad. She'll never be able to challenge it; I've made sure of that.'

'You had the marriage annulled?'

'I'm Catholic. You can buy anything if you have the money. Funny, Rita converted so that we could marry. I think she liked the wealth of the Church. She said that Methodists were cheapskates. The woman had no principles.'

Sylvester Sturgess sat back in his chair. His whole body was shaking and his face had gone a chalky white.

'Is there anything more that you can tell us?' asked Reggie.

'Just that I feel sorry for her poor little daughter. I never saw a child so timid and browbeaten as Dolores. There was no light in her eyes. She just did what she was told. She was seven years old. She'd be in her thirties now. I hope she got away; I really do.'

They got up to go.

'Happy New Year, Mr Sturgess,' said Dotty.

'For you, perhaps, but for me there is little to look forward to. Death will be a welcome release.'

Chapter Thirty-Seven

There were two notes on Reggie's desk when he returned to work after a brief holiday over the Christmas period. The first one made him smile. It was from his editor giving him permission to pursue the case against Rita Bracegirdle. The second evoked a different response. He scowled as he read it. The message was from O'Flanagan. It was dated the 29th of December, 1923. Over a week ago.

'Damn.'

The detective was planning to interview Henry Stout on suspicion of murder. He'd uncovered the fact that Henry had been seen opposite the Punt Road property in late 1922, before the body was discovered. Obviously, Frank Feely had been re-interviewed and revealed that piece of evidence against Lily's twin brother. In his note, the detective stated that Reggie should hand over any evidence he'd uncovered regarding the Cornelius Stout case.

It was obvious to Reggie that O'Flanagan was fishing for any information that might strengthen his case against Henry. It was also apparent that he now realised that leaving Reggie out of the loop had been a tactical mistake, and he was trying to draw him back in.

'Not so fast, Mick,' the reporter muttered. 'You don't have enough evidence to prove murder.'

He considered the case against Henry, what little there was. Cornelius had disapproved of Henry's career choice—a clerk with the Railways—and had wanted him to carry on the family business. This had caused friction between them. Stanley Duggan, Henry's friend and nephew of Horace

Striker, had been made bankrupt after getting involved in a financial scheme initiated by Cornelius Stout. Henry's support for his friend had riled his father and led to him being disinherited, although Lily had overridden Cornelius's wishes when he died. Henry had been seen near the terrace house, thus had prior knowledge of where his father had been murdered, but the evidence was circumstantial; there was nothing of a physical nature that tied him to the basement and, therefore, the crime scene.

Lily's lovely face came to mind. If Henry went to jail, Reggie's future with the beautiful heiress was over. O'Flanagan could wait. It was time to draw the net around Rita Bracegirdle.

Chapter Thirty-Eight

Leggett's Ballroom looked a treat. Crystal chandeliers sparkled from the ceiling of the main auditorium, climbing roses wound their way through the latticed windows leading to the conservatory, and pretty coloured lights twinkled between the leaves of ferns that filled a plethora of hanging baskets. Being a special event—the Cabaret Ball—numbers had been restricted to five hundred people but, fortunately, Reggie had obtained tickets from one of his contacts.

Reggie and Dotty sat at one of the dainty supper tables, which lined the edges of the ballroom, chatting as the dancers glided past. Their conversation focused on how to orchestrate a meeting between Reggie and Rita.

'I'll bump into her,' suggested Reggie.

'That's ridiculous,' said Dotty. 'Once you've knocked her over, she'll really want to dance with you. I have a better idea.'

'Well, what is it?' he asked sharply.

'It's better if I don't tell you. Your reaction won't be natural otherwise. Just trust me, Reggie. How long do you need with her, do you think?'

'Twenty minutes.'

'I'll meet you near the cloakroom afterwards. Have you got your story ready?'

'Of course. I'm experienced at this sort of thing.'

Dotty arched an eyebrow. 'Catching a murderess?'

Reggie sniggered. He stood and held out his hand. 'Is the *signorina* ready?'

Dotty grinned. '*Si, signore.*'

A ten-piece orchestra was playing at the far end of the auditorium. Reggie led Dotty onto the dance floor, and soon they were blending in with the others.

Being a special event, everyone was in their Sunday best. The men were wearing evening dress, with their hair slicked, and their shoes highly polished. The ladies' frocks ranged from the simple to the fantastic, an abundance of lace, silk, and feathery concoctions, designed to enhance the wearer and captivate the men.

Dotty was certainly not out of place. She had found a dress in the back of her wardrobe that had been made for a friend's wedding, a high-class affair at The Hotel Windsor. Fortunately, it still fitted. It was in the palest pink with beading at the hemline, set off by a scarf that skimmed her neck and wafted ethereally behind her.

Reggie, his hair shining from the application of a liberal amount of hair oil, was immaculate in a black dinner suit, new sparkling white dress shirt, satin waistcoat, and white bowtie.

It wasn't long before Reggie sighted Rita. She was standing on the sidelines, swinging her hips to the music, a big smile on her freshly painted ruby lips. Her dress was a sheer crimson design with an underskirt, and a cross-over bodice that followed her curves and accentuated her breasts. The skirt fanned out over her large hips, allowing her to move freely when she danced. She wore a glittery headpiece with a jaunty crimson feather above one ear.

A small elderly man, with hollowed cheeks and thinning white hair, approached her and asked her to dance. She flashed a toothy smile at him, and held out a gloved hand. He took it and guided her onto the dance floor, looking like the cat that ate the canary.

Dotty and Reggie were soon caught up in the good humour and excitement that the cabaret ball was designed to evoke. They danced well together, Dotty moving in unison to Reggie's lead. Rita was just in front of them, heading for the conservatory.

'Don't lose sight of her,' whispered Reggie.

Rita and her partner found an empty supper table and were chatting together like they were old school friends. Reggie and Dotty moved up close

165

to them, trying to maintain a spot not far from their table.

'Pretend you're saying something to me,' Dotty whispered to Reggie, as they drew close to Rita again.

He bent down and murmured in her ear.

'How dare you!' shrieked Dotty. She slapped Reggie hard. He pulled away, a look of horror on his face. His eyes watered, and a red welt soon appeared across his left cheek.

'You wealthy men!' she cried, a look of indignation on her face. 'You're all the same. You think you can buy anything. But you can't buy me!'

She stormed off, in the direction of the foyer. A small circle of people had stopped dancing and were staring at Reggie. He backed away and sat at the next table to Rita. She whispered to her partner and came over to Reggie, sitting in the empty chair opposite him. She leaned over and touched his arm.

'You poor man. What a bitch. Fancy making a scene like that.' Her face was a picture of concern.

'She was wrong to say that,' said Reggie, touching his cheek, staring in the direction of the retreating Dotty. 'I would never disrespect a woman.'

'Of course, you wouldn't. I can see that. You are a cultured man. A handsome one, too. She is not worthy of you.' She pulled her chair around so that she was closer to him.

Two employees of Leggett's approached them. 'We believe you've been causing trouble, mister. Come with us.'

Rita spoke up. 'No, no. He's with me. He is a friend. That woman, she is the problem.'

One of the men winked at her. 'If you say so, Rita.'

The other looked doubtful and addressed himself to Reggie. 'We don't want no trouble tonight, you understand?'

'Of course,' replied Reggie, straightening his bow tie.

The two men walked away, one of them looking unconvinced.

'Thank you,' Reggie said, smiling at Rita. 'You saved me from an embarrassing situation.'

'Come, let us dance.'

CHAPTER THIRTY-EIGHT

'But your partner?'

Rita made a pooh-poohing noise. 'He is no one to me. You, on the other hand, need what only a woman can give: affection and understanding.'

Reggie nodded slowly. 'You obviously know what men need. Your name is Rita?'

'Yes. Rita Savage. And you are?'

'Reggie Costigan.' He took her hand and led her onto the dance floor.

Her previous partner was not slow to appraise his change in circumstances and, with one final look at Rita, stalked down the side of the hall in search of a replacement.

Despite her garish appearance and uneducated speech, Reggie found Rita to be good company. She listened carefully to his opinions, and complimented him frequently on his appearance and expertise on the dance floor. She laughed at his jokes, made sympathetic noises when he complained about the price of a good suit, and seemed to have eyes only for him. Reggie felt quite disconcerted being someone's sole focus of attention. It had been a long time since that had been the case. He was also finding it hard to believe that this woman, who seemed so besotted with him, could be a cold-blooded murderer.

The band struck up a tango and immediately the dance floor emptied by half. Rita smiled seductively at Reggie. 'You like to try?'

'Of course.'

Tango was a favourite of his. Although he did not like to admit it, he sensed that his Italian heritage, and his father's flair with the violin, played a part in his appreciation of music and dance. The mood of the tango—melancholic, sensual, and romantic—evoked an emotional response in him that he did not see in the more knockabout, uncultured Australian men of his acquaintance. More importantly, he knew that he looked good dancing the tango, and that women noticed him. All he needed was an accomplished partner to show off his prowess, but they were few and far between, including, no doubt, this rather garishly dressed, older woman who stood in front of him.

'Let us begin,' he said.

He took Rita in an embrace, his left hand clutching her right, his right arm around her with his hand on her left shoulder blade. His head held high, his spine straight, he stepped forward. Rita mirrored his moves, her head tilted back and to the side. He had to admit, it was a promising start.

As the music swelled, they snapped their heads around to look at each other. Rita's face was a study in concentration, her lips pursed, her cheeks aflame, her eyes smouldering. Reggie realised with a shock that she was not only good, she was very good.

A circle of dancers had paused and stood watching them.

Reggie moved into the *corte*. Their torsos rotated towards his left, with both bodies tilting into a lunge, his right leg and her left one straight. Then, unexpectedly, Rita wrapped her right leg over his hip, and brought her face around so that her eyes stared up into his. It shocked and excited him. They held the position until the music released them.

He executed a dip. Rita leaned back, supported by his arms. Her throat and upper chest were exposed, signalling her abandonment to him. 'I am yours,' her eyes seemed to say, as she gazed up at him. There was a burst of spontaneous applause from the onlookers as she bent her left leg and raised it, still reclining in his arms.

Reggie had never felt the passion of the tango until this moment. The music inhabited him, its rhythm intense and staccato, the melody moody and melancholic. It drew him in, made him forget about the past and the future, for it was only this present moment that existed. His back was wet with perspiration, as he responded to every sensual, sultry step, every kick of her heels, every smouldering look, that this woman brought to the dance. And, even then, he knew that she was making him look better than he was, such was her skill. It was exhilarating and exhausting, and he wished that it would never end.

When the music ceased, they were greeted with expressions of admiration. Rita moved provocatively towards him. He could feel her breasts and hips pressing against his body, as she kissed his cheek. He took her hand and led her over to a table at the side.

'That was superb,' he gushed, wiping his forehead with his handkerchief. 'I haven't danced like that for years.'

'Thank you,' replied Rita, smiling seductively. 'I am so glad that I could keep up with you. You are a Prince of Dance. The time flies when I am with you.'

Her comment startled him. He checked his watch and realised that he *had* lost track of the time. Dotty would not be amused.

'I'm sorry. I must go.'

'Why?' Rita was pouting, out of sorts.

'I have to work tomorrow. I'm in property. Investment. I have my fingers in a few pies.'

She relaxed, looking at him appraisingly. 'I will see you next Friday, perhaps?'

'I'd like that,' he replied, trying to calm his emotions. He realised that he wanted to see her again. He had felt so alive, so exhilarated, and so absurdly aware that he was a man and she was a woman as they danced together.

He walked away, then turned back in time to see her approach the little elderly man she had deserted for Reggie. She was smiling down at him and he was gazing up at her.

Dotty was waiting for Reggie at the cloakroom. 'You took your time,' she muttered, checking her watch.

'Time got away from me.'

Dotty studied him. 'You look different. What's going on, Reggie? Has something happened?'

'I'm just not sure, anymore. She's not what I expected.'

It was hard to put into words the emotions that Rita had evoked in him. He couldn't explain it to Dotty because he couldn't explain it to himself. On the surface, Rita was most assuredly not his type. She was not sophisticated, cultured, or well-groomed. Her speech was uneducated, her make-up was overdone, her perfume reeked, her clothes were cheap, and her body was old. Worst of all, she was a major suspect in a murder investigation and he couldn't afford to forget that. And yet, there was something about her that he had found alluring. The fact was that he had wanted her.

Dotty took his arm and guided him out into the street. 'Fresh air, that's what you need. And a dose of reality.'

They sat in the Citroen, staring out at the darkened sky. 'Tell me what she was like.'

'She was actually interested in me. She made me feel like I was important. I don't think I've ever met anyone like her before.'

'Remember what Arthur Bakewell said? "She could charm the birds from the trees."'

'She doesn't act like a murderer.'

'What does a murderer act like? I doubt if any of her victims thought she was.'

'You can't understand the effect that she has on a man.'

Dotty wasn't having any of it. 'Listen to yourself, Reggie. She's a fifty-three-year-old woman who has worked her way through at least six men we know of. She used the same technique on each. Charm, flattery, her feminine wiles. Mr Sturgess thought she was trying to poison him. He got better when he left her. He was lucky. Her second husband, James Hardcastle, is dead. As is her fourth, Clyde Bracegirdle. She had an affair with Cornelius Stout and he was murdered. She manipulates men and uses them for her own ends. If they don't give her what she wants, she kills them. *You* told me this, Reggie. *You* talked me into going to Castlemaine to prove a case against her and now *you* are suffering the same fate as all the men that came before you. You're under her spell.'

Reggie had gone red in the face as Dotty catalogued the very arguments that he had used to convince her that Rita was a murderer. 'It's not the same.'

'Of course, it is. You're deluded if you think she likes you. She thinks you have money. Just like the others she had relationships with. I'll guarantee that she tries her act on a number of men then sees which one comes back for more. Once you walked away, she'd probably forget about you and move on to the next man. For goodness' sake, wake up!'

Reggie took a deep breath. 'You're right. She did go back to the man she was with before me. But Rita has a way about her that's hard to resist. I'm going to have to keep my wits about me when I'm with her.'

Dotty nodded her head, her eyes appraising her companion. 'It will be a challenge for you. Be careful or you'll rue the day you decided to trap her.'

Chapter Thirty-Nine

Henry Stout was sweating. He wiped the perspiration off his brow with his handkerchief. It felt like the pale green walls and the barred windows of the interview room were closing in on him. Opposite sat O'Flanagan.

The detective leaned closer, cracking his knuckles. 'What do you have to say for yourself, Mr Stout? What were you doing on the street opposite where your father's dead body was found? We have a witness who can place you there.'

'I've told you already,' said Henry, his eyes wide with fear. 'I knew that Dad had been visiting that woman, so I went there after he disappeared. I was sure that she was involved.'

'What woman?'

'The woman he was having an affair with. Rita Bracegirdle.'

O'Flanagan tried to keep the surprise out of his voice. 'He was having an affair with Clyde Bracegirdle's wife?'

Henry's thick eyebrows knitted together. 'That reporter, da Costa. He knew. He told Lily.' He shook his head in disbelief. 'You call yourself a detective?'

O'Flanagan recovered quickly then leaned forward, his finger stabbing in Henry's direction. 'Don't use that tone with me. How did you know where she lived?'

'I followed Dad to her place.'

'You went inside and confronted them?'

'Don't be ridiculous. Dad would have torn me to shreds if I did that.'

'You were angry with him and you wanted to make his life miserable. Create a scene with his lover, and make it hard for him. Just like he made life hard for your friend, Stanley Duggan.'

'I'd never do that.' Henry put his head in his hands, then raised haggard eyes to O'Flanagan. 'My father was a difficult man. I don't deny that. I was angry about Stanley but I would never have hurt Dad. Why don't you ask Lily? She'll tell you.'

'Your sister doesn't come into this.' He thrust his face further forward and eyeballed Henry. 'You hated your father. He left you out of his will. You were angry. You followed him to Punt Road and you killed him.'

'I never did. It was that Rita woman.'

'Just because her name was on the ring doesn't mean she killed him.'

'But she lived there. Where he was found. Rita Bracegirdle. Have you even interviewed her? If anyone had a reason to kill him, it was Rita. Dad stopped seeing her. She was the one who was missing out on the money, not us. She's the one with the motive. I still get half of Dad's money, because of Lily.'

O'Flanagan sat back and took a deep breath. When he'd called Henry Stout in for an interview, he had predicted that the young man would crack during the interrogation and admit his guilt. But instead, Lily's brother had given him information that he should have known, and which threw a completely different light on the case. O'Flanagan had lost control of the interview and he wanted it over.

One significant piece of information had changed the focus of his enquiries, in the blinking of an eye. It raised so many questions that needed to be answered. Had Rita Bracegirdle still been married when she was in a relationship with Stout? How did they meet and where was she now? And, most significantly, was Rita the killer of Cornelius Stout? He sighed heavily. This case was going nowhere. His interrogation of Henry Stout had fizzled out, and he feared that he might have to explain the gaping hole in his investigation to the Chief Commissioner.

Inwardly, he remonstrated with himself for not following up Reggie's suggestion to investigate Rita, but it begged the question: how did Reggie know about the Rita-Cornelius relationship? The reporter had kept it from him and now O'Flanagan was looking like a fool in front of his main suspect.

There was no time to waste. He shuffled some papers on his desk and addressed Lily's brother one last time. 'You can go now, Mr Stout, but I'm onto you. I'll have you for the murder of your father before the month is out.'

It was an idle threat, but he didn't want to lose face in front of a suspect. As Henry was escorted from the interview room, O'Flanagan reached for the telephone.

'Tell Reggie da Costa at *The Argus* to get himself here immediately.'

* * *

'You've been holding out on me, Reggie.' O'Flanagan scowled at the crime reporter who was now sitting in the same chair where Henry Stout had sat, only hours before. 'Withholding evidence is a crime.'

'Really, Mick? Treating me with contempt hardly encourages me to confide in you. You promised that we would work together to solve this crime, that we'd be partners, but you kept me in the dark.'

Threatening Reggie was not going to work, O'Flanagan realised. He should have known better. He softened his expression. 'I was wrong, but it's frustration. There's so much on my mind at the moment: Squizzy; Angus Murray and the Berriman case; the Flagg and Stout murders. The gangs are causing havoc and our manpower is down. Help me here.'

'You first.'

'Alright.' He paused. 'I'll admit that Armitage Flagg fits the same demographic as Cornelius Stout, but I'm buggered if I can find a connection. There's also a missing person—Julius Mathieson—who disappeared in 1916. Separated from his wife, living on Richmond Hill. Wealthy, elderly, alone. Shades of Edmund Stout. It seems like too much of a coincidence. I like Henry Stout for his father's murder, but I can't ignore Horace Striker or Stanley Duggan either.' O'Flanagan rubbed his chin. 'But this woman, Rita Bracegirdle—'

'You finally found out who Rita was. You took your time,' interrupted Reggie. 'I've been trying to tell you to investigate her, but you ignored me.'

'I'm not ignoring you now.' O'Flanagan lay his large hairy hands on the desk. 'What do you know?'

'Rita Bracegirdle was Stout's housekeeper.'

'How did you find that out?'

'Stout kept everything. Including his advertisement for a housekeeper and replies from the women who wanted the job. One applicant was Rita Bracegirdle. Add to that Lily Stout's letters to her father, where she talked about their relationship, and you have enough evidence to implicate her. Stout and Rita became romantically involved before her husband died. Stout refused to marry her once she was free, and she was angry. It's highly likely she lured him to her flat and killed him, then stuffed him in the trunk.'

'How would a woman do that?'

'She's big, he was small. And she has a daughter who lives with her so that's the accomplice she needs.'

'How did you find that out?'

Reggie smirked. 'Simple police procedure. I uncovered that Rita Savage, as she was called then, had an illegitimate daughter at the age of sixteen. She's been married four times since; widowed three.'

'Interesting, but that doesn't mean she's a murderer.'

'Really, Mick? I'd suggest that two of those deaths are suspicious.' Reggie smirked. 'Why don't you check out whether Edmund Stout, Flagg, and Mathieson liked to dance?'

O'Flanagan frowned. 'What does that mean?'

'You find out. If there's nothing more, I have work to do.'

'I'm warning you, Reggie. If you withhold evidence—'

'You'll what? Lock me up?' Reggie stood and put on his hat. 'Look at the evidence. It's pointing fairly and squarely at Rita Savage. Savage by name, savage by nature.'

O'Flanagan shook his finger at the reporter. 'Don't get in over your head, my friend. You haven't told me all you know, and that will get you into trouble.'

Reggie smirked. 'I can look after myself, Mick. Just watch me.'

Chapter Forty

Reggie was at home, in the dwelling above the grocer's shop, sitting in an armchair next to the glow of the lamp, a cigar in one hand and a glass of fine whisky in the other. It was twilight outside and the cicadas were chirruping in the garden on the other side of Swan Street. The semi-darkness took the edge off the room, giving it a comforting and friendly atmosphere.

Mildred Bardsley Smith's and Dotty's words had resonated with him. He had responded by writing to his mother, sending her best wishes for the new year. It was all he could do in the circumstances. The last thing he wanted was to run into his father or to engage in another argument with Mavis.

A reply was forthcoming within days. His mother had become accepting of his absence and acknowledged that it was perhaps for the best, given that his father was still living in the family home. She had no wish to quarrel with Reggie, and asked if they could meet at some stage in the near future, perhaps in a park or a café. With time, she hoped that Reggie might consider returning to the family nest—there was always a bed there for him—if he could come to accept Mario's return.

Going home was no longer an option. His father's presence precluded that. But there was now a more important reason in play: Reggie was beginning to like the independence that he had living above the grocer's shop. The housekeeper cum cook came in three days a week, and he took his clothes to the Chinese laundry, when necessary. Life in his new home was not onerous at all.

On the work front, Melbourne was abuzz with crime, a situation that warmed the cockles of Reggie's heart. Squizzy Taylor and his gang, the upcoming trial of Angus Murray, a jewel robbery in Kew, the drug trade, and the corruption that percolated around the brothels bordered by Little Lonsdale, Spring, Lonsdale, and Exhibition Streets, provided him with plenty of fodder for his articles.

But the identity of Cornelius Stout's murderer remained unresolved. O'Flanagan was holding to his conviction that Henry Stout was the culprit, but was still unable to construct an ironclad case against him. Reggie had withheld from the detective what he had learned about Rita's whereabouts, not only as payback but also because he wanted to solve the murder himself, and thus endear himself to Lily Stout.

But his time in Rita Bracegirdle's company had implanted an element of doubt in his mind. If he considered, objectively, what he knew about her, he would say that the case was almost airtight. Here was a needy, manipulative woman, who was well-versed in the arts of seduction and who married for personal gain. If her desires were thwarted, what then?

She could turn on the charm, that was true, and she had an animal magnetism that apparently attracted lonely men who craved companionship and sex. But was she capable of murder? Was she mercenary enough to eliminate a man once he had written his will in her favour, or be prepared to kill him, if he didn't?

Dotty Wright had challenged his response to Rita Bracegirdle that night at Leggett's. She suggested that Rita's appearance of solicitude, empathy and interest were all part of a deadly game she played to attract and trap men. He, Reggie da Costa, had been blinded by her charms, said Dotty, and that accusation had resonated with him.

One way or the other, his future meetings with Rita Bracegirdle would prove her innocence or guilt. But next time he would ensure that he would not fall for her tricks. It came down to this: Rita's guilt would prove Henry's innocence, giving him the chance to win Lily's hand.

He poured another whisky and held it up to the light, admiring the richness of its amber glow. His plan was straightforward. He had to convince Rita that he was interested in her, so that she would show her true colours. He needed evidence against her, and this could only be gathered by seeing her *in situ* with her daughter. If he could draw information from both Rita and Dolores that would implicate them in the murders of Stout and Bracegirdle, then he could hand the case to O'Flanagan as a *fait accompli*, but not before he had informed the public of his role in snaring a killer of rich, lonely men.

The important thing was not to excite Rita's suspicions. He would have to play along with her, pretend to desire her, earn her trust. It would be challenging, but he didn't doubt his ability to play that role. Forewarned as to her true nature, he believed that he held all the cards in this game of cat and mouse. And, when the contest was over and she was exposed as a killer, then he would claim his trophy: Lily Stout.

He closed his eyes and stroked his moustache. Lily. That stylish young woman, his future wife. Beautiful, ambitious, an heiress. What more could any man want?

Chapter Forty-One

The Citroen purred up the driveway, its headlights illuminating the thick bush and prickly pear, which grew unchecked around the little weatherboard house. A small pathway had been cleared leading down towards the river but, apart from that, little had been done to improve the property. The house looked neglected. The paint was peeling around the windows and the corrugated iron roof was rusting.

Rita sat next to Reggie, her perfume wafting through the car, its sweetness cloying. He had spent another evening in Rita's company at Leggett's, and had offered to drive her home.

He was amused and, if he were honest, flattered by the look on her face two hours earlier, when she had seen him making his way through the crowded dance floor towards her. Her smile was broad, the crimson lipstick slashed across her mouth and upper teeth. The elderly gent who was clutching her suddenly found himself partnerless.

This second evening with Rita had been quite different. Dotty's pep talk had had an effect. He had not felt that desire for her that he had experienced the night they danced the tango. She was bolder and brassier, whispering comments that smacked of innuendo. He found her common. As the evening wore on, an endless round of foxtrot, waltz, and one-step, Rita's attempts at conversation appeared to be little more than a concerted effort to compliment Reggie into submission.

'You are a marvellous dancer, Reggie!' she said. 'A natural. You and I, we move together as one.' She clutched his shoulder even harder and placed her cheek against his chest. He wondered whether her lipstick was going to leave a smear on his clean white collar.

She plied him with questions. Was he married? Did he have a lady friend, because surely, someone so attractive must have a woman in his life? Was he close to his parents? What was his house like? Did he travel much?

He answered her, giving her what she wanted to hear. No, he was neither married nor in a relationship. He was lonely. ('That is hard to believe, a prince like you, alone.') His parents were dead. ('Oh, you poor man!') His house in Toorak was being refurbished so he was living in rented accommodation. ('Then you must come to my place where I will give you a delicious, home-cooked meal.') He loved to visit Italy. ('You are such a cultured man. Such taste. You must take me some time.')

But when it came to questioning her, Rita's answers were brief and revealed little. She was a widow, she said, and very lonely too. Leggett's was a wonderful place where she could meet people, dance, and have a good time. Otherwise, her life had little to offer unless she was making a man happy. 'A man such as you, Reggie.'

During the evening, they had watched a demonstration of two dances: the Charleston and the Samba. Rita stood behind Reggie, occasionally pressing her breasts against his back. He found it disconcerting that a woman in her fifties, a woman who was uncouth, overblown, and uncultured, should be trying so hard to woo a man twenty years her junior, a man of style and taste. In truth, he wondered how he could ever have been captivated by her. She was so gauche and ill-bred. She was old enough to be his mother. And yet, the question remained unanswered, 'Was she a murderer?'

It was with relief that Reggie had walked her to his car, knowing that the evening was almost over. He had decided that even if she made the first move towards him, he would be cautious when responding to her. What he wanted was for her to talk to him, particularly about her past. Tonight, he would drop her off at home, but appear keen about seeing her again, somewhere other than Leggett's Ballroom. He'd had enough of the place, and had become fearful that he might be recognised and his cover blown. Besides, he had his pride and being seen with Rita was not what he wanted. What would people think?

And now, standing on the front porch of her home in Mary Street, Rita smiled seductively at him. 'Would you like to come in?' she asked.

'It's late. I have an important meeting tomorrow morning, early.'

'Again? On a Saturday?'

'I'm afraid so. Business doesn't stop for a weekend. We could meet again in a few days if that suits you? I do so enjoy your company, Rita.'

She beamed at him, placing her hand on his arm. 'I am flattered that such a handsome man as you should choose the company of little me. You are a prince among men. I would consider it a privilege to wait on you, if you would come to dinner here. I would pamper you. And, in the morning, I would serve you a sumptuous breakfast.'

Reggie raised his eyebrows, unable to suppress his surprise. 'I really must be going. However, I am free Thursday night. Would that suit you?'

'That suits me well. I like a man who knows what he wants. Come at six o'clock and we'll have time to get acquainted.' She winked at him, knowingly.

'Lovely. I'll see you then.'

He was about to give her a peck on the cheek, when she turned her head at the last moment and kissed him full on the mouth. He managed to stifle the feeling of repulsion that overcame him by giving her a broad smile. It worked. She beamed at him in return and waved as he started the car.

'Goodbye, my dear Reggie,' she called after him.

As he drove away, he wiped the lipstick off his mouth. It was hard work maintaining his composure in the face of such an onslaught. Was it any wonder that men had succumbed to Rita's dubious charms in the past? He had to keep his head if he were going to prise information out of the woman. It would require great skill and careful questioning, as well as resisting her attempts to get him into bed. She was a brazen woman with few scruples. The mask had slipped and it was evident that she had set her sights on him. It was what he had wanted, but now he felt a niggling doubt about how to ensnare her. It occurred to him, as he parked outside the grocer's shop fifteen minutes later, that Dotty might have some ideas on how to tackle Rita Bracegirdle.

* * *

It was late. Dotty was up preparing some lessons for the Grade Sixes when she heard the knock on the door. She was surprised to see Reggie standing there.

'I saw your light on,' he said. 'I hope you don't mind me coming in at this hour?'

'Not at all. I'm still on holidays and I could do with a diversion. You're dressed to the nines. Where have you been?'

'Back at Leggett's. With *her.*'

'Rita?'

Reggie nodded. He followed her into the sitting room and leaned against the mantelpiece.

'I really think you should put this in the hands of the police,' said Dotty, returning to her armchair.

'I don't have enough evidence. It's all circumstantial. I need proof.'

'What sort of proof?'

Reggie sighed with frustration. 'I don't know. Just proof. I'll know it when I see it. Or hear it.'

'How did she behave this time?'

'You were right about her. Big, blowsy, dressed in bad taste. That's what she is. She tries to win you over with an onslaught of praise.'

'I thought you would have liked that.'

Reggie smiled despite himself. He was beginning to appreciate Dotty's gentle, and not so gentle, jibes.

'She's invited me to dinner on Thursday night. The problem is that I'm not sure how to deal with her when I get there. I won't go into details but she is rather forward, if you take my meaning. Let's just say that I would find it difficult to be romantic with her.'

'You might need to,' said Dotty, matter-of-factly. 'If you don't, she may become suspicious. I suspect, from what you've told me, that she wants what men can give her—money, presents, attention—and in return she gives what she thinks men want: good cooking, her undivided attention, compliments, and sex.'

Reggie was shocked. 'Really, Dotty. I wouldn't expect a woman like you to speak like that.'

'I'm a teacher, not a nun. I understand how the world works. It doesn't mean that I live that way.'

'How do I get her to confide in me? Do you have any ideas?'

'Take her a present. Something small, but personal. Flowers. Compliment her on her dress. Tell her what a good figure she has.'

'You are joking?'

'You asked my advice. It will relax her. Put her off her guard.'

'I suppose you're right.'

Dotty sat quietly for a moment, gathering her thoughts. She leaned forward. 'Be a good listener. Don't dominate the conversation. Ask her about the men in her life but couch it in general terms. Be sympathetic. Build up her trust. She might let slip some things from her past. Share some reminiscences of your own. Whatever you do, don't elaborate too much. Or exaggerate. If she knows too much about you, she might check whether you're telling her the truth. That would be very dangerous.'

'What about her daughter? If she's there, what do I do? Should I ignore her?'

'You may need an ally. Be nice to her. Polite. But don't be overly friendly. Rita may feel threatened if you show too much interest. The girl is more your age, remember.'

Reggie listened, a thoughtful expression on his face. 'What you say makes sense.'

The clock on the mantelpiece chimed midnight.

'It's late and I'm being selfish, keeping you from your bed. I'll go now. Thank you so much for your advice. I appreciate it.' He picked up his coat and hat.

Dotty touched his arm. 'Be careful, Reggie. If she really is a killer, she's no fool. She's managed to get away with it before. Whatever you do, take it slowly otherwise she'll get suspicious.'

Reggie nodded and touched his hat. 'Good advice. But don't worry about me. I can take care of myself.'

As he pulled the door shut behind him, Dotty looked thoughtful. 'I don't like this,' she whispered. 'Not at all.' She shook her head, turned off the light and walked down the hallway to her bedroom.

Chapter Forty-Two

Dolores Savage melted away into the shadows, silently watching from the kitchen door. She was a big woman, like her mother, but without the accoutrements of jewellery and makeup. She had thick brows and thick lips, with dark hooded eyes that showed little of her feelings. Her dress was shapeless, of a brown colour. If you saw her in the street, you probably would not notice her. And that's the way her mother liked it.

The table set, the meal cooking, and the bottle of wine uncorked, all was in readiness for the arrival of Rita's latest gentleman caller. She had been instructed to stay out of the way, preferably in the kitchen or her bedroom. Conversation with the guest was to be minimal. Dolores knew the rules.

For some reason, Rita had lit a fire, even though the evening was a warm one. Perhaps it was so that she could wear another flimsy dress which showed off her curves, Dolores thought. Her mother was obsessed with her appearance, actually convinced that men found her desirable.

What a joke. She was a painted trollop, a dangerous painted trollop. Dolores had watched a succession of men come and go, the occasional one falling prey to Rita's charms, if you could call them that. Incessant compliments; smarmy and suggestive conversation; touching and smiling. All designed to trap the unwitting. And there were plenty of stupid men out there to be trapped. But the story had a sameness. A couple of dinners, the promise of sex, a few nights with a stranger under her roof, and then the inevitable departure.

But there had been exceptions: naïve men who had believed Rita's

185

declarations of love, brought her presents, accepted without questioning that she was the answer to their loneliness, and then had succumbed to her charms. The relationships were always short-lived, in more ways than one.

And she, Dolores Savage, had been a constant in her mother's life, but unappreciated. Except when she helped her mother dispose of men who had outlived their usefulness.

Each time it happened, she thought it would be the last, but her mother's vanity and obsession with money inevitably led to yet another man standing on the doorstep, oblivious to what might happen if he didn't submit to Rita's whims. Inwardly, Dolores seethed with resentment, but her mother was blind to her moods. She would always be the shadow in the doorway, the daughter who was little better than a maid, unloved, and taken for granted.

A new man was in the house, an unlikely prospect who looked far too worldly and intelligent to fall for Rita's tricks. He was immaculately dressed and, from Dolores's observation, didn't need a woman like Rita. He would easily attract women of his own age and social class. To put it succinctly, he was not the usual type: elderly, lonely, needy. Surely her mother was suspicious?

'It's warm in here,' he had said when he entered the sitting room.

'Let me take your coat.'

He protested that it wasn't necessary, but Dolores came forward and took it from him.

'Your daughter?' he had asked.

'Dolores. She won't bother us. Pretend she's not here.'

Dolores went into the kitchen. Her fingers rifled through his jacket pockets looking for identification. It was part of her job, checking the identities of Rita's lovers to ensure that there was no mistake as to whom they were, and how much money they carried. The wallet was in the inside pocket. Within were five one-pound notes, a ten-shilling note, and his press card.

'I knew it,' she whispered. 'It had to happen.'

She sat at the kitchen table, listening to the rise and fall of the conversation from the next room, her mother's girlish giggle, her interminable compliments, and the brief replies from the intruder who had lied to her mother and who planned, no doubt, to expose her.

Rita entered the kitchen, carrying the flowers that he had brought with him. The smile left her face. She stared at her daughter, sitting inert at the table.

'You lazy girl. Is dinner almost ready?'

'Five minutes. Do you know who you've got in there?'

'Of course, I do.'

Dolores paused, enjoying the moment and her mother's look of discomfiture. 'No, you don't. He's not a financier. He's not wealthy. He's probably married. He's a crime reporter. Reginald da Costa from *The Argus*.'

'What?' Rita's face froze, all excitement and sparkle fizzling out in the blink of an eye. 'Let me see.' She grabbed the press card from her daughter and studied it. 'The bastard.'

'You misjudged this one,' Dolores said. 'A blind man could see that he's not your type. Too suave, too sophisticated, too young for you.'

Rita gave her daughter a black look. 'Watch your mouth.' She looked back in the direction of the sitting room. 'He must know something. But how? I'm always so careful. We need to get rid of him, permanently. You know what to do.'

Dolores frowned. 'Don't be ridiculous. This is different. You can't kill him and expect to get away with it. Who knows who he's told? They'll come after you. I've warned you before, but you never listen.'

'If you don't like it, you can leave. No one's stopping you.'

Dolores was silent.

'I thought so,' said Rita. 'You couldn't survive without me.' She took up the bottle and two glasses. 'Fix his dinner. A fatal dose. When I tell you to do something, you do it.'

Rita gave her a long look, then stalked out of the room.

Dolores gazed after her, muttering to herself. She stood and took the packet of rat poison from under the sink. Then she turned back to the pot simmering on the hob, took the ladle off the hook and tasted the stew. Potatoes, meat, turnips, carrots, onion, and beef stock, thick and flavoursome. Just right to mask the bitter taste of strychnine.

Chapter Forty-Three

Reggie glanced around the room while Rita was in the kitchen. On the mantelpiece was an odd collection of cheap, porcelain dogs and some framed photographs of Rita at various events, dressed to impress. The curtains were shabby and faded. The couch was threadbare, its antimacassars, greasy and stained. Reggie watched as the fire spat out embers, adding to the burn marks on the carpet, while a thin pall of smoke hugged the ceiling. It was all quite depressing and tasteless.

Reggie was straightening one of the cheap framed prints on the wall when Rita returned from the kitchen. He turned back to face her, and caught her giving him an odd look.

'I like things symmetrical,' he explained.

She pulled a face and stood before him. She really was a sight. Her hair was tied back into a bun, with a strange tiara-like contraption across her head. Lots of cheap bangles dangled on her wrists, while her nails were painted a tawdry red, to match her lipstick. A thick layer of blue eye shadow covered her eyelids, her cheeks tinged with bright pink rouge, and her face, heavily powdered. Worst of all was her dress, made of thin satin, which hid very little, given that she appeared to have forgotten her undergarments. Reggie wondered how he could ever have found her attractive.

He forced a smile. 'You look very striking, Rita. One could not forget you in a hurry.'

'Thank you. I do my best with what I have.' She ran her hands over the front of her dress, smoothing out the wrinkles in the fabric. 'You are a man of good taste. You don't think this is too much?'

Reggie shook his head. 'Unforgettable.' He looked around. 'You have a comfortable home, Rita. Is it just you and your daughter?'

She raised an eyebrow. 'Most of the time.' She came up closer and flicked a piece of fluff from his collar, the smell of her cheap perfume wafting unpleasantly around him.

'Sit, Reggie. Dinner is ready.'

He sat at the head of the table, with Rita to his left. Dolores came in with two plates of stew, placing them in front of Reggie and her mother.

'Isn't Dolores eating with us?' he asked.

'She ate earlier. Do not concern yourself with her.' She eyed his meal. 'Please, do begin. I do not like my food so hot. I have sensitive lips.'

Reggie raised his eyebrows. This was going to be an interesting meal, he thought. He took a mouthful and was surprised that it was edible, tasty in fact. He nodded in the direction of the daughter. 'Very nice.' She shrank back into the hallway, watching.

'Why don't you tell me about yourself, Rita? You intrigue me.'

'Do I, indeed? You are all kindness and consideration.' She paused, moving the lumps of meat around the plate with her fork. 'Eat, please, and I will tell you my story.

'Many years ago, I lived in a small country town. It was a quiet place. Very dull. My parents were strict. They were church people; they did not know how to enjoy themselves. They were hard on me. All the time, do this, do that. I wanted to move away, meet interesting people, like you.

'I was a good daughter. I cared for my sick mother when my brothers and sister wouldn't lift a finger. But there came a time when I needed to get away.'

She popped a piece of meat in her mouth and savoured it before swallowing, watching as Reggie made short work of his meal.

'I came to Melbourne when I was still young. I had nothing, and no one helped me. I survived, despite what others did to me. I learned to be strong. I learned that no one cares for me but myself.' She paused, looking at him intently. 'In my life I have met many men. Some were weak; some took advantage of my generosity and goodness; some lied to me. They think I am stupid, but I am not.'

'Why did they think that?'

'Because they only saw what was on the surface, not what was below. Men tried to use me, but I know what's what. I used them. You understand, Mr da Costa?' She laughed, watching Reggie closely.

Reggie put down his knife and fork and pushed his plate away. 'Costigan. I am Reggie Costigan.'

'See, you think I am stupid too. It's you who are stupid.' She wagged her finger at him. 'You come here under false pretences, trying to trap me. You are one of those men who lie to women. But it is I who trap you, Mr Reporter.'

Reggie tried to play the innocent. 'I'm not trying to trap anyone. I'll be honest with you. I'm writing a series of articles about interesting people in the everyday world. When I met you at Leggett's, I thought that you would make a good subject. Larger than life. Vibrant. I wanted to know your story, but I thought you wouldn't be willing to talk to me if you knew who I was.'

'I interest you, yes? That is the effect that I have on all men.' She ate a mouthful of stew, then put her knife and fork down. 'I will tell you more. That's why you're here, isn't it?'

Reggie nodded and took a sip of wine. It was going well. She was about to spill the beans on her criminal escapades.

'I was made pregnant by a man who used me up, then left me on my own to raise a child. My parents threw me out of home. I had no help. I pleaded with them to take me back, but they refused. I was left to fend for myself in the city.' She tapped her head and nodded. 'I am very smart, Mr Reggie da Costa. These rich men, they want a woman to cook and clean and go to bed with them, all for nothing. But I took what I could get. It was only fair.'

'Who were these men?' asked Reggie. 'What were their names?'

'All in good time. I am hungry. Let me eat.' She coated a sizeable piece of beef with gravy and ate it quickly. 'You want to know their names? I will tell you. My first husband was Sylvester. He was lonely, much older than me, but his mother interfered with my plans. She whispered in his ears, filled him up with lies about me. She came between us. But I won in the end. He gave me this house. So convenient being near the river.' She chuckled. 'But you will know about that soon enough.'

Reggie leaned forward. 'Perhaps I have misled you. You interest me because I know that there is more to you than meets the eye. I have researched you, Miss Savage. I know that two of your husbands—James Hardcastle and Clyde Bracegirdle—died from natural causes. Is there anything that you might like to tell me about their deaths?'

'You mean the truth? You probably know it anyway. I treated them like princes, but they were greedy. They wanted everything that I could give them, and they offered nothing in return. All I wanted was a roof over my head and money to buy nice things. Surely that is fair?'

'It depends on what you did to them in the end, doesn't it?'

'Nothing less than they deserved.' She looked at him, concerned. 'You look pale. Are you feeling ill?'

'Just a slight stomach ache, nothing serious. Please continue.'

'I met men at Leggett's, just like you.'

'Such as Edmund Stout?'

'You know about him? Edmund was not a nice man. I asked him to help me. Just a little bit of money from one who had so much. When he said no, I got angry. It was his fault that I did what I did. I am usually so sweet, so caring. I took one look at him and knew his days were over.'

'You killed him?'

Rita shrugged her shoulders. 'Not my fault. He should have been more considerate of my situation.'

'You stole from him?'

'I took what he owed me. Nothing more, nothing less.'

'Where is he now?'

'He took a little trip, down the river. It's close to here, you know.' She laughed out loud, as she took in the expression on his face. 'I'm surprised it took so long for him to sink.'

'What about his brother?'

'Now that was a strange coincidence. Edmund talked about Cornelius, but I never met him. That is, until I saw his advertisement for a housekeeper.'

She laughed. 'His house. Full of rubbish. But he was nice to me. Very generous. He appreciated me.'

'You gave Cornelius a ring? A gold signet ring?'

'Really, Mr da Costa? Men give *me* presents.'

'And then he died?'

'That is true.' She pulled a face. 'It made me sad. I am sad about you, too. I thought you were a nice man, but you deceive me like the others. You don't look well, Mr da Costa. I hope the stew does not upset you. Dolores added something special just for you.'

Reggie looked down at his plate, the significance of her words slowly dawning on him. He clutched his stomach and doubled over, as cramps seized him. He looked up at her and saw the look of delight on her face.

'You're actually enjoying this,' he said as he straightened up in his chair.

'Even as I speak, the poison is moving through your veins. It is very gratifying to see someone suffer for their sins. You have lied to me. You would put me in prison, even though it was those men who did the wrong thing. How dare you judge *me!*'

Reggie tried to stand, but it was as if the strength had gone out of his legs. He fell back into his chair, as the realisation of what she had done to him sank in.

'What did you give me?'

'Strychnine. It's very powerful and, I might add, quite painful too. Just surrender to it. It's easier that way. It will take you on a journey to the deepest parts of your being.'

She took another large mouthful of meat and chewed it thoughtfully, before swallowing it. She nodded to her daughter. 'Delicious.'

Reggie sat back in his chair, the blood draining from his face. He could hear his heart thumping against his chest.

'I will tell you more of my story. This is what you came for, isn't it, Mr Reporter?' She smiled and took a sip of wine. 'You've heard about Armitage Flagg? Another miser. I should have brought him back here to dispose of him. The ground was hard at his place. It was difficult to dig a grave.'

'Julius Mathieson?' Reggie felt his vision blurring, but he had to know.

'The one at Richmond Hill? He hit me, then he gave me money to shut me up. I showed him.'

Reggie bent forward; his arms locked across his chest. He felt weak and giddy. Another spasm took hold. He tried to take a deep breath, but it made him gasp in pain. He gripped the arms of his chair, but there was no relief. All he could hear was the pounding of his heart and Rita's voice droning on in the background.

'I am good at predicting how men will act, but there was one who surprised me. I was housekeeper for a grocer in Richmond. Things were rather tight money-wise and I needed some extra cash. He wasn't interested in sex. He was different that way,' she added matter-of-factly. 'I liked to look through his personal things when I was cleaning his bedroom. Interesting what you find. Turns out he was a Kraut pretending to be one of us. I asked for money. A little bit of blackmail. Nothing bad. It was a bit of a shock when he killed himself.'

Reggie found his voice. 'Eric Smith?'

'You know about him?' Rita laughed and pushed her plate away. She swallowed another mouthful of wine and stood up, looking down on him.

'It's nearly time. Nothing can save you now. You're dying, Mr da Costa.'

As she spoke, her eyes widened and her face became deathly pale. She doubled over and clutched her stomach. She looked around wildly, her eyes moving from her plate to her daughter.

'What have you done? Stupid cow.'

Dolores stepped into the light. 'You are the stupid one. You and your men.'

Rita started to twitch, her face contorting. She let out a bloodcurdling scream.

'You've poisoned me!' she cried. 'Me. Your mother.'

'You stopped being my mother a long time ago.'

Rita moaned, 'So sore. So sore. I can't breathe.' She rubbed her jaw and neck vigorously. 'Why? Why would you do this to me?'

'You've made me do things that no daughter should ever have to do. Those poor men.' Dolores took a deep breath. 'I had to stop you. No one else can.'

Tears flooded Rita's eyes, her mascara forming thick black rivulets of wrinkles down her cheeks. 'I gave up everything for you.'

'You gave up nothing.' Dolores spat out the words. 'It was all for yourself.'

'Do something. Get me to a hospital!' She collapsed onto the floor, writhing in agony.

Reggie clenched his fists and bit his lip. Another spasm was building. It was taking hold of him. His insides felt like they were being wrenched and twisted. He bent over and tried to breathe, but the pain of drawing in air made him stop. He was holding his breath, what little oxygen he had left in his lungs. Beads of perspiration popped out on his brow. His lips were drawn back, white against his gums. There was a peculiar metallic taste in his mouth.

A strange tremor passed through him, as the pain began to build towards a crescendo. He collapsed to the floor, doubling up, struggling to remain conscious in the face of the paroxysm.

And then, as quickly as it came, it was gone. He sucked in deep breaths of air to his starved lungs and lay back, feeling weak, but relieved.

Next to him, Rita started to convulse, throwing her body around erratically, like a rag doll. A violent seizure surged through her body, forcing her head back in the direction of her buttocks, so that it looked as if her spine would crack. It was horrible to watch. She let out a blood-chilling cry and then fell unconscious.

From the corner of his eye, Reggie could see Dolores standing in the doorway, watching.

'Am I going to die, too?' he whispered.

She turned to him, registering his question. 'We're going to the hospital.'

'Her too?'

Dolores shook her head, almost preternaturally calm in the presence of her mother's stricken body.

Rita's eyes opened wide, glazed and unseeing, her chest heaving as she scrabbled for breath, spittle mixing with her deep red lipstick. Reggie watched in horror as she succumbed to her death throes. Her muscles began to spasm, so that her body involuntarily jerked and thrashed, the violence of her paroxysms increasing with each minute that passed. She no longer looked like the person he had met at Leggett's two weeks ago: the woman who had danced and preened herself and hung on every word he uttered. Her body was no longer hers to control. She was possessed by a force that would bend her and shape her, and ultimately take her to her death.

Reggie could feel all hope ebbing away as he lay on the floor. Dolores had not moved from the shadows of the doorway. She was watching; he could feel her eyes upon him. Never again would he see the face of his devoted mother, or experience the promise of a future with Lily. All that he had done in his life would end here, on the floor of this dilapidated little weatherboard house next to the river. All his hopes and dreams were being consumed by the strychnine that was flowing through his veins, contaminating all in its wake. No one would cry at his funeral; no mother would weep over his casket. His body would be consigned to the frigid waters of the Yarra River.

But suddenly, he felt Dolores's powerful arms drag him up off the floor. She looped his arm across her shoulder, and half-carried him out the front door. Outside the northerly wind had come up, the branches of the trees moaning as they swayed. Reggie's back was drenched in sweat, his shirt sticking unpleasantly to his body, and his collar rubbing against his neck. He groaned and leaned heavily against her.

At the side of the house, not far from Reggie's Citroen, was a rusting Ford truck.

'Get in,' she said tonelessly, pushing him up into the passenger seat. She slammed the door shut and he slumped against it, watching as if through a fog as she stood in front of the vehicle and cranked the engine. It roared into life. Back in the cab, Dolores released the handbrake, adjusted the throttle, and pushed down on the pedal. The truck responded, the noise of the engine engulfing the silence of the night. The Ford edged forward down the dirt driveway, slowly gathering speed.

They headed out through the gate, the narrow wheels catching in the ruts of the road. Trees screened the Yarra River from view, but as they turned into Mary Street, Reggie saw a glint of water, caught in the headlights of the truck. Dolores drove slowly, negotiating her way around the potholes that punctuated the road. Each bump resonated with Reggie, sending stabbing pains through his weakened body.

At times, Reggie became aware that Dolores was talking to herself, catching fragments that made no real sense to him. At other times, he was in a world of his own, drifting between blissful unconsciousness, interspersed with moments of excruciating pain.

They turned up towards the city, the engine struggling as it tried to crest Richmond Hill. To the left, Reggie recognised the imposing bluestone edifice of St. Ignatius' Church, standing against the night sky. It occurred to him that it was too late now to make his peace with God.

He began to panic. The poison was taking hold again, moving slowly through his gut and contorting his insides. He could feel his throat constricting and his jaw tightening as he struggled to breathe. His back arched involuntarily, pushing him hard against the door of the truck. He grabbed the handle and turned it. The door swung wide and he could feel himself falling towards the road. But, at the last moment, a strong hand grabbed him back, anchoring him to the seat. The door slammed shut again, from the force of the wind.

'Let me die,' he whispered.

'No,' replied Dolores, above the roar of the engine. 'You're not going to die tonight.'

Reggie cried out, tears running down his cheeks. He felt as if he were on an endless journey to oblivion, steered by a strange woman whose motivation he could not fathom, but one who had been a willing partner in murder and had now, apparently, poisoned her own mother.

He began to hallucinate, as panic and pain engulfed him. In his mind he imagined his funeral, a large affair in St. Paul's Cathedral. The choir sang as an orchestra played Mozart's *Requiem in D minor*. His casket, a highly buffed mahogany coffin shrouded in pure white lilies, lay before the high altar. The church was full of mourners, his mother sobbing in the front pew, his colleagues from *The Argus* lamenting his loss. Dotty and Lily were wailing, their cries blending in with the music, growing louder and louder and louder, until they merged with the roar of the truck's engine.

Through the fog in his brain, Reggie could just see O'Flanagan standing at the pulpit, speaking of Reggie's service to the police and the posthumous award of a police medal to honour him. Kramer followed, reflecting that the world of journalism had lost one of its favourite sons. And then came his father, playing Chopin's *Funeral March* on the violin.

Tears began to thread their way down Reggie's face, as he imagined a world without Reggie da Costa, a world which would be so much poorer without him.

He was blinded by a light. He must be crossing to the other side, he thought. He raised his face to meet it, but there was only darkness.

Chapter Forty-Four

'Reggie. It's me. O'Flanagan.'

The voice was coming from far away and, as it came again, it seemed closer. Reggie opened his eyes. The blind was drawn, shutting out the bright sunlight, but he could see the outline of a large bullish man against stark white, unadorned walls. He looked down. He was wearing a hospital robe.

'Where am I?'

'Melbourne Hospital. You've been here for three days. The doctor says you're making a good recovery. Luckily, the dose of strychnine you were given wasn't fatal.'

Reggie shut his eyes and opened them again. 'I'm still alive?'

'Indeed, you are.'

'I'm so sore. Everything aches.' He leaned forward, trying to focus on his surroundings. 'My Citroen. Where is it?'

'One of my constables drove it back to your place.'

'That's a relief.' He fell back against the pillows. 'Is she here?'

'Who?'

'Dolores.'

'She's dead.'

Reggie closed his eyes. 'She saved me,' he whispered.

O'Flanagan spoke slowly. 'We know she brought you here. She told the doctors that you'd been poisoned, and then she left. You're one lucky bastard. They gave you tannic acid as soon as you were admitted. The strychnine was neutralised. Then they anaesthetised you until the effects of the strychnine wore off.'

Reggie opened his eyes wide. 'Dolores is dead?'

'She is. Same as Rita. Strychnine. We think Dolores carried her mother into the bedroom, then took the poison herself. We found them together on the bed. Mother and daughter lying next to each other.'

Reggie screwed up his face. 'How horrible. How did you know where they were?'

'The doctor on duty contacted the police after Dolores brought you in. Your friend Dotty had already gone to the police station when you didn't come home on Thursday night. She was worried. She asked for me. She remembered what Sylvester Sturgess said about Rita's house—Mary Street near where the road meets the river—and we followed her directions and found the bodies.'

'This isn't the way I thought it would end.'

O'Flanagan reached into his coat pocket and took out a notebook and pen. 'Fill me in on the details. Take your time.'

Reggie took a deep breath. 'Help me sit up, then get me some water.'

The detective sergeant listened carefully as Reggie recounted how he had met Rita at Leggett's Ballroom, after Lily reported seeing her there.

'It was Rita's happy hunting ground, Mick. It was where she found her victims, when she wasn't using the Classifieds. I danced with her, and it went from there. Over dinner at her place, she admitted killing Cornelius and Edmund Stout, Bracegirdle, Mathieson, and Flagg. Sylvester Sturgess was lucky he didn't meet the same fate.'

'Why did she kill them?'

'Money, mainly. Anger that they didn't give her what she wanted. She was a cold-blooded killer. You should have seen the look on her face when she watched me succumb to the strychnine. She was enjoying it.'

'You should have got out once your cover was blown,' commented the detective.

'It was too late. I'd eaten the meal by then.'

'Sturgess made it hard to track her down when he gave her the house near the river,' said O'Flanagan. 'It was in his name, not hers. That made our investigation of Stout's murder difficult to solve.'

'Your investigation? You didn't have one that involved Rita. Admit it, Mick. You got it wrong. It was my investigation that tracked her down.'

O'Flanagan put his pen and notebook away. 'You could have died,' he growled. 'You should have told me everything.'

Reggie looked him in the eye. 'I would have told you if you hadn't played games with me. You didn't play straight with me, Mick, so don't pretend you did.'

'I'll concede that you have a point,' the detective admitted, 'but you don't know everything, Reggie.

'You see, there's more. We've been digging up the block where Rita lived. The house by the river. So far, we've found four bodies. We think one of them is Mathieson. There's another adult male who's unidentified.'

'It's not Edmund Stout,' said Reggie. 'Rita put his body in the river. Who were the other two?'

'Newborn babies. Whether they were Rita's or her daughter's, we'll never know.'

'That's awful.' Reggie sank back, exhausted. 'So that's the end of it. The murder of Cornelius Stout solved.'

'A feather in your cap. I have to admit that I never considered Rita Bracegirdle a genuine suspect. We'll need to exhume the bodies of Hardcastle and Bracegirdle. See if the post-mortem shows evidence of strychnine. In all my days, I've never seen anything like this.'

'You've dropped your investigation into Henry Stout?'

'He's been informed that he's no longer a suspect. I guess that it won't be too long before he and his sister pay you a visit.' O'Flanagan winked at Reggie. 'She'll be very grateful, I should think.'

He got up from the chair. 'I might need some more information from you, but we can wait a few days for that. Your mother is outside. I believe she's been here every day, waiting for you to wake up.'

'Could you ask her to come in? We have a lot to talk about.'

Chapter Forty-Five

Reggie was to remain in hospital a further five days, while checks were made that he had not suffered kidney damage, and that he was strong enough to return home. Reggie became convinced that Dolores had laced his stew with enough strychnine to bring on symptoms of poisoning, but not kill him, while serving up the fatal dose to Rita.

His brush with death made him rethink his relationship with his mother. Perhaps he'd been too hasty cutting ties with her after his father's reappearance?

Their reconciliation was an emotional one. Tears flowed on both sides when she sat on the edge of his hospital bed and drew him to her. She had been so scared that she might lose him, she said. To think that they might have been estranged when he died. It was too terrible to contemplate. She pleaded with him to come home, so that she could nurse him back to health. On that point, he remained unmoved. He had no wish to live under the same roof as his father.

Half-heartedly, Mavis mentioned that the man himself was outside in the corridor, waiting to speak to him. Reggie had shaken his head and replied with a definitive 'No.'

Resigned at last to his determination to live away from her, and assured that he was making good progress, Mavis left him, promising to return the next day.

After she was gone, Reggie lay back exhausted. O'Flanagan's interrogation and his mother's visit had worn him out. The doctor stated that no further visits should take place that day; the patient needed to rest. It was only later that Reggie was told that Lily Stout had been waiting to see him but, sadly, was sent away.

Lily. He closed his eyes and let his thoughts drift. The way she had clung to him as they waltzed around the dance floor at Leggett's. Those languid grey eyes, staring up at him, admiring him, captivating him, promising him everything he could ever wish for. Her boyish figure, perfect for Paris fashions. The fragrance of her perfume: tuberoses.

And now, with the mystery of her father's death solved and the estate in her hands, Lily would be free to choose the partner of her dreams. The one she had asked coquettishly, 'Why haven't you contacted me? I thought you liked me?' The one who had saved her brother from being hanged for murder.

He drifted off to sleep, weary but content.

Chapter Forty-Six

CORNELIUS STOUT MURDER SOLVED
SHOCK DISCOVERY:
MOTHER AND DAUGHTER MURDER-SUICIDE
Deadly Intent: Savage by name, savage by nature!

By REGGIE DA COSTA, Senior Crime Reporter

In an astonishing development in the Cornelius Stout murder, detectives went to a home on the leafy banks of the Yarra River and discovered the bodies of a mother and daughter. They have been identified as Mrs Rita Bracegirdle and Miss Dolores Savage. It appears to be a case of murder-suicide.

It is more than three months since the body of Cornelius Stout, a wealthy widower, was found in the basement of a Punt Road terrace house. Police detectives had been unable to crack the case.

Mr Reggie da Costa, crime reporter with *The Argus*, had been investigating the murder since his discovery of Stout's body. He discovered that Mrs Rita Bracegirdle (née Savage) killed Stout after he terminated his relationship with her.

Mrs Bracegirdle, formerly of Castlemaine, was married four times. Police now suspect that she murdered two of her husbands and attempted to poison a third.

Strychnine in the stew!

On Thursday night last, Mr da Costa was invited to Mrs Bracegirdle's home for dinner. Suspicious of his motives and fearful that she was about to be exposed as a killer, she directed her daughter to serve him a stew laced with strychnine. During dinner, she confessed to him that she was responsible for the deaths of several of her suitors and husbands. For reasons unknown, Mrs Bracegirdle's daughter, Miss Dolores Savage, poisoned her mother's meal too.

The bodies of mother and daughter were found in the house. Mr da Costa is now recuperating in a Melbourne hospital.

More bodies found in yard!

Further investigations reveal that the bodies of two men and two babies were buried in the backyard. The identities of the deceased have not been made public. Detectives also searched the house and found a box containing bearer bonds and bundles of money, to the value of £2,300. Their origin is unknown.

Detective Sergeant Michael O'Flanagan issued the following statement:

'I am pleased that the file on the Cornelius Stout murder is now closed. I wish to commend the efforts of Mr Reginald da Costa, of *The Argus*, in attempting to bring this woman to justice.'

The bodies of both mother and daughter have been removed to the Morgue. A post-mortem examination will be held today. It is expected that the coroner will hold a hearing into the case.

[*The Argus* February 1, 1924]

Chapter Forty-Seven

Reggie smiled to himself as he read the article that he had dictated to Kramer from his hospital bed. His part, in solving the Cornelius Stout murder and the disappearance of men who had been victims of Rita Bracegirdle, would cement his name as the foremost crime reporter in Melbourne. He had been promised a pay rise and his own office. His only misgiving was that work might interfere with his pursuit of Miss Lily Stout, who had since spent considerable time at his hospital bedside.

It was enjoyable reliving the look on her pretty face when she had finally been allowed to see him. Her beautiful grey eyes had lit up with delight as she entered the room. 'Thank God you're alive. I've been so worried about you.' The pressure as she took his hand and squeezed it. The feel of her lips grazing his cheek. The long look as she took in his condition. 'You poor man. How you must have suffered.'

She was all concentration as he recounted his experience with Rita, and how he had escaped death through the unexpected intervention of Dolores Savage.

Then there were the endless questions. 'Did she confess?' 'What did she say about Dad?' 'Did she say why she killed him?'

Her conversation was peppered with compliments about his skill in drawing out Rita's confession, and little shrieks of dismay, as she listened to Reggie tell of his close call with death.

Finally, her curiosity assuaged, she put her arms around his neck and whispered in his ear, 'I'm so glad you're alright, Reggie. It means a lot to me.'

Her eyes drifted towards the door. 'I must go. I can't tell you how happy I am that this whole terrible business is over. You put yourself at risk to save my brother. I'll make it up to you.'

That promise resounded in his head. He had to admit that he was head-over-heels in love with Lily Stout. It was only a matter of time till he secured her hand in marriage.

* * *

That afternoon had also brought another visitor: Dotty Wright. He was glad to see her, not only because she had worked closely with him on the case, and thus understood how integral he had been in exposing Rita's criminal activities, but also because she had brought his shaving kit and brushes, pyjamas and dressing-gown, and a change of clothes for when he would be released from hospital. Her thoughtfulness more than made up for her lack of taste in selecting a shirt that didn't coordinate well with the trousers she had chosen, but who was he to be critical? Her visit was, in the end, most welcome.

After inquiring about the state of his health, she had been keen to learn more about Rita. She wanted to know what impression she had left on him.

'Rita was cool and calm. Quite cold-blooded. She claimed that it was the men's fault that she killed them. Imagine that?'

'She confessed to the murder of Cornelius Stout? And the others?'

'She did.'

'Has Detective Sergeant O'Flanagan seen you?'

'He has. Twice. The second time to tie up some loose ends. You know that she killed two babies?'

'How horrible. They probably didn't fit with her way of life. Dolores was useful to her, whereas young children would have got in the way. She seemed to have no conscience.'

'Good riddance.'

'You nearly died, Reggie. Why weren't you more careful?'

'How was I to know that she'd found my press card?'

'The fact that she had tried to poison Mr Sturgess should have alerted you.

Yet you ate the dinner without thinking. You were too confident in the end.' Her face softened and she took his hand. 'I would have been so sorry to lose you. You've become a friend to me.'

'What about Dolores? Imagine her saving my life?'

'Dolores must have hated her mother, making her do her dirty work for her. But she couldn't live without her. It's so tragic to think that she would kill herself in such a terrible way, suffer so much, and then lie down next to Rita to die.'

She rose to go. 'I understand that you had a visit from Miss Stout.' She tapped her ring finger and grinned. 'No more grocer's shop for you.'

'That reminds me,' said Reggie. 'There's something more I have to tell you.'

Dotty sat down again, putting her handbag on the floor. 'Go on.'

'Your grocer. Eric Smith.'

'What about him?'

'Rita cleaned for him. She was the woman you saw a few months ago.'

'I never recognised her from Leggett's.'

'She was dressed to kill there.' He chuckled softly. 'Anyway, according to the woman herself, she answered Eric Smith's advertisement for a housekeeper. Being Rita, she went through his private papers and saw the old photographs and newspaper articles. She became suspicious. Somehow, she uncovered his secret. A secret that was fodder for blackmail. She threatened him with exposure, but he reacted in a way that she didn't expect: he killed himself. He must have realised that nothing was going to satisfy her and that she would bleed him dry. Or that he would be thrown into prison. He chose to end it all.'

Dotty shook her head sadly. 'What an incredible coincidence. Rita and Mr Smith, too. The poor man. She really knew how to manipulate men, didn't she? I don't think the world will miss her.' She picked up her handbag again. 'But I'll miss you as a neighbour. You've certainly brightened up my life since you moved in. Much more exciting.'

As she reached the doorway, she turned back. 'I meant to tell you. They're burying Rita and her daughter on Friday morning. I'm going to the funeral. Call it curiosity.'

'They say I'll be out of here by then,' said Reggie, 'but I don't have the stamina to go. Can you let me know what happens? I'd be curious to hear what's said about her. Take note of who's there, if you don't mind.'

'Of course. I'll drop in on the way back. I'm making up a big pot of stew for you on Friday.' She laughed.

Reggie pulled a face. 'Not stew. Anything but stew!'

Chapter Forty-Eight

Dotty stood on the steps of St Ignatius' Church on Richmond Hill. It was an impressive building, composed of bluestone with white Sydney stone dressings, in the style of French Gothic of the thirteenth century.

The funeral was over, a brief affair which glossed over much of Rita's chequered history. It would be some time before Dotty could get the vision of those two wooden coffins, lying side by side in front of the altar, out of her mind. Rita and her daughter, Dolores, were joined together in death as well as life.

The priest had preferred to dwell on Rita's belief in the Roman Catholic Church. Paradoxically, Rita Bracegirdle had been a staunch Catholic, never missing Mass, and insisting that Dolores attend, too. She had not avoided the Confessional, although what the priest must have thought of her utterances there was not revealed. She was certainly an enigma, a woman of conflicting opinions and actions, who somehow had rationalised her sin away as being a valid response to the ill-treatment of the men in her life. Dotty had come away perplexed.

She had made a mental note of the attendees, as Reggie had requested. There was a smattering of regular parishioners, those who had made Rita's acquaintance or had heard about her exploits in the newspapers. There were the voyeurs, who were curious about a woman who had made a habit of poisoning her husbands. And, there were the newspapermen, who had turned up in the hope that some extra juicy morsel might come up at the funeral which would make good copy in the next day's press.

Dotty had noticed the formidable presence of Detective Sergeant Michael O'Flanagan, sitting in the back pew of the church. At the end of the service, Dotty approached him.

'Sad, wasn't it?' she had asked.

O'Flanagan raised his eyebrows when he saw who was addressing him. He doffed his hat. 'Miss Wright. I'm surprised to see you here today. No doubt you're filling in for Reggie. I guarantee he's asked you to take notes.'

Dotty laughed. 'You know him well. Only a good dose of strychnine would have kept him at home.'

The detective chuckled. 'How right you are. But he put himself in serious danger to prove Mrs Bracegirdle's guilt. I regret that. I confess I had not considered her seriously as a suspect. I was wrong. Despite her faith, she was an evil woman who thought that the world, and men, owed her a living. Who knows how many more might have died if Reggie hadn't stepped in? I will never forgive myself for being so offhand when he suggested that she might be responsible.'

'She's dead, Detective Sergeant. Remember that.'

The policeman lowered his head and rubbed his eyes. 'Not my doing. That's the problem.'

'You've closed the cases now? How many deaths was she responsible for?'

'We've exhumed the bodies of Cornelius Stout, Armitage Flagg, James Hardcastle, Julius Mathieson, and Clyde Bracegirdle. Traces of poison were found in all of them, except Stout. It appears that she must have lashed out at him, striking the fatal blow. Edmund Stout is missing, presumed dead, but Reggie informs me that Rita Bracegirdle disposed of his body in the river. We still haven't identified the second adult male in the backyard of her house. Perhaps we never will.

'I'm combing through missing persons files to see if there are any others who fit the profile. I have to hand it to Mrs Bracegirdle: she was a manipulative schemer. She met her victims at Leggett's or through the classified advertisements, then turned on the charm till they succumbed. Her intentions were deadly.'

'At least your desk is cleared of a few cases. Her poor husbands.'

'That reminds me. Did you see him, Miss Wright? Sylvester Sturgess, her ex-husband?'

'He was here?'

'Not for long. I spoke to him briefly. He told me that he paid for Dolores and Rita's funerals. Despite everything that happened between them, he felt that he owed her and her daughter a decent send-off.'

'That I don't understand. She tried to poison him.'

'I don't understand it either. In over thirty years of policing, I still find it hard to understand human behaviour. People are strange. Anyway, I must get back to work. Crime stops for no man.' O'Flanagan grimaced. 'At least not while Squizzy Taylor continues to evade the Law. That little hoodlum will meet a bad end, either through my intervention or through the efforts of his enemies.'

Dotty fixed the detective with a shrewd look. 'Don't be too hard on yourself about Rita, Mr O'Flanagan. You're an honest policeman and you did your best.'

The detective tipped his hat to her. 'Thank you, miss. I wish I could believe that. Tell Reggie that I'll look forward to seeing him well and back at work.'

She watched him as he walked away. His shoulders were stooped. He looked like he was carrying the weight of the world on his shoulders.

Mingling with the onlookers outside the church after the service, Dotty was on the verge of leaving when she overheard one parishioner comment that it was unfortunate that Rita's fiancé had died just before their planned wedding. It seemed to contradict what she had read in Reggie's recent article, and it needed to be checked. Had Stout and Rita broken up, or hadn't they? Rita's motive for murder was dependent on the answer.

Chapter Forty-Nine

R eggie settled back into life in the dwelling above the shop. He organised for the housekeeper to come more frequently and to prepare most of his meals. Sunday lunches were spent at Dotty's, with her consenting to him bringing a bottle of wine, as long as he didn't overindulge. She was a good cook, and he had to admit that he enjoyed their conversations.

After another week off work, he returned to *The Argus* and wrote up the final stages of the Rita Bracegirdle case for his devoted readers. The fact that an older woman had made a habit of poisoning rich, vulnerable men, and got away with it, attracted much attention. His role in her exposure enhanced his reputation as an investigator, and his near-death experience aroused the public's interest.

Now, cleared of any permanent effects from strychnine poisoning, Reggie felt that he could move on with his life. However, there were moments when even he had to question the wisdom of his decision to apprehend Rita Bracegirdle, single-handed. He could have died. But those thoughts were never voiced out loud, even though Dotty challenged him on it.

The weeks passed. His relationship with his mother resumed, with him meeting her on a regular basis, when he could be certain that his father was absent. Squizzy Taylor still provided him with enough material to fill his crime reports, and there were the usual robberies and murders to occupy his time, but one subject remained unresolved: his relationship with Lily Stout. Her inheritance had come through, the sale of her father's mansion completed, and her brother and she had moved into an elegant house in

East Melbourne. Despite his best efforts, Reggie was unable to persuade her to commit to an engagement, even though she seemed attracted to him. She explained her reluctance by saying that she needed to come to terms with the resolution of both her father's and uncle's deaths. The whole experience had taken a toll on her, she said, and she had been affected badly by the fact that her twin brother had been a suspect.

'We are so close, Reggie. Henry is finding it difficult to return to a normal life and I must be there for him. Be patient. I will always be grateful to you; don't you forget that. You have everything a girl could want. Why wouldn't anyone want to marry you?'

Patience was not one of Reggie's strengths, but he had no choice but to take a step back and give her time to come to her senses. It was an unfortunate fact that her wealth gave her the upper hand in their relationship. In fact, he felt quite touchy on the subject when Dotty raised it with him over Sunday lunch.

'If she loves you, why aren't you engaged?'

Reggie had been forced to defend her, even though he couldn't hide his wounded feelings. The truth was that Dotty was asking the same question that he asked himself. The conversation came to a dead stop.

'I'm sorry,' she said, noting the change in his demeanour. 'I didn't mean to hurt your feelings.'

They moved on to other topics, but the damage was done. Reggie took his leave from her as soon as was polite, but the whole subject left a bitter taste in his mouth.

Chapter Fifty

One evening, in early March, Reggie had an unwelcome visitor. On the threshold stood Mario da Costa. His thick, greying hair was slicked back and his three-piece suit, in brown houndstooth, featured the latest wide-cut trousers. He was, as usual, impeccably groomed.

'Not you,' Reggie said. 'I don't want to speak to you.' He went to shut the door, but his father's foot was wedged firmly in the gap.

'I'm leaving your mother.'

Reggie released the door and stared at his father. 'What?'

'You were right about me. I'm not sick. In fact, I'm in excellent health.' He stroked his moustache and smiled. 'Can I come in? I promise that I'll never bother you again.'

Reluctantly, Reggie stood aside and watched as his father ascended the staircase to the sitting room above the shop. He followed, and leaned against the bookcase as his father sat down.

'A bit shabby, but no doubt you'll change that,' said Mario, glancing around. 'Not quite up to my standards.'

'You can leave if that's all you have to say.'

'Sit down, my boy. I have something to tell you.' He waited, but Reggie showed no desire to do as he was told. 'As you wish. The fact is that I have told your mother I'm going. I haven't told her why, because it might hurt her, and I don't want to do that.'

'That would be a first for you.'

Mario raised his hand. 'It's true, I have hurt her, hurt her badly. And you. I've never been a good husband, or father. It's fair to say that I don't take

215

well to responsibility. That's what I am. There are names for people like me. Cad. Bounder. *Bon vivant.* I came back because I was short of money, and Mavis has never been able to refuse me. However, things are looking up. I'm heading off. The truth is that a nice quiet middle-class life doesn't suit me. A home in the suburbs. Meals on the table seven nights a week. Luncheons with the Bardsley Smiths, the Wellington Browns. Associating with people who have no idea what fun is. Frankly, Reggie, I can't stand it anymore.'

'You came here to tell me that? Do you think I care?'

'Go and see your mother. She will need you. Move back in, if you wish. I've packed my bags and I'm off tonight.'

Reggie couldn't help himself. 'Where are you going?'

'Back to Italy. The Italians know how to eat and drink. And love. I miss that. I feel so restricted, so confined by this life your mother has chosen to live. Everyone is so polite. So good-mannered. So *bourgeois.* No one enjoys themselves. It's so boring. In the time I have left, I want to embrace life again.'

'How will you live?'

'I met a nice woman. With lots of money. She finds me amusing. And I will be for her.'

Reggie scowled. 'So that's it? Is that what you came to tell me? That, after using Mother up, you're moving on?'

'Partly. But there's something I have to say to you that can't be said in a letter. I need to say it face to face.'

'What?'

'It's about Miss Stout.'

'What can you possibly have to say to me about Lily?'

'I met her when we were in the hospital waiting-room. The doctor said that you weren't having visitors so I asked her to have a drink with me. We had a good chat.' Mario's expression was uncharacteristically serious. 'I'll say this to you bluntly. She's not what you think.'

Reggie clenched his fists. 'She'll be my fiancée soon. How dare you talk about her like that!'

'I'd expect you to feel that way. But ask yourself. Why would she be interested in you? Certainly, you have looks and charm, but you can offer her nothing more.'

'How is that different to your situation?'

'My lady and I are honest about our relationship. Marriage isn't discussed. I know we won't last, and so does she. And there's the difference. Miss Stout is rich. She's beautiful. She could have anyone she wants, but she chose you. Or so you think. Ask yourself why?'

'Because we're similar, that's why.'

'Don't take offence, son. I'm not saying this to hurt you. I understand that I owe you something for the years of damage I did to your mother and you. That's why I'm here. To warn you.'

He continued. 'I can recognise a con man or a hustler when I see him, or her. It's like looking at yourself in a mirror. She's not genuine. She'll never marry you. Admit it, she's putting off getting engaged, isn't she?'

Reggie's mouth went dry. 'She's upset about her father's murder. She's worried about her brother.'

Mario rose to go. 'Ask yourself what she really wanted from you.'

He picked up his hat and stood, looking back at Reggie. 'I speak to you as your father. I'm someone who can recognise a kindred soul, someone like Lily. Be careful. She'll hurt you. I repeat: she's not what you think. This is my parting gift to you.'

He raised his hat in farewell and walked down the stairs, out of Reggie's life.

Chapter Fifty-One

Doubt started to gnaw at Reggie, as the days went past without any word from Lily Stout. Finally, he visited her new home in an attempt to invite her out for dinner. But, according to Henry, Lily was not there. She had gone with friends to their beach house in Portsea, and would not be returning for a few days.

Reggie kept turning Mario's words over and over in his head. What had he meant when he implied that Lily had her reasons for pretending to be attracted to him? No woman could be so calculating, he thought, when there appeared to be no reason for artifice. He was attractive. Handsome, in fact. He was charming. He was well-known in his profession. He brought all that to the relationship while she provided the money. There was no doubt that he would be an asset to her now that she could claim her rightful place in society. Still, he found it unsettling that she should be away with friends, not with him.

Unexpectedly, it was his mother who offered him a distraction from his preoccupation with Lily's social life. Arabella Axworthy, the daughter of one of Mavis's friends, had announced her engagement to Hamilton Hatcher of 'Seven Hills,' Wagga Wagga. A soirée was to be held in Elsternwick, at 'Rippon Lea,' a splendid Victorian mansion in the Romanesque style, which had immaculate and extensive pleasure gardens. All the best people would be there, his mother said. It was a social *tour de force*, that she had engineered an invitation for them both. Black tie. Hors d'oeuvres. A string quartet. Very classy. Very select.

The days dragged as the event grew closer. But, at last, it was Saturday.

His dinner jacket cleaned and pressed, his hair and moustache trimmed, his automobile polished and gleaming, Reggie collected his mother from her Richmond home.

The street lights seemed to twinkle, as he parked his car outside the Elsternwick mansion and escorted his mother, past the gatehouse, to the front entrance of the house.

Reggie straightened his white bowtie and checked his silver fob watch. Half-past eight. He had heard that it was the 'done' thing to be fashionably late. But when he entered the ballroom, after the maid had relieved him of his hat and coat, he discovered that he had miscalculated. The room was already overflowing with expensively dressed and immaculately groomed men and women. Champagne glasses in hand, scoffing hors d'oeuvres from silver platters borne by waiters dressed in white jackets, red cummerbunds and black trousers, the guests were laughing and chatting with each other, comfortable in the knowledge that they were amongst their peers. Immediately, his mother made a beeline for her Brighton friends, leaving Reggie all alone, as the cream of Melbourne society mingled around him, their faces recognisable from the social pages of the daily newspapers.

To his left were the Fitzhuberts, owners of several expensive Brighton properties. To his right was Mrs McQueen, doyenne of Melbourne society. By the grand piano was the Chief Commissioner of Police, Mr Nicholson. Over near the fireplace was Sir John Flinders Smyth, property developer and speculator, chatting to Major-General Edward Black, visiting from London.

Reggie took a glass of champagne from a waiter and sipped slowly, looking left and right for a familiar face. Joining his mother would be an admission of social failure, so he stood on, watching and smiling, as if he were enjoying the proceedings.

The crowd parted momentarily and Reggie experienced a rush of delight, mixed with relief. On the other side of the room, he spied none other than Lily Stout. She was holding forth to a small select circle of admirers, who were laughing in response to some joke she had just made. She looked dazzling. Her silk dress was deep purple, the bodice embroidered with tiny silver stars. She wore a finely wrought tiara on her shiny black bob. Next to her was her brother, small and wiry, watching his sister with a mixture of adoration and deference.

Reggie started to push his way past a group of youthful revellers, when Lily turned his way. He stopped, smiled, and raised a hand in recognition. Her eyes rested on him for a moment. He waited for her face to light up at the sight of him, for a sign that he should join her and her friends. But, to his surprise and horror, Lily lowered her eyes and turned away, giving her full attention to some young buck with large teeth and a braying laugh. It was mortifying.

Just when he thought it couldn't get any worse, Mavis and a few of her old school chums accosted him. 'Reggie, dear, tell my friends about your dinner with Rita Bracegirdle. They're dying to know.'

He rallied, but his heart wasn't in it. Rather than savouring being the centre of attention, enjoying every wide-eyed look of shock, every *ooh* and *aah*, he felt only emptiness as he recounted his brush with death. And then there were the questions, which seemed inane and insensitive.

'She fed you strychnine? What did it taste like?'

'She went into convulsions? Did she froth at the mouth? I had a polo pony that did that.'

'I heard that she killed seven husbands. A female Bluebeard.'

'They found her naked. Is that true?'

At last, he made his escape and went out into the garden. All he wanted was some peace and quiet, and a chance to collect his thoughts. But who should be out there, having a cigarette, but Henry Stout and a couple of his mates? Reggie turned to go, but Henry had seen him.

'Reggie. Nice to see you. Must say that I didn't expect to see you here. Thought you were more into chasing down the criminal classes rather than mixing with members of the upper crust. Lily and I are off to Portsea tomorrow. Lots of champagne and so on. You know how it is.'

And there it was: his humiliation at the hands of the Stout twins was complete. It seemed that his father had been right after all. His dreams, of a future with Lily Stout, evaporated into the chill night air.

Chapter Fifty-Two

The subject came up unexpectedly at Sunday lunch with Dotty, a week after the party.

'You seem rather subdued, Reggie,' she had commented. 'Is it the aftermath of this whole Rita Bracegirdle business? Now that it's over, you feel a bit lost?'

'I wish it were. That might make sense.' He paused, at first unwilling to admit his true feelings in case Dotty might laugh at him. But one look at her face, full of concern for him, convinced him that she could be trusted. 'It appears that I was wrong about Lily. She snubbed me at that soirée. I was ready to buy an engagement ring, you know.'

'Do you love her?'

'I thought I did. Now I'm not sure. I really thought she liked me, that she might even love me. I think I was mistaken.'

'From what you told me, I thought she was very interested in you.'

'My father suspected that she didn't really care for me.'

Dotty put down her knife and fork. 'Your father came to see you?'

'Before he left.'

'Really? Tell me about it.'

Reggie described Mario's visit to his house, and his parting words: 'She's not what you think.'

'What on earth did he mean by that?' Dotty asked.

'I've been trying to work that out. He told me to be careful. But coming from him, I was ready to ignore it.'

'If what your father said is true, what could Lily have wanted from you?'

'The obvious thing was for me to investigate her father's murder.'

'But she didn't need to put on an act to get you to do that. You're a crime reporter. That's your business. Imagine if a relative were murdered and you couldn't get the police to track down the killer. You'd be desperate to get someone on your side.'

'She was very insistent that I hand over the information to the police. In fact, she was irritated when I told her it was too soon.'

'That's understandable. She wanted someone to be found guilty of her father's murder. I'd be impatient too.'

Reggie scratched his head. 'I suppose you're right. But I thought she was attracted to me. Separate from the investigation. To put it bluntly, once I proved Rita killed Stout, Lily lost interest in me.'

'Why would that be so?'

'I don't understand it. My father seemed to be suggesting that Lily had an ulterior motive for befriending me in the first place.'

'I'm so sorry,' said Dotty, touching his arm. 'I know you liked her very much.'

Reggie pushed his plate away. 'If I'm honest, I'm hurt at the thought that she was never attracted to me at all.'

'That couldn't be true,' Dotty assured him. 'You're very attractive.'

'You're not … interested in me, are you?'

Dotty laughed. 'You should know that by now. You're not my type.'

He sniggered. 'That's good. It would make life complicated if I were. You won't repeat what I just said, about being hurt?'

'Of course not. Friends don't reveal confidences. You can trust me.' She looked at him thoughtfully. 'Can I ask? Did Rita actually admit that she murdered Cornelius Stout?'

'In a manner of speaking.'

'What does that mean?'

'She said that his death was sad.'

'Sad? That's a funny way to put it. Not what your normal murderer would say. When I was at her funeral, I felt like the priest was talking about someone else. Not the Rita I know of. She was certainly a strange one. Very religious, yet prepared to kill to get what she wanted. I forgot to tell you that I overheard one of the parishioners at the funeral talking. She mentioned that Rita was planning to marry. Was she talking about Cornelius Stout? I've been wondering ever since why Rita would kill him, if that were true.'

Reggie looked up sharply. 'But Stout called it off!'

Dotty took up the plates and carried them out to the kitchen. Reggie poured himself another wine and filled up Dotty's glass of apple cider.

She sat down again. 'Why don't you tell me exactly what Rita said about Cornelius Stout? Try to remember her actual words.'

'That's not easy. I was getting sick by then.'

'Do your best.'

He paused, trying to recall their conversation. 'Rita said that she killed Edmund Stout. That she threw his body into the Yarra.' His eyebrows knitted as he concentrated hard. 'She never actually said that she killed Cornelius. She never mentioned that they broke up. I said something like "He was killed" and she agreed with me. That's odd, isn't it? She said that he was different to Edmund. Generous. He appreciated her, she said.'

'So why kill him? What else did she say?'

'I asked her about the signet ring that Cornelius was wearing when he died.'

'The one with "Rita" engraved on it?'

'That's right. Now that was odd.' He smoothed his moustache. 'She didn't seem to know anything about it. She said that men gave *her* presents.'

'She doesn't admit to killing Cornelius even though she confessed to the other murders. Why would that be?'

Reggie thought carefully. 'I don't know. Maybe it was a mistake. Maybe she didn't mean to kill him.'

'Detective O'Flanagan said that she lashed out at Mr Stout. Maybe she was angry with him. Perhaps it was an accident, not murder.'

'That's still possible.'

Dotty leaned forward and laid her hand on Reggie's arm. 'Or maybe *she* didn't kill him.'

Chapter Fifty-Three

Mavis da Costa was celebrating her birthday. Reggie, aware that his father's departure would impact her happiness, contacted Mildred Bardsley Smith and asked, given the circumstances, if she could make a fuss of his mother to keep her spirits up. Dotty's aunt had instantly agreed and organised a light luncheon. All of Mildred's social set would be there, she assured him, and they would shower her with gifts and good wishes.

He had taken his mother to the dressmaker, and had her fitted for a new dress. It was in the Parisian style, made of fine wool in a midnight blue, with a dropped waist, long sleeves, and a collar of broderie anglaise. Around her neck was a string of pearls, Reggie's gift to her.

'You look wonderful, Mother,' he said.

Her eyes shone as she looked at her reflection in the mirror.

'Thank you, Reggie. I do look nice, don't I? You are such a good son.'

'How are you, really?'

A shadow passed across her face. 'If I'm honest, I saw it coming. I knew he was getting bored. I knew then that he wasn't ill.'

'What will you do if he comes back?'

'Take him in, of course. He's still my husband.' She sighed. 'Let's forget about it just for today.'

He gave her a hug, then stood back to look at her. 'You're a strong woman. I admire you. Now, let's go.'

The drive had been a pleasant one; Mavis in a state of excited anticipation about the social event to be held in her honour.

'The pearls are lovely. I've always enjoyed my birthdays because I have such a generous son.' She beamed across at him as he drove the car down Point Nepean Road towards Brighton.

He was feeling oddly sentimental. 'Remember when I took you to see *Cousin Kate* for your birthday? Marie Tempest and Graham Browne were wonderful.'

Mavis shook her head. 'Don't be ridiculous, Reggie. That was in July. Really, your memory is slipping.'

'Are you sure?'

'Of course, I am. You took me to that lovely little restaurant near the Exhibition Buildings for my birthday. I had the fish, don't you remember?'

Reggie frowned. 'That's right. I don't know where I got that idea from.'

He headed down New Street, past Brighton Grammar School, and turned right into Grosvenor Street. The impressive iron gates of 'Glenrothes' were open. Reggie drove up the circular driveway and parked the Citroen near the stables. He escorted his mother to the door and, after thanking Mildred for her kindness, left Mavis to enjoy her birthday celebration, as a bevy of Brighton matrons clustered around her. Satisfied and content that his mother would have a marvellous time, Reggie headed home to Richmond. There was something that he needed to check.

The box containing Cornelius Stout's private papers was out in the shed. Reggie carried it upstairs, depositing the contents on the floor. He poured himself a whisky and set about going through them, searching for the pile of letters bound with a blue ribbon.

The letters from Lily Stout were towards the bottom. He turned his attention to the first one.

May 16, 1921

Dear Dad,

Seeing Cousin Kate with you was wonderful. Thank you for inviting me. It was such an enjoyable production. However, I do wish that Henry had been there with us. It would have meant so much to him.

It is nearly six months since you last spoke to him. I know that you are bitter about what he said to you, but he was being loyal to a friend. I ask you to reconsider your attitude to him. He loves you and I know that you love him. He is your son. Can't you find it in your heart to restore our family to what it used to be? We were close once and can be again.

Please make our family whole again. Don't cut Henry off in this way.
Your devoted daughter,
Lily.

He re-read it then turned his attention to the second one.

May 22, 1921

Dear Dad,

I am so unhappy that you and Henry have not repaired your relationship. Both of you are strong-willed and have chosen different paths in life. Henry loves his job with the Railways, just as you love being in finance. Can't you see past your differences of opinion and make up? I love you both and regret that our family has come to this, particularly after Mother died so tragically.

I think that Rita played a part in alienating you from Henry. I think she was jealous of us. Now that you and Rita are no longer together, perhaps the three of us could rediscover the bond that once existed between us. I would love to see Henry become part of the family again, and that you restore his inheritance.

Give it some thought, please. It's very important to me.
Your devoted daughter,
Lily.

Reggie put the letters aside and poured himself another whisky, trying to come to terms with the implications of what he had just read.

'Bloody hell.'

He looked at the mantel clock. If he left immediately, he could get into the city and then out to Brighton in time to pick up his mother at four o'clock. He drained the rest of his glass, put the letters in his pocket, and rushed out the door.

The offices of *The Argus* were always open—the news didn't adhere to a five-day-a-week timetable—and Reggie was soon entrenched in the newspaper archive.

'I don't believe it.' Reggie stared at the newspaper. 'Surely not?'

* * *

The drive home from Brighton was different, to say the least. Reggie listened with half an ear to his mother's chatter, as he turned over what he had just learned. It couldn't be, he thought. But what other explanation was there?

'Reggie, are you listening to me? Mildred gave me not one, but two, bottles of scent. And Myrtle gave me a lovely silk scarf that she bought in the Block Arcade.'

'That's wonderful, Mother,' he murmured.

He let her talk on, while he nodded and made the occasional remark to keep her happy. But when he finally dropped her off at home, there was only one person that he wanted to see, and on whose opinion, he had come to rely.

The light was on in the front room of Dotty Wright's small weatherboard house. He parked the car in the back laneway, then went around and knocked on the door.

* * *

'Explain it to me again.' Dotty leaned forward, her face a picture of concentration.

'*Cousin Kate* wasn't on in May. It was playing in mid-July.'

'So that means—'

'That the letter wasn't written in May 1921.'

'I'm still not following you.'

'Lily wrote a letter, dated May 16, 1921. In it, she says that she and Cornelius went to see the stage production of *Cousin Kate*. But I've checked the archives of *The Argus* and it didn't begin in Melbourne until July. I took my mother to see it then.'

'*Cousin Kate* wasn't on when the letter was written,' said Dotty, nodding her head slowly. 'That means that she wrote it *after* her father went missing.'

'That's right,' said Reggie.

Dotty frowned. 'The letter is a fake. Lily planted it after her father's death. But why would she do that?'

'If the first letter is a fake, then the second must be too. Lily says that Cornelius and Rita had broken up. What if they hadn't? What if they were going to get married?'

'Then Henry and Lily wouldn't inherit their father's estate.'

'Exactly. What if Cornelius was going to change his will so that his new wife would inherit everything? What if Henry and Lily found out? If that isn't motivation for murder, then I don't know what is.'

Dotty sat quietly, absorbing what Reggie had just said. 'The letter has another purpose. It gives Rita a motive for killing Cornelius. If Cornelius supposedly terminated his relationship with Rita, it would make her angry. She would want revenge.'

Reggie frowned. 'Those letters were designed to put me off the scent. You need to ask the question: who would benefit from Cornelius's death? Henry and Lily, that's who. The irony is that they didn't know that Rita really was a killer. How convenient for them. By chance, they chose the right person to pin Cornelius's murder on. They also could never have predicted that Dolores would poison her mother. Fortunately for them, Rita will never have to defend herself in court. She will never testify that she was innocent or that she and Cornelius were planning on getting married.'

'But this is all conjecture.'

'But think about it, Dotty. What if Rita was really planning to marry Stout? She told me that Cornelius's death was *sad*. She never said that she killed him and she didn't seem to know about the signet ring.'

CHAPTER FIFTY-THREE

'So, Rita didn't do it?'

'Unfortunately, the only suspects appear to be Henry and Lily. They killed their father to keep his money.'

'But they didn't know about the Punt Road terrace where their father was found.'

'But they did. Lily admitted that Henry had followed Rita home. Frank Feely recognised him from a photograph. He said he saw Henry out on the street, watching the house.'

'That changes things. Is Lily capable of murder? You don't think she'd kill him with her own bare hands, surely?' Dotty was horrified at the thought.

'Maybe not. But she has a twin brother who's in awe of her. I watched him at the soirée. He idolises her. That woman is a manipulative little minx.'

'But how would Lily know you'd read the letters?'

'Henry directed me to the box. He told me to take it home and go through it. And, I remember O'Flanagan saying he must have missed the letters when I mentioned them. They probably weren't there when he looked. They were planted in time for me to find them.'

'But what if you hadn't read them?'

'If I missed the fake evidence pointing to Rita's involvement, I'll bet that Lily or Henry would have found some way to draw my attention to them. They knew that I would never have thrown the letters out, because they could be used as evidence in a court case.'

'This is unbelievable. How will you prove it? The letters aren't enough on their own. You'll need evidence.'

Reggie nodded his head. 'You're right. As far as O'Flanagan is concerned, the case is closed. He'd think I was crazy if I went to him right now. Perhaps I should confront Lily and Henry.'

Dotty shook her head. 'Very unwise, Reggie. They'll cover their tracks if they know you suspect them. Anyway, I'm not totally convinced. It's circumstantial and hearsay, if they're the right expressions. A couple of letters and the words of a dead woman, who has been proven to be a liar and a killer. No one will believe you.'

'I'll think about it. It's hard to say who's telling the truth here. Rita made a habit of misleading men for her own gain. I feel that Lily has a lot in common with her. Can I count on you to help me find out the truth?'

'Of course. Like I said before, life's much more exciting with you around. By the way, I meant to tell you that Eric Smith's estate has been settled. The title to the shop is being transferred to me next week.'

'What are you going to do with it?'

'I've already had an enquiry from a shopkeeper who wants to lease it. But he doesn't want to live in the dwelling. I was wondering if you were going to move home, now that your father has gone.'

'If you don't mind, I'd like to stay on. This independent living is rather nice. I please myself when I come and go, and don't have to report to Mother.'

Dotty looked pleased. 'The only thing is that I'd need to charge rent. It would give me an income apart from my teaching.'

'Of course. I'll make a few changes; bring the place up to my standards. It's convenient to my work and to Mother.'

Dotty smiled. 'We'll work out a figure that's agreeable to both of us. Let's make it a gentleman's agreement, Reggie.' She reached out and shook his hand.

'You're definitely not a gentleman, Dotty.'

'And you are?'

Reggie chuckled. 'Not always.'

Chapter Fifty-Four

Later that week, Reggie charmed his way past Floyd Kramer's secretary and entered the inner sanctum of *The Argus*'s sub-editor. He had armed himself with a raft of arguments to convince Kramer that his investigation into the Cornelius Stout murder should be re-opened. But his pleas fell on deaf ears.

Floyd Kramer fixed Reggie with a withering look. 'Bloody hell, Reggie, I've promoted you. What more do you want? Rita Bracegirdle was the killer of six or seven husbands. I've lost count! And you want to quibble about one victim? Drop it. Do you hear me?'

'Boss, I'm sure that Lily Stout is behind the murder of her father. Give me a chance to follow it up.'

'The strychnine's affected your brain. Take a holiday. Go to the seaside and let the breeze blow away those silly ideas of yours.'

'You think about it. Rita Bracegirdle always used poison. She never whacked a victim on the back of the head.'

'Maybe Stout wouldn't die?'

'But there were no traces of strychnine in his body.'

'I don't care, Reggie. Leave it alone. You've solved seven crimes! What more do you want?'

'Justice. I want justice.'

'What rubbish. What's got into you? You're a reporter, not a lawyer. I won't argue with you anymore. Your priority is Angus Murray. He's being hanged next Monday at the Melbourne Jail.' Kramer pushed his glasses up onto the bridge of his nose and glared at Reggie. 'Now, get out there and file a report.

'And Reggie,' he added, tapping the desk with his pencil, 'if I hear anything more about Lily Stout or her brother, you'll be out the door. They have friends in high places and I don't want them upset. Understand?'

'Bastard,' Reggie snarled under his breath. 'I'll show you.'

* * *

But it wasn't that easy. The execution of Angus Murray now occupied Reggie's full attention, whether he liked it or not. The bank robber had been sentenced to death for the murder of Thomas Berriman. Despite 70,000 people signing a petition asking for a reprieve, the Executive Council had recommended that the hanging should proceed.

On the Sunday following Reggie's meeting with Kramer, demonstrations against Murray's execution were held outside the Melbourne Town Hall and Exhibition Buildings. Moving between the two, Reggie recorded the gist of the speeches and the arguments put forward to oppose capital punishment. He knew from the witnesses' reports, before and at the trial, that Murray may not have pulled the trigger. He was more likely an accomplice to the gunman, who had disappeared without a trace. Despite those arguments, the jury had not been swayed and, after deliberating for two hours, had found him guilty. Here was a man who might be innocent of murder, thought Reggie, yet he was facing death at the end of a rope.

The vagaries of the Law struck him. Class and privilege made all the difference when you were in the dock. Murray, a man from a disadvantaged background, whose father, uncle, and aunt had all committed suicide, had been condemned to die, while Lily Stout, spoilt society favourite, would avoid the hangman's noose by virtue of her wealth, connections, and beauty. Reggie's socialist leanings, gone silent in the last few years, were showing signs of resurrection.

By Monday morning, a crowd of several thousand people had gathered outside the Melbourne Jail, on the corner of Russell and Victoria Streets. Reggie and his photographer, Sid, joined them, recording the scene. Working-class women were in the majority. They had walked down from their cottages in the inner suburbs of Melbourne to join the protest. By nine o'clock the crowd was singing 'Nearer my God to Thee,' after which some sank to their knees, praying and sobbing. The mood was becoming dangerous, and the police were hard-pressed to keep the protesters away from the jail's main gate.

Reggie checked his suit. It was perfect for the occasion: a subdued grey check with cream shirt and purple tie. Not exactly funereal, but respectfully low-key. A man was being hanged, after all.

Leaving Sid behind to document the demonstration in photographs, Reggie entered the large bluestone archway that formed the entrance to the jail. He passed through the inner courtyard of the administration block and waited, as his credentials were checked. The gate swung open to the main cell block, where the other witnesses were waiting between the two stone staircases, which led to the upper cells. He looked up and there was the scaffold, its oregon beam supported by metal brackets. It was a sobering sight. The sheriff stood to one side while the hangman checked the apparatus. The time was nearing for the condemned man to emerge from his first-floor cell and take his place on the scaffold.

Reggie gazed at the thick, bluestone walls and felt the hard, cold slate beneath his feet. An involuntary shiver passed through him. Grim and forbidding, the Melbourne Jail was an institution that cast a shadow over those who lived within it. Thin rays of light filtered in through the skylights of the central nave, but nothing relieved the gloom.

This was Reggie's second hanging, so at least he knew what to expect. He looked around him, making a mental note of those who had come to witness the execution. There were members of the press and the governor of the prison, Mr J.M. Burke, himself.

It was almost ten o'clock. The door to the condemned cell opened. Angus Murray stepped out onto the scaffold, followed by an Anglican chaplain. With his hands and ankles in shackles, and a cloth cap draped on the back of his head, Murray addressed the witnesses who were standing below.

Reggie took out his notebook and pen. He jotted down a brief description of Murray's demeanour, which he later described to be neither anxious nor angry. The condemned man stated calmly that he didn't deserve the sentence of death, but still asked for forgiveness from those he had injured. Turning to the hangman, he said simply, 'Pull it tight.'

The hangman pulled the mask down over Murray's face. He placed the noose around his neck. A hush fell over the assembled witnesses. Later, Reggie realised that he'd been holding his breath. The hangman pulled the lever to release the trapdoor. Angus Murray fell through the gap, his body jolting as the rope stopped his descent. An audible gasp went up from the assembled witnesses, and then there was silence. Angus Murray's neck had broken, his death mercifully instantaneous.

Reggie turned to the man standing next to him. 'It was a good death,' he whispered. The man nodded; his face as white as a sheet. Casting one last look at the hanging man, Reggie shook his head and made his way out into the courtyard. He felt wrung out, but there was still a report to write up.

The crowd was back in full voice, but it was not to last. A proposal to march on Parliament House demanding the resignation of the Government was put forward, but it seemed like the protest was running out of steam, now that Angus Murray was dead. As Reggie and Sid watched on, the crowd slowly dispersed and returned to their homes.

'Thank God that's over,' said Sid. 'Hard to believe that someone could be hanged as an accomplice to murder. It must be the first time.'

'You're right,' agreed Reggie. 'There are some out there who get away with murder and are living the high life.'

Sid looked at Reggie, quizzically. 'Squizzy Taylor?'

'Him, too.' He frowned. He couldn't leave it alone, he thought, no matter what Kramer said. He'd build a case against Lily and Henry Stout, even if it meant his job.

Chapter Fifty-Five

T he Easter holidays were over. Dotty Wright sat in her armchair, knitting a cardigan for herself. April was giving way to May, and the nights were getting colder. She looked around her, feeling contented now that the business with Eric Smith had been resolved, and that her inheritance was no longer in question. She could accept what chance had given her with a clear conscience, although she wished that she could have helped Eric in his time of need. But that was the past, and there was nothing she could do about it.

She put her knitting aside and stared out the window into the dark street. If she didn't know any better, she would have thought that all Melburnians spent their nights in quiet contemplation or gentle conversation. But Reggie had introduced her to an underside of life: one that was based on greed, revenge, and murder. It might be improper for the senior mistress of a school to admit it, but she found the subject both intriguing and stimulating.

Thoughts of Reggie and his preoccupation with the Cornelius Stout case roused her from her chair. She sat down at her desk, one of the little treats she had bought for herself, now that the future looked more financially secure. It was a lovely piece of furniture, in walnut, with a set of drawers down one side. In one of the compartments were some of her students' work, which she had finished checking the previous night, whilst in another was stationery. She took out a fresh sheet of paper, put a new nib in her pen, dipped it into a bottle of black Indian ink, and began to write.

If Reggie were to successfully mount a case against the Stout twins, he needed to document the evidence against them and pursue possible lines of enquiry. Dotty smiled to herself; she was starting to sound more like a crime reporter every day.

She underlined her first heading: 'Case against Lily and Henry' and began to write:

- Motive for murder? Greed? Henry and Lily inherit the estate. If Rita and Cornelius marry, Henry and Lily lose inheritance.
- Lily and Henry knew about the basement. Henry followed Rita home.
- The letters: Henry suggested that Reggie take the boxes, containing the letters, from Stout's house. Detective Sergeant O'Flanagan doesn't remember the letters, so they were planted <u>after</u> the police investigation.
- Date is wrong for *Cousin Kate* production, so letters must have been written <u>after</u> Cornelius's death.
- Were Rita and Cornelius still in a relationship when he died? We only have Lily's letters to suggest that they had parted. Why would Rita kill Stout if they were to marry? No financial incentive for murder.
- Parishioner at Rita's funeral mentioned upcoming nuptials. (Interview priest.)
- Signet ring: If Rita didn't know about the ring, who gave it to him? Who bought it? From which jeweller? Was the engraving ('Rita') a red herring to point police in her direction? The attempt to saw the ring off Stout's finger points to Rita's involvement. A distraction from the real killers (Lily and Henry)?

She sat back. This was going well, and she was merely an apprentice in the investigation game. Would Reggie appreciate her efforts, or would he sneer at her amateur attempts to construct a case? What did it matter, she thought? It was an enjoyable distraction from her day-to-day tasks of planning lessons and correcting spelling. She chided herself; what a terrible thing to say. She loved teaching the children and helping them find the way to being better people, but sometimes—

Dotty got up and made herself a cup of tea. Then she turned her attention back to the task at hand. Her next heading was: 'Case against

Rita Bracegirdle.' She had to be fair, after all, and present an unbiased view of the Stout murder.

- Rita lived in the terrace house where Stout was found.
- She was Cornelius's housekeeper and became his lady friend.
- If their relationship had ended, as suggested in Lily's letters, then her motive for murder would be revenge.
- Rita murdered Bracegirdle, Flagg, Edmund Stout, Hardcastle, Mathieson, and an unidentified man. Attempted to kill Sylvester Sturgess and Reggie. Obviously capable of murdering Stout.
- The signet ring incriminated her. Did she try to saw it off Cornelius's finger to remove evidence against her?
- Daughter was accomplice to murder.
- Killed her own babies? Shows that she was cold-blooded.

Dotty folded up the sheet of paper and put it in one of the small compartments of her writing desk. Then, after she'd washed up her cup and saucer, she prepared for bed. As she stared at her reflection in the mirror, she thought about the way she had spent the last hour. God forbid that any of her colleagues, or indeed the headmaster, should discover that she was living a clandestine life!

Chapter Fifty-Six

Reggie put aside the book he had just finished reading: 'Dramatic Days at the Old Bailey.' Not all criminals profited from their crimes, the author argued, because some languished in prison, or committed suicide, or died in poverty. How right he was, Reggie agreed, when he compared the treatment dished out to Angus Murray with the fate of the Stout twins, who appeared to have got away with murder.

He stood and re-tied the belt on his crimson velvet smoking jacket, then poured himself a whisky. Outside, on Swan Street, the street lights cast a milky glow over the puddles accumulating on the road and footpaths, as the rain tumbled down. He watched for a while, then turned away, his attention taken by the file lying on the table. Cornelius Stout's murder had become an obsession with him.

If Henry and Lily Stout had been involved in their father's death, then it was unlikely that they would face the same fate as the criminals he had just read about. The social pages of the newspapers confirmed that the twins were living the high life, entertaining lavishly, and being entertained in return. The connections they were creating, with those in the more privileged stratum of society, would undoubtedly protect them from scrutiny.

'Lovely Lily,' as she was now called, could be seen on the arm of this man or that, at society dinners, the opening of stage shows, and at social events involving the rich and famous. She was dressed in the latest Paris fashions, with a touch of Hollywood thrown in. And Melbourne's eligible bachelors were lining up to be seen with the beautiful, independently wealthy, young woman. Henry, too, was benefitting from his new-found wealth, basking in the company of society debutantes and other affluent, pleasure-seeking young men.

Innocently, Reggie's mother had asked after Lily and the progress of their relationship, until he had been forced to give her an edited version of the truth, if only to stop her questions. In private, he cringed at the thought that Lily had played him for a fool. She had used him to track down Rita and collect evidence against her, a crucial factor being that he was seen as impartial, given that he would not benefit from Rita's conviction or Stout's wealth. He would be seen as a crime reporter chasing a story. In the back of his mind, his father's words haunted him: 'She's not what you think.' Although he hated to admit it, it was becoming highly likely that his father was right.

He checked the letters and the newspapers again, but the contradiction remained: the stage production of *Cousin Kate* was performed in July, not May. There was no alternative to the conclusion that the letter was a fake. Memory was unreliable, he knew, and obviously Lily had made a mistake when she thought that the play had been performed before her father's disappearance. Whichever way Reggie looked at it, the letter was designed to mislead him, by suggesting that Lily was the devoted daughter, whose sole aim was to reconcile her brother with her father. In truth, he had no idea how well the twins and their father had really related to each other, given that he only had Henry and Lily's word for it. The one certainty was that Henry and Cornelius had been estranged, with the former being disinherited. The will had been read, Lily had inherited the entire estate, and she was now at liberty to share it with her twin brother. The only conclusion he could draw was that Henry was being rewarded for his participation in the murder.

And, if the first letter were a fake, then the second must be, as well. The likelihood was that Lily Stout had written both of them at the same time. He examined them carefully. They were both written on the same creamy parchment, using the same ink. The choice of a blue ribbon to bind them could only be construed as an attempt to draw his attention to them.

Rita had been accepted as the murderer of Cornelius Stout, and Lily was free to enjoy the fruits of the inheritance, without being scrutinised by the authorities. Fortuitously, Rita was dead, meaning that she could not contradict any statements made by the Stout twins, or the findings of the police and the coroner. It was the perfect crime.

If it were the last thing he would do, he'd track down the evidence needed to convict the twins. In theory, they had put his life in danger. Lily had encouraged him to pursue the case against Rita, which had resulted in his poisoning.

If Lily were the mastermind behind her father's death, he'd prove it and have her punished. If she weren't, then he promised himself that he would never again succumb to a woman's charms without being absolutely sure of her attachment. No woman would ever make a fool of him again.

The coroner's report lay on the table. O'Flanagan had extended an olive branch and provided him with a copy. Traces of strychnine had been found in the exhumed bodies of Armitage Flagg, James Hardcastle, Clyde Bracegirdle, Julius Mathieson, and the unidentified body in the garden of the Mary Street home. In one fell swoop, the deaths of five men had been explained, with Rita Bracegirdle, the culprit. But, not one drop of poison had been detected in the body concealed in the trunk at the Punt Road terrace house.

Reggie frowned. The police would never re-open the Cornelius Stout case. They would react in much the same way that Kramer had when Reggie had accused Lily Stout of being the guilty party, rather than Rita. And how on earth was he going to prove Lily's guilt or innocence, if his boss had forbidden him from pursuing the investigation?

Chapter Fifty-Seven

The priest of St Ignatius' Church beckoned for Dotty Wright to come inside. Father Clements was a giant of a man, his cassock covering a barrel chest and a gut to match. His face was blotchy, covered in fine spider veins.

'What brings you here today, miss?'

'My name is Miss Wright. I attended the funeral of Dolores Savage and Rita Bracegirdle.'

The priest shook his head. 'A sad business.'

'I should explain. I have a friend who was instrumental in exposing Mrs Bracegirdle's crimes but, since then, he has received certain information that suggests that she may not be responsible for Mr Stout's death. Would you mind answering some questions for me?'

'It depends what those questions are.'

'Someone at the funeral said that Mrs Bracegirdle was intending to marry Mr Stout. Is that true?'

'That is true. She mentioned it to me after Mass one day. She asked if I would perform the ceremony. I told her I would need to speak to her fiancé. As far as I know, he wasn't with the Church.'

'But she was adamant that she was going to marry?'

'Oh yes. She said that Mr Stout was a widower and that he was very kind.'

'Let me clarify something, Father Clements. Mrs Bracegirdle told you, about a month after her husband's death, that she intended to marry Mr Stout. You didn't question the timing?'

'If you must know, I thought she was very lonely, being a widow again

241

after the death of her husband. In hindsight, I suppose that I have been rather naïve.' Father Clements looked uncomfortable. 'Particularly given what I've read in the newspapers about her recently.'

'Did she ever admit her crimes to you?'

He raised himself up to his full height. 'You've overstepped the mark, Miss Wright. If you were Roman Catholic, you wouldn't ask that question. There is the seal of the confessional. I'll just say this. Mrs Bracegirdle was a good Catholic. It's time for you to go. I have parishioners to visit.'

Red-faced, Dotty let herself out of the rectory. She'd offended the priest and she regretted that, but now she had confirmation of Rita's intention to marry Stout. If that were so, what possible motive would Rita have for murder?

* * *

Over Sunday lunch, Dotty told Reggie about her conversation with Father Clements.

'Why didn't you tell me you were planning to meet the priest? You should have asked me.'

Dotty flushed. 'I thought I was helping you. My conversation with Father Clements proves that Lily's second letter was fake too. Rita didn't have a reason to kill Stout. You should be pleased that I showed some initiative.'

Reggie raised his hands as if to fend her off. 'I suppose so. You've proved that Stout and Rita hadn't broken up. But don't expect to get a medal.'

'There's something else. I want to show you this.'

She took from the desk the lists that she had made a few days before. 'You'll be impressed.'

Reggie skimmed the document then laid it aside. 'Really, Dotty? Case against Lily and Henry? Case against Rita? Leave it to the experts. You're a teacher, not a detective.'

She blushed, disappointed but defiant. 'I am perfectly capable of logical thinking, so don't patronise me. What's wrong with them, then?'

'It's simplistic. It outlines arguments, but doesn't present a course of action or enquiry.'

'Do you disagree with any of it?'

'No,' he replied, begrudgingly. He re-read the lists. 'I admit that your arguments have some merit.'

Dotty was slightly mollified. 'Good. So, let's put together a course of action. I've interviewed the priest. What's next?'

'I would have thought that was obvious. We need to check with Cornelius Stout's solicitor and find out if Stout discussed the possibility of changing his will in Rita's favour.'

Dotty nodded in agreement. 'Don't forget the ring. Who paid for it? Who had it engraved? Who was the jeweller who sold it to either Rita or Lily?'

'That's not easy, Dotty. There are so many jewellery shops in Melbourne.'

'Rita lived in Richmond. Lily lives in East Melbourne. Couldn't we start there?'

'That's still a large area to cover. Perhaps we can narrow it down further. Think about it. Rita wouldn't want to spend too much on a man. She'd be looking at pawnbrokers rather than fashionable jewellery shops. And, if it were Lily, she'd want to keep her activities under wraps. She would most probably go the same way. She wants a ring that points to Rita's involvement. She doesn't want to waste money on an expensive piece of jewellery. Second-hand dealers would be the preferred option.'

'I have to hand it to you, Reggie, I never would have thought of that.'

Reggie smiled and stroked his moustache. 'Experience, my dear.' He pointed at Dotty's list of evidence against Lily and Henry. 'You left out one important point. Poison was Rita's *modus operandi*. Cornelius was bludgeoned to death, not poisoned.'

'Of course. It's obvious when you think about it.' She picked up a pencil and added it to her list. 'What do you want me to do? Do you want me to check the pawnbrokers?'

'Too time-consuming. You'll be at school this week. And I can't be seen doing this in my working hours. I'd lose my job. I need to come up with a solution that will shorten the process. I'll think of something. I always do.'

Chapter Fifty-Eight

Fate smiled on Reggie da Costa in the form of Squizzy Taylor. Two days before Angus Murray's execution, detectives and plain-clothes constables had raided the establishment of one George Foster, who was then charged with running a common gaming-house. Forty-six men were arrested, including the bane of Detective Sergeant O'Flanagan's existence, Leslie 'Squizzy' Taylor. The little gangster was released on bail of fifty pounds.

The raid was the result of an anonymous tip-off, but Reggie had heard from his sources that Squizzy believed that Horace Striker was the informant. It was the usual case of crime boss versus crime boss, each trying to steal the other's territory. As soon as the charges were heard and he was out on the street again, Taylor intended to get his revenge on his enemy. The ensuing battle would be a bloody one.

Reggie considered the situation carefully. He knew that he could turn it to his advantage, if he took the trouble to make some enquiries. By digging around and listening to the talk on the streets, Reggie uncovered the truth behind the raid. It would be a risk, but he needed to apprise Squizzy of the truth, and hopefully put the diminutive gangster in his debt.

Reggie was well-known to the members of the various 'pushes,' or gangs, that made up Melbourne's underworld. Some even sought him out, to clear up a misunderstanding about their role in a crime, or to ask that he go easy when he reported their activities in the newspaper. Occasionally, there was the odd criminal who craved publicity, and was only too happy to grant Reggie an exclusive interview, as long as the reporter played the game and wrote about him in the way he wanted. One of these was Squizzy Taylor, who made for good copy with his loud clothing and aping of the American bootleggers. Since their last meeting, the little gangster had refined the art of the standover merchant, blackmailer, and jury-fixer, the latter role being particularly useful when it came to his own court appearances.

Taylor, the leader of the Richmond gang, was a fixture at the gambling dens and racecourses of Melbourne. Near to the Fitzroy Town Hall was 'The Narrows,' an assortment of claustrophobic lanes, cobbled streets, and dingy houses. It was into this hostile environment that Reggie set foot one day in mid-May, in a bid to meet with Joseph Theodore Leslie Taylor, alias 'Squizzy' Taylor.

He was met at the door by a couple of thugs, who patted him down then directed him into the inner sanctum. The usual suspects were preoccupied playing 'two-up,' gambling on the fall of two pennies, heads or tails. Others sat around tables drinking illegal booze. Through the cigarette smoke, Reggie could discern the recognisable form of the little gangster, surrounded by his henchman and assorted admirers.

As usual, Squizzy was dressed as a toff. His suit was of the finest quality broadcloth, set off by a silk shirt and patent leather shoes. Diamonds glittered on his fingers and in the pin of his silk tie. He leaned on a silver-knobbed walking stick, which had become part of his wardrobe since he was shot in the leg. Compared to Squizzy, Reggie looked positively austere.

Seeing the crime reporter across the room, Taylor strode forward and shook his hand, flashing a gold-toothed smile.

'Reggie, my boy,' he said, 'what brings you into my world?'

'Information.'

'For you or me?'

'You.'

'Come with me.'

Squizzy led him to a back room and waved away two of his stooges, who were hovering close by.

'Have a seat.'

'How have you been, Leslie?'

'You should know. If it's not one trumped up charge, it's another. It's a crime.' Taylor offered the reporter a cigar, then lit up his own.

'I've been fitted up by the coppers. How was I to know that Angus Murray escaped from the Big House? The jury knew I was telling the truth. Next thing, I walk out of court and they arrest me for running some dame over. I done nothing. No one's identified me. And no one will. I tell you, Reggie, Detective O'Flanagan's a disgrace. It's harassment, that's what it is.'

Reggie nodded in agreement. 'O'Flanagan is like a dog after a bone.'

'That's true.' Taylor took another puff of his cigar. 'What's this information that you're talking about?'

'That business about the raid on George Foster's establishment. You weren't set up by Horace Striker. I have it on good authority that one of your own gang squealed.'

Squizzy frowned. 'And who would this little rat be?'

'Someone with aspirations to take over from you.' He leaned down and whispered a name.

Squizzy's eyes narrowed. 'I thought as much. Makes sense. Thought he could put me away and take over? We'll see about that.' He looked at the reporter keenly. 'You don't get something for nothing. I assume you want a favour in return?'

'You remember the Cornelius Stout murder? Rita Bracegirdle was fitted up for it. She's dead so she can't prove her innocence. I have someone in the frame for it, but I need proof.'

Squizzy cocked his head to one side. 'Why bother?'

'I was played for a fool. It's payback time.'

'Understandable. You just saved me from a gang war. Tell me what you need.'

Over the next five minutes, Reggie told Taylor about his suspicions.

Squizzy whistled. 'That dame? The one in all the papers? More likely she went to Richmond if she's avoiding the coppers. East Melbourne's for toffs. She'd be known there. I know some blokes in the jewellery trade. I'll see what I can do.'

Reggie nodded. More likely those blokes in the jewellery trade, to whom Squizzy was referring, were receivers of stolen property rather than legitimate businessmen. But he wasn't going to argue. Squizzy's reach extended far, whereas Reggie's didn't. He butted out his cigar and put on his hat.

'Thanks, Leslie. Keep me in mind if you have anything newsworthy for me. Your boys are my bread and butter. I scratch your back, you scratch mine.'

Taylor smiled and flicked his cigar ash onto the floor. 'I'll get one of my men to show you out.' He tapped his walking stick on the floor. Immediately, one of his goons put his head around the door.

'Yes, boss?'

'Make sure Mr da Costa gets a glass of the best whisky in the house before he leaves.'

Reggie went out into the smoke-filled room and downed the proffered glass. He felt no guilt about informing on Squizzy's 'snitch.' He'd been one of the gangster's most violent enforcers for some time, and he deserved whatever was dished out. Reggie looked about him. The clientele of 'The Narrows' was endlessly interesting. Petty thieves, gamblers, drug dealers, Taylor's cronies. Here was the stuff of a hundred different crime stories in one place. And he was just the man to document it.

Chapter Fifty-Nine

The solicitors who dealt with Cornelius Stout's estate were only a few blocks away from Reggie's usual haunt on Wednesdays: Fasoli's Café, whose signature dishes of rich soup and highly-seasoned pot-cooked meat ragout made Reggie's taste buds tingle.

After a most pleasant hour spent savouring their fare, Reggie put his mind back to the task at hand: had Cornelius Stout planned to change his will in Rita Bracegirdle's favour? It would confirm that they had intended to marry. If Lily and Henry had discovered this, it would give them a powerful motive to do away with their father before he led Rita down the aisle.

Wellington & Sons, Solicitors, was situated in William Street, in the legal district of Melbourne. The brass plaque outside their offices had been polished to a high sheen. Reggie took the steps that led up to the substantial oak door and turned the handle.

Inside was another world, a dimly lit room with dark wood wainscoting and high windows that allowed only a modicum of sunlight to penetrate the gloom. Behind a large desk a small woman hovered, searching for some document or other in the pile of papers that overflowed the metal baskets on each side of an ancient typewriter. She looked up in shock when she saw a stranger watching her, and quickly pushed the folders back into place.

'You have an appointment, Mr—?'

'Reginald da Costa. To see Mr Fawcett.'

She smiled bleakly and disappeared into the deepening shadows behind her. A deep, booming voice told her to send him in.

'Mr Fawcett will see you now, sir.'

He nodded and entered the solicitor's office. The door was shut behind him.

The introductions complete, Reggie was invited to sit down. It was better lit than in the outer office; a large pendant light hung down from the ceiling, illuminating a room whose walls were dominated by oak shelving, packed with legal tomes in different coloured leathers. Behind a monstrous desk, with a green leather top, sat a very small man, the owner of the booming voice. Mr Aldous Fawcett was wearing a shiny black suit that was nearing the end of its life, and a ridiculous black wig, which was slightly askew. It occurred to Reggie that a solicitor, who represented the interests of the moneyed classes, should invest a little more in his choice of clothing. Appearance should never be underestimated.

'How can I help you, Mr da Costa?'

'I am senior crime reporter with *The Argus*. I am tying together some loose ends in my investigation of Cornelius Stout's death.'

Fawcett rested his hands on the edge of his desk. 'Ah, yes. I've read your reports in the newspaper. A sad case. Mr Stout was a valued client.'

'I have one question for you. A simple yes or no will suffice.'

'And what would that question be?'

'Did Mr Stout ever express the desire to make a new will?'

'It is common knowledge that Miss Lily Stout inherited the estate.'

'But did Mr Stout ever suggest that he might wish to change his will?'

'In the interests of client confidentiality, I cannot answer that question.'

Reggie took out his pocket book and slipped a one-pound note across the desk, in the solicitor's direction.

'Let's say, hypothetically, that a man of means, with a son and daughter, meets a woman that he intends to marry.'

'Yes?'

'Hypothetically, he wonders if he should protect his new wife's interests, rather than those of his children.'

Reggie took another one-pound note and placed it on the desk. 'Does the man consider making a new will?'

'Hypothetically?' Fawcett's hand grasped the notes. 'Indeed, this man might consider such an action, but perhaps he never had the opportunity to follow through with his intention. Death comes to us all.'

'But perhaps a little sooner than he hoped?' Reggie stood. He leaned over and shook Fawcett's hand. 'I'll show myself out. I trust that this conversation will not be repeated outside these four walls?'

'Indeed, no,' boomed the little man. 'It was, as you say, a hypothetical discussion.'

Chapter Sixty

Armed with the information that Rita and Stout had planned to marry and that Rita was to be made the beneficiary of the will, Reggie knew that there was one last piece of evidence outstanding to prove that the Stout twins were killers. If only Squizzy would come through with the name of the second-hand dealer.

The days passed slowly until Reggie found the much-anticipated envelope on his desk. Inside, there was a slip of paper with the address of a pawnbroker.

Reggie shook his head in wonder. He had come to question whether he had given Squizzy Taylor an impossible task in locating the seller of the gold signet ring found on Cornelius Stout's finger. Indeed, he had even wondered if Squizzy would honour his side of the bargain. It had taken all of three weeks for Taylor's men to track down the pawnbroker.

He was in high spirits when he drove home that Tuesday. As he got out of the car, he saw that Dotty was home.

'Squizzy's letter has arrived,' he said, as Dotty invited him in. 'This is what I've been waiting for. Definitive proof that Lily and Henry Stout planted evidence to point the finger at Rita.' He waved the envelope in the air. 'The pawnbroker isn't far from here. I'll leave work early tomorrow, before the shop shuts.'

'Wonderful! But how will you prove the identity of the person who bought it?'

'I have a photograph of the Stout twins with their father. That will seal their fate.'

'I finish work at four o'clock. Could I come with you?'

'I'll pick you up outside your school. Make sure you're ready.'

Dotty grinned. 'Wouldn't miss it for the world!'

* * *

The next day dragged for Reggie. He had reports to file on a bigamist farmer in Western Australia, and the arrest of a young man for stealing a tray of diamond rings from a jewellery shop in Hawthorn. He watched the hands of the clock as they moved slowly around the dial. At half-past three sharp, he picked up his hat and walked out of the newsroom, informing the receptionist that he was going to conduct an interview with a magistrate from the Children's Court. In actual fact, he had organised that interview for the next day. If Kramer knew what his true destination was, there'd be hell to pay.

Dotty was waiting at the school gate when Reggie pulled up outside Richmond State School. A couple of parents raised their eyebrows at the sight of Miss Wright, Senior Mistress, getting into a very flashy yellow and black Citroen driven by a man who could only be regarded as flamboyant. It would be a talking point among the mothers for weeks to come.

It took about fifteen minutes to reach Church Street, weaving past horse-drawn carts and buggies, bicycles, and slow-moving cars. Finally, they found the premises of 'TH White, Licensed Pawnbrokers and Second-hand Dealers. Fine gold jewellery a specialty.'

The man behind the counter was separated from them by an iron grille. He smiled in a bleak fashion and asked, 'Can I help you?'

Reggie stepped forward. 'My name is Reggie da Costa. Leslie Taylor sent me.'

The pawnbroker's expression changed in an instant.

'Mr da Costa. I've been expecting you,' he said, smiling broadly. 'Mr Taylor's assistant said that I was to give you my full co-operation.'

It was the first time that Reggie had heard one of Squizzy's henchmen referred to as an 'assistant.'

The pawnbroker reached below the counter and extracted a large ledger. 'I've marked the spot. June 1921.'

'You keep records?' asked Dotty.

The man appraised the school teacher coolly, then answered. 'Unlike some of my colleagues, and I use that term loosely, I run a legitimate business. I document every transaction. My customers can be sure that their pledges will not be disposed of before their time is up. If they return within the agreed time, they can redeem the item for the amount of the loan plus interest.'

'The signet ring?' asked Reggie, impatiently.

'Of course.' He cleared his throat. 'According to my records, it was received in February 1920 from a Mr Francis James. I sold it on the 2nd of June, 1921.'

'Do you have the buyer's name?'

'I do. I was also asked at the time if I could engrave the ring, but I do not offer that service. I recommended a jeweller down the street.'

'The name?'

'Coincidentally, I saw a photograph of the lady in a newspaper recently. And a photograph of the gentleman with her.'

Reggie drew out the photograph with a flourish. 'This is the couple you saw? Henry and Lily Stout?' He brandished the picture in front of the pawnbroker.

'Indeed, no. It was the gentleman with them. Their father, Cornelius Stout. And his killer, Rita Bracegirdle.'

Chapter Sixty-One

It was a week before Reggie could bring himself to admit his mistake. He had been wrong about Lily and Henry. It was mortifying. He was the senior crime reporter for *The Argus*, after all. A junior reporter may have jumped to such conclusions, but he should have known better. At least he had not made his suspicions public, which was a blessing.

As the days passed, he grew to accept the truth that Rita Bracegirdle had murdered Cornelius Stout, despite evidence to the contrary, and how much he would have liked it to be so. However, there remained some questions that required answers. Swallowing his pride, he drove to East Melbourne, and parked outside Lily and Henry's fashionable terrace house in Hotham Street. He rang the doorbell.

'Reggie, can't you take the hint? It's over.' Lily Stout stood in the doorway, frowning at her visitor.

'I need to speak to you.'

'You're an attractive man, you're diverting, but I have bigger fish to fry.'

'Fry away, Miss Stout. I couldn't care less about you.'

Lily looked puzzled. 'Then why are you here?'

'Let me come in and I'll tell you.'

He followed her into the drawing room. It was elegantly furnished, with a marble fireplace, and a settee and chaise longue in red velvet, with matching drapes. The polished boards were covered by an elaborately woven Turkish rug, in muted reds and greens. Reggie sat on the couch and put his satchel on the floor.

Lily was silent, watching him. 'Well?' she said, at last.

'I find myself in a quandary, Miss Stout. I would have liked nothing better than to find you guilty of the murder of your father, but it seems that all the evidence points to Rita Bracegirdle. I'd like a clarification of a few things, so that I can put you firmly in my past. To begin: Why did you contact me, in the first place?'

She sat opposite him, her hands in her lap. 'It's simple. I wanted someone to prove that Rita was guilty. You were perfect. Vain enough to believe that I might be interested in you, and good enough at your job to track down a murderer. And you were free of charge.'

'Go on,' said Reggie. 'You're nothing, if not blunt.'

'Henry and I knew that Rita must have had a hand in Dad's death, but we couldn't prove it. Two and a half years without a body. Seven years before we could declare him dead and claim his money. We were desperate. And then you found him by chance. Henry and I never thought that Rita would have put his body in the basement of her rented apartment. It's amazing that it wasn't discovered earlier.'

'What aroused your suspicions?'

'We were worried when he took up with that trollop. Typical rich man, weak when it came to flattery. We employed a private detective to find out about her. Rita had a history of dead husbands. Wealthy ones. I tried to tell Dad, but he wouldn't believe me. I can only assume that he found out the truth for himself and decided that it was all over with her. He never deigned to tell us why they broke up. Said it was none of our business. At least we no longer had to worry about losing the estate.'

'Did you ever consider killing your father?'

Lily shrugged her shoulders. 'I don't see why I can't tell you now. I confess that it crossed my mind, when I thought the marriage was going ahead. We were his children, and she was little more than a money-hungry whore. It would have been justified. The trouble was that Henry would never have had the guts to do it, and I didn't like the idea of employing a third party. That can get messy. Then Dad and Rita split up, and he went missing. We knew Rita lived in Punt Road. Henry went there a couple of times with the intention of confronting her. The second time, he saw the new tenant living there and knew she'd gone. Where we didn't know. It was like she'd disappeared off the face of the earth, just like Dad.

'Our money had run out before you found his body. We couldn't afford to employ someone to find Rita. The will would take time to be processed. Our problem was that the police thought we were involved. The inheritance, you know.' She waved her hand around the room. 'Lovely, isn't it? Money is so necessary to appreciate the good things of life. You can never have enough.' She frowned. 'It was pure chance that I saw Rita at Leggett's. You did a wonderful job contriving a meeting with her and exposing her criminal history.'

'I nearly died.'

She shrugged her shoulders. 'But you didn't. You got a good story for your paper. You came out of it well. But you didn't get the girl.' She laughed, a deep throaty laugh.

Reggie was unmoved. 'Why did you plant the letters, if you didn't do it?'

'I don't understand.'

Reggie took the letters out of his satchel and passed them to her.

Lily undid the ribbon and read them. 'I'd forgotten these.'

'You admit they're fakes?'

Lily shook her head. 'They were real.'

Reggie tapped his finger defiantly on the table. '*Cousin Kate* was performed in July 1921, not May. I took my mother to see it. It was at the King's Theatre.'

Lily sighed. 'Silly boy. You jump to conclusions. The Green and Tan Dramatic Club also performed it at The Playhouse. That was in May 1921. They're a theatre group of former students from University High School. My brother went to school there. That's why I wrote that I was sorry he didn't go.' She pointed at the letters and smirked. 'How's that for you?'

'Even so, you used me. You lied to me.'

'I did, didn't I? But you were a willing partner.'

'Only because I thought you were interested in me.'

'The fruit doesn't fall far from the tree. You're like your father. I met him. He likes women with money too.'

Reggie was furious. 'I am nothing like my father!'

Lily stood defiantly; her arms crossed. 'It's time you went. Don't come back again.'

Reggie picked up his satchel and studied her. 'You're unscrupulous, Lily. Hopefully, one day you'll get treated the same way that you treated me.'

Lily scowled. 'Get out.'

Reggie walked down the path and paused next to his motorcar. He looked back at the woman hovering in the doorway. How could he have thought that he was in love with her? How could he ever have thought that she was beautiful?

As he drove home, he remembered an expression used by one of his colleagues at *The Argus*, a soldier who'd survived the Western Front. He'd told him that he'd dodged a bullet in the War. Until now, Reggie hadn't realised the implications of those words.

In fact, he had dodged two bullets. If he'd gone public about his belief that the Stout twins had killed their father, his reputation would have been in tatters. He would have lost all credibility with O'Flanagan, Kramer and his readers, and Lily and Henry would have called on their connections to have him sacked. Rita *was* Cornelius Stout's killer. She had bought Stout the ring, despite her suggestion to the contrary. She had wanted to marry him, and had been angry and vengeful when he called the marriage off. She had tried to saw the ring off his finger, because it implicated her in his death. It was probably as O'Flanagan had suggested: Rita lashed out and struck Stout in anger, rather than relying on strychnine to do the job.

The second bullet was harder to come to terms with. Lily Stout had appeared to be the ideal wife: beautiful and rich. He had believed that he was in love with her, and she with him. But he had been given a glimpse of what lay behind the façade, and he didn't like what he saw. Beneath the appearance of charm, sophistication, and glamour lay a cold-hearted woman. He realised that he had never really known her; he had just been infatuated with what she appeared to offer him. No one would know how wrong he'd been about Lily. Except Dotty Wright. And he trusted her to keep his confidences.

Rita and Lily were cut from the same cloth. Both wanted money; both told men what they wanted to hear; both used men for their own ends. Deception and lies and greed were part and parcel of whom they were. And then it struck him. Was he like that too? Using women for his own ends to give himself the lifestyle he craved? Like his father? That was something to contemplate over the coming weeks, not now while he was coming to terms with so much else.

Whether he liked it or not, he was getting older, but was that such a bad thing? With age came wisdom, he'd been told. The facts were that he was still alive, despite Rita's best efforts, and that he had a comfortable home, a good job, and a wardrobe full of beautiful suits, the envy of all and sundry. Most importantly, there were a select few, such as Dotty, Captain Jack, and his mother, who liked him for what he was, and whom he liked in return.

The roar of the engine of his Citroen 5CV 'Torpedo' tourer, with its yellow boat-tail and black mudguards, intruded on his reflection. He smiled. He'd forgotten to mention the car. Flashy yet classy, he thought, much like himself. All in all, he was a lucky man.

Half an hour later, he pulled up outside the grocer's shop and knocked on the front door of Dotty's house.

'What is it, Reggie?' she asked him. 'You look different.'

'I'll tell you all about it later. Fix your hair. Put on your best dress. I'll be back in twenty minutes. We're going out for dinner, then we're going dancing.'

'Where?'

He smirked. 'Leggett's, of course.'

A Note from the Author

I have retained Australian spelling, punctuation and word usage, where possible. However, in an effort to avoid confusion, I have opted to use 'jail' rather than 'gaol'. I apologise to my colleagues at the Old Melbourne Gaol!

Acknowledgements

Writers Victoria has been instrumental in my development as a writer. Their workshops and manuscript assessments have proved invaluable to me. Dr Kate Ryan's editing skills helped me polish the manuscript and prepare it for publication.

Researching the historical and social background to this book has been aided by the National Library of Australia's research portal, *Trove*, using their digitised newspapers from the past. In particular, I drew on reports in *The Argus* and *The Age* to describe the Police Strike of 1923. These were also the years of the gangs of Fitzroy and Richmond, when Squizzy Taylor and his criminal exploits made headlines. The description of the hanging of Angus Murray at the Melbourne Gaol was also drawn from my knowledge as a volunteer guide at that prison museum, as well as from accounts in the newspapers of the day.

My sincere thanks must go to the Dames of Detection—Harriette Sackler, Verena Rose, and Shawn Reilly Simmons—of Level Best Books, for their continued faith in me as an author. I am extremely fortunate to have them as the editors and publishers of my work. I also wish to acknowledge the support of the other Level Best authors in welcoming me into the fold.

My love and gratitude go to my family for their belief in me. And where would I be without the encouragement of my friends, as well as my golfing buddies at the Victoria Golf Club, who have enthusiastically supported my writing? Finally, there is my wonderful husband, Bob, who has patiently supported and encouraged me throughout this foray into becoming a novelist.

About the Author

Laraine Stephens lives in Beaumaris, a bayside suburb of Melbourne, Australia. With an Arts degree from the University of Melbourne, a Diploma of Education and a Graduate Diploma in Librarianship, she worked in secondary schools as a Head of Library. On retirement, Laraine decided to turn her hand to the craft of crime writing.

SOCIAL MEDIA HANDLES:
  Laraine Stephens | Facebook

AUTHOR WEBSITE:
  https://lainestephens.com

Also by Laraine Stephens

The Death Mask Murders: A Reggie da Costa Mystery